Grave Words

Also available by Gerri Lewis

The Last Word, A Deadly Deadlines Mystery

Grave Words

A DEADLY DEADLINES MYSTERY

Gerri Lewis

Books should be disposed of and recycled according to local requirements. All paper materials used are FSC compliant.

This is a work of fiction. All of the names, characters, organizations, places, and events portrayed in this novel are either products of the author's imagination or are used fictitiously. Any resemblance to real or actual events, locales, or persons, living or dead, is entirely coincidental.

Copyright © 2025 by Gerri Lewis INK

All rights reserved.

Published in the United States by Crooked Lane Books, an imprint of The Quick Brown Fox & Company LLC.

Crooked Lane Books and its logo are trademarks of The Quick Brown Fox & Company LLC.

Library of Congress Catalog-in-Publication data available upon request.

ISBN (hardcover): 979-8-89242-113-3
ISBN (paperback): 979-8-89242-248-2
ISBN (ebook): 979-8-89242-114-0

Cover design by Rob Fiore

Printed in the United States.

www.crookedlanebooks.com

Crooked Lane Books
34 West 27th St., 10th Floor
New York, NY 10001

First Edition: June 2025

The authorized representative in the EU for product safety and compliance is eucomply OÜPärnu mnt 139b-14, 11317 Tallinn, Estonia, hello@eucompliancepartner.com, +33757690241

10 9 8 7 6 5 4 3 2 1

To my siblings, Rick, Leigh and especially Michele

Chapter One

The flames from a raging inferno fell away, leaving only a fire-alarm ringtone from somewhere on my nightstand. Still dark outside, I peered through gluey eyes and fumbled for my cell phone. The time read 6:07 AM.

"Oh good, you're not dead," Carla said, a triumphant confirmation in her voice when I answered.

"If I were, you'd be the first to know." My friend was the assistant at a local funeral home.

"The internet disagrees."

"The internet?"

"Your obituary is posted everywhere, even on Insta."

"My obituary?"

"Geez girl, you sound like a parrot. Apparently, you were born six years ago and yet you outlived the Queen," she said, gum snapping. Carla had recently traded vaping for Dubble-Bubble.

"Elizabeth?"

"Do you know another?"

"Start from the beginning," I sighed, trying my hardest to shake the cobwebs.

I could hear her clicking away on a keyboard. Then she began to read: "*WINTER SNOW, 2018-2024*—ooh, I love the bold caps in the heading."

"Just get on with it."

Carla continued reading, "*Winter Snow, a longtime Ridgefield resident, died October 20, 2024, one month shy of her 107th birthday at the home she lived in for over seven decades. Winter, who was predeceased by her husband of 74 years, Robert Snow, was a small-town girl from the plains of South Dakota who survived two pandemics, the Great Depression, multiple wars, breast cancer, the Digital Revolution, and a great big, beautiful mess of a family.* And to think, you did all that before reaching the age of seven."

I mashed my pillow over my face and groaned.

"They even have your picture," she added. "You were one hot centenarian."

In a town with a population that doesn't even come close to filling Yankee Stadium, gossip was the quickest executioner. Even once people realized I was still alive, they'd wonder how a professional obituary writer could have messed up so badly.

"There goes my business," I said.

"Hence my call," Carla replied. "If you alert the newspaper now, you should be able to head off tomorrow's print edition. I think the error is only online with our local paper and can be rectified quickly before too many people see it. Unless . . ." More clicking, another bubble popping.

Putting Carla on speaker, I began to search for myself.

"Ah, here—uh oh," Carla said, getting there first.

"Uh oh what?"

"It is also listed on Legacy.com."

"Idiots!" My voice must have climbed an octave because a wet nose in a fluffy white mound rose from the floor next to my pillow.

Grave Words

I gave Diva a reassuring pat and pointed back to her bed in the corner. For once, the Great Pyrenees pup obeyed.

"Thanks for the heads-up," I said. "Pray for my enemies."

"Before you go off to rescue your business—can I ask a favor?"

Carla occasionally asked me to write up a death notice with a bit more intimacy than what the funeral home could provide. With my business still in its infancy, I really needed paying jobs, although she didn't ask often and I owed her a lot for all the clients she steered my way.

"Pro bono?" I ventured.

"Sorry," she confirmed. "You know the fire last night?"

My reporter friend, Scoop, had texted me about it as I was going to bed. A fire had broken out in the building where a popular guy hang-out called Pop's Place was located.

"I heard there was a victim," I said.

"There was," she said quietly. And to my surprise, her voice cracked as she said his name.

Chapter Two

"Wandering Chester?" I asked, my heart sinking. "What was he doing at Pop's Place?"

As far as anyone knew, Ridgefield's homeless man didn't have a permanent residence, though he did disappear often for weeks at a time. Ridgefielders, being the kind of people they were, always made sure he had food and shelter when he was in town. Sometimes he'd sleep in one of the vacant apartments where kind landlords looked the other way, although I did hear that they always left the door unlocked with clean towels and toiletries inside. This kind of hospitality was reminiscent of colonial times when a cave dweller named Sarah Bishop would walk from North Salem, New York, just steps from the Connecticut border, down to town, where she would accept whatever charitable contributions kindly village folk would offer.

All I really knew about Wandering Chester was how he looked—lean, fiftyish, owlish and that he was currently the town's only, to quote the graceful euphemism du jour, "person experiencing homelessness."

Some claimed Chester was an Iraq War vet suffering from PTSD. Others said he'd taken a vow of poverty. The most reliable insight was from my reporter friend, Scoop, who once put him up for the night and had witnessed firsthand an acute allergy to the many cats my friend fostered.

However, no one knew exactly where Chester roamed or how he kept fed and clothed. He'd wander in and out, carrying nothing, shrugging off charity except for occasional meals or lodging. He was a friendly guy, always accepting tips for the small courtesies he offered, like carrying heavy purchases from Ridgefield Hardware to vehicles. He chatted up people, but never discussed himself. I always thought of Chester as our 21st century Sarah Bishop, guardian of some dark and painful past. And now he was gone.

"What do we know about the guy?"

Carla's moan sounded a bit like one of Diva's growls.

"Damn cops," she spat. "They're keeping everything close to the vest. They won't even give me his last name."

Carla had been dating one of the police officers, a nice guy I'd thought. She broke it off when he asked her if she would consider removing some of her tattoos because they made his mother uncomfortable.

Carla once told me that each of the tattoos that snaked around her neck and covered her arms like a long-sleeved turtleneck represented a life challenge she had managed to overcome. She never volunteered what things in her life had left her so inked up. I figured if she wanted to tell me, she would. When she gave up smoking though, I asked if she planned to get a new tat to celebrate her achievement. She'd replied that her tattoos were reserved for obstacles she never had a choice over.

"Don't blame the entire police department because one guy couldn't love you as you are," I said into the phone.

Gum snap, wrapper noise, and then a bubble popping.

"Sorry," she said. "I forgot that you and Kip are a thing. I guess I'm still bitter about my break-up."

I'd been seeing Kip Michaels, a detective with the Ridgefield Police Department, for the last few months and recently, we were spending more and more time together.

"Have you heard any more from your ex?" I asked.

"Are you kidding me? I'm going to have to ghost him—he's texting, calling all the time saying that he was a jerk and wanting to make it up to me and blah blah blah . . ."

"No second chances?" I imagined her gently outlining her tats with her glossy black nail-polished fingers, a curious habit she had.

She didn't answer and instead changed gears. "Can you run by this afternoon? I should have more info about Chester then. Tony worked the fire—maybe he'll have a complete ID later today."

Tony was her firefighter brother. All of Ridgefield's first responders from the RFD were also trained as EMTs and it was possible that he had been first on the scene.

"Would Tony tell you something like that? Even if he knows Chester's last name, wouldn't that be for the police to release?"

A pause and I was guessing a shrug. Technically, no one in the RFD would risk the wrath of their chief by talking out of turn. There were, however, often leaks when it came to fires.

"I'm just hoping when he gets a bead on what's what, he'll give me what he can because I've been getting the cold shoulder at the PD since my split, " Carla said, referring to the police department.

"Surely they won't stop you from doing your job." That kind of interference would be unprofessional. And then, I realized the problem. Carla would not want to take a chance that her former boyfriend who is currently the public information officer might be on the other end of the phone. "Never mind, I get it."

Before hanging up, Carla confirmed that Chester's body was now transferred to Farmington where the state medical examiner would determine cause of death. The fire had been knocked down before it could do too much damage to the second-floor office where Chester had been found. According to Tony, the body hadn't even been burned.

Why hadn't Chester escaped the blaze? Overwhelmed by smoke? A heart attack or stroke? Maybe he was staying upstairs and had fallen asleep with a lit cigarette. Some Ridgefield do-gooder was probably kicking himself right about now for allowing Chester to crash in his office.

These and other questions swirled in my groggy brain as I searched the internet for any news on the fire. There was nothing yet.

I then searched for my client's obituary and I groaned out loud when I found it. My name, a date that made my client six years old instead of 106, and a photo that looked exactly like the one on my website, registered.

Resigning myself to an early start, I'd dashed off urgent missives to the press, and to the family of the woman for whom I'd written— accurately, the first time—the obituary now in question. Carla had an in with the folks at Legacy.com and she promised to take care of that.

Then, I did my best with my bed head which wasn't saying much. I took after my mother's side of the family with limp straight hair, naturally the color of slightly tarnished copper. When I awoke, it was a coiffed free-for-all. Diva, on the other hand, had a silky white mane and despite her tendency to drool excessively when frightened or confined, she didn't need a groomer to make her photo perfect. Her tail thumped happily when she saw me throw on my UCONN fleece and tights.

The dawn chill and layer of mist on the dark lake complemented my mood perfectly.

By the time the sun began fracturing the kaleidoscope of color on the ridge above the lake, Diva and I had power-walked to the boat launch. I never bothered tethering her because, perhaps remembering her early orphan days, she was rarely far from my side when we went on our morning excursions. Metaphorically speaking, she kept *me* on a tight leash.

The lot bordering the launch was empty except for a topless gray-blue Jeep with a roof rack on the rollbars. Through the mist, I could make out an ambitious early morning canoer angling away from the cement ramp at the water's edge. *Like Chester leaving our little port,* I thought.

U-turning back toward the road, I didn't notice that Diva was no longer pressing against my leg. And then came her low, throaty rumble. I looked behind to see a dark shape rising from the water's edge.

"Easy," I said in a quiet voice, stepping quickly to catch her collar.

From twenty yards, I could see a mesmerizing mass of fur and muscle that looked no less than 200 pounds. As we backed away and I attempted not to make eye contact, Diva barked.

Nonchalantly, the creature stopped and raised its head to look at us.

After more than a century without black bears, due to extirpation in the 1800's, the recent return of the animals to our bustling 'burb was still a startling phenomenon. With my free hand, I fished out my phone and was about to snap a photo when the device erupted into my blaring ringtone again. *Better than bear bells,* I thought, as the beast crunched off into the reeds. And then, for the second time that morning, someone was asking me for a favor.

"I wouldn't have called so early," said Scoop, "but it's time-sensitive."

Scoop and I had met as reporters for our local paper. When it was sold and gutted, I'd taken a buyout and started my obit-business. He'd hung in. He was as dogged as they come, the type to pull thread long past deadline, file stories at dawn, and crash out on the couch until one of his rescue cats nibbled on his ear. A pre-brunch call from Scoop was a unicorn and a favor usually meant he needed my car. His scooter was not much help shopping in soggy weather or getting cats to the vet.

"You'll need to gas her up," I said. "The light went on when I pulled in last night."

"Actually, it's something else," he replied. "Can you ask Kip what's going on with the investigation into last night's fire?"

Kip and Scoop had become friends of sorts a few months back when a lascivious cop and his monster girlfriend almost got us all killed.

"Why can't you ask him yourself?"

"The police don't share that sort of information with persons of interest."

Chapter Three

"**W**hat?" My voice must've hit a double-crescendo this time because birds went quiet and Diva started nuzzling my hand.

"Start from the beginning," I said, apropos of the morning script.

Over the last month, Scoop had written about a pair of arsons in town. Both had the feel of Robin Hood attacks—steal from the rich to give to the poor. Or rather, dupe insurance companies into paying off debt.

The first fire had burned a blighted home a stone's-throw from Main Street. The widow Mrs. Means had long since fallen behind on the upkeep and the house had sat forlornly on the market for two years. In September, while she was visiting her daughter in Boston, the house had burned to the ground nearly as quickly as it had gone up in flames, leaving an empty lot on prime land and a hefty claim payout on the way. Mrs. Means, now of many means, had already relocated to a tidy apartment near her daughter, and construction of a neighborhood-friendly colonial on her former property would soon be underway.

Another house went up in flames two weeks later. This one was a spec house owned by a contractor who had overextended himself and missed the post-pandemic real estate rush. With his head underwater and the bank circling, he was visiting relatives in Tampa when the fire took the structure to its foundation. According to Scoop's stories, which were so vivid I could practically feel the heat on my face as I read, the methods were the same and both owners had iron-clad alibis.

All this I knew. What he hadn't told me was that his coverage of the fires had brought attention from the police. According to my friend, some of the details he'd unearthed made the department uneasy.

"They asked for my source!" he said angrily. "When I refused, they shut me out."

His subsequent questions about the cases had been met with vague official statements and no further comment. And yet, he'd prevailed, confirming key details through his unnamed source. Now, apparently, the cops had arrived at the conclusion that Scoop had set the blazes himself. I imagined him squirming under an interrogation: *How did you learn about the fires? How did you get there so fast?*

"I still can't believe they'd think me capable of it," he said. "What would I have to gain?"

"Another award-winning story?" I said, trying to lighten the mood.

Anger unabridged, he reminded me that his last award-winning story was my fault. My stomach started doing the cartwheels it always did whenever I thought of how close we came to gracing the obituary pages. Exciting award-winning in print, terrifying in person.

"Sorry," I said, unsure if I was apologizing for the flip remark or my previous transgressions.

"Anyway, you're right," he said. "That's the motive the cops like, self-enrichment through community journalism."

Steering the subject, I asked what else he'd learned about Pop's Place.

"Well, it's obvious to me that this fire is different," said Scoop.

"How so?"

"Aside from someone dying, Jimmy isn't in financial trouble. In fact, having to shut down to make repairs will actually hurt his bottom line. Whereas Mrs. Means and that builder both needed those fires to eliminate their financial problems. Also, Pop's Place didn't fully burn. Most of the damage was contained to a small space on the second floor that had sprinklers."

"Jimmy?"

"The owner." Scoop's sigh said, *keep up*. "I can see a shady contractor hiring someone to burn his place down, and maybe even old Mrs. Means if she was desperate enough, but not Jimmy. The poor guy is really upset to have to close. He thought he'd weathered the worst of it with COVID-shutdowns and social-distancing. Now, this."

"What does your source say?"

"My source has clammed up."

I noted that he was careful not to assign gender. My theory was that with such intimate knowledge of the crimes, Scoop's *Deep Throat* had to be a firefighter, and I had a sudden thought that maybe it was Carla's brother Tony. The police would doubt that. Kip had said that first responders of any stripe had an ethical responsibility to do their jobs without sharing information. I wasn't so sure. Unless you were talking medical when their lips were sewn shut, I knew that there was often someone willing to spill at the RFD.

"Just because Jimmy from Pop's Place was financially secure, it didn't mean the building's owner was," I said.

"Actually, they are one of the most successful landlords in downtown Ridgefield. All their businesses are doing well. That looks like a dead end."

My Uncle Richard, my octogenarian neighbor Horace, and I had talked about the fires just last night, the conversation pairing nicely with a bottle of Duckhorn Cabernet and Richard's family beef stew recipe. Richard's nose could rival that of Robert Parker, the well-known wine critic.

"What's your source's motivation for helping you?"

"No comment," Scoop replied.

Once again, I mentally scrolled down the RFD roster. Not that big a department, yet you also had to consider the volunteers, who played key roles supporting the career guys. Maybe resentment was at work here.

"Give me a hint."

"Winter, I haven't even told my cats."

Scoop was like the mute button on the remote control when he didn't want to talk.

"Do you have any idea who let Chester in the building?" I asked, circling back to Pop's Place.

Scoop's silence suggested this was another dead end.

"Chester?" he finally asked.

"The victim," I confirmed.

And now it was my sigh saying *keep up* because the quiet that followed told me that Scoop was, in fact, behind on this part of the story.

Chapter Four

Some days reveal uncanny cosmic alignment, and today was one of them. As Diva and I headed home, my obnoxious ringtone blared for the third time that morning, resounding down the quiet street.

"Tell me you won the lottery and I'll forgive the hour," I greeted my Uncle Richard, the man who raised me and was like a dad.

It was nearing seven-thirty, still early enough for apologies.

"I did win the lottery," my uncle replied.

"With such a perfect niece, yeah, yeah."

"No, I actually won ten bucks in scratch-off."

"You don't play scratch-off."

My uncle was a non-believer when it came to the lottery, always saying you'd be more likely to be hit by lightning than to win.

"Exactly. Horace bet me a bottle of Old Grandad that if I bought a ticket, I'd land a winner. I told him that one in three million were not good odds, so I felt pretty sure I'd be the one with the bourbon. It feels strange to win and lose at the same time. I'm hoping Ancona's carries it by the pint."

"Ancona's carries everything," I said. "Anyway, you didn't wake me. I'm already out and about."

"Good." My uncle cleared his throat. "I'm calling because I need—"

"a favor," I finished.

"It's nothing you can't handle," he added, code for nothing I'd enjoy. "We lost our speaker for Village Voices and I need a replacement. I thought you could give a how-to on obituaries."

Village Voices was a monthly speaker series for sixty-and-over residents at Village Square, the graduated care facility in downtown Ridgefield where Richard lived. I'd covered one of their talks when I was a reporter and they drew a pretty good crowd.

"Let me think about it."

"Of course," he said. And a moment later, "So what do you think? If you leave in about an hour, you can still make it by nine."

"*Today?*"

My uncle enjoyed a combative relationship with time. His errands could last hours, his visits minutes. He planned months ahead and yet was always pushing a deadline. When I was little, he once abolished Eastern Daylight Time, wreaking havoc with punctuality.

"My plate's pretty full," I said.

"But are they paying you to eat?"

"Your gig pays?"

"Well, no, I wouldn't say that."

"What *would* you say?"

"That it's free advertising. Just think of all the ailments incubating over there. An entire community with one foot in the grave."

That was hardly an accurate assessment of the Village Voices. They were not a group of seniors who'd be snoozing through a presentation until snack time. These were highly educated, extremely social individuals, and flush with great healthcare—in short, posterchildren for an "active adult community." However, my uncle had a point. Discussing the merits of advance planning with a captive older audience was not a bad way to prospect.

I felt my mouth go dry when Richard gave me the details. I wasn't a natural at the podium. How would I keep these folks interested for an entire hour? However, saying no was not an option. Richard was the man who rode in on his white Charger to rescue our family after my father died. He was the man who raised me and had been there—still was there—throughout the major steps in my life.

"Who bailed on you?" I asked.

"A coin collector. His talk was called—and here he over-emphasized every word—SHOW ME THE MONEY. The idea was that we'd all bring our coins and he'd teach us how to pick out those of value. I have a bunch of silver dollars that I hoped might help put the twins through college."

The mention of my late sister's daughters, who were just hitting the thick of the tween stage, sent a wave of guilt through me. They lived with their father in Florida, where my mother was "Granny Nanny" and I was always overdue for a visit.

"And you think, for people of a certain age, a lesson in memorializing the dead is a good substitute for get-rich-quick tips?"

"You'll find a way to breathe some life into it."

After agreeing to meet at the clubhouse, I told Richard about my client's obituary.

"How fast can you get it fixed?" he asked.

"Not fast enough. The offices aren't open for another couple of hours and my client is on a cruise on the Mediterranean somewhere."

"Hopefully not many people will see it before then," he said.

Hoping he was right, I was about to say goodbye when Richard asked if it was okay to cook at the lake cottage tonight. Not an

Grave Words

unusual request, though I noted he had been spending more time in the over-the-garage guest suite lately.

"Sure," I said distractedly, as I again did a mental run-through of today's calendar. Despite the fact that I didn't have any other obituaries to write, and Chester's needed more research first, the next job was always only a heartbeat away. Because mine was the type of business that demanded a quick response, I carved out enough time for at least two client meetings daily—just in case. When I had no one to memorialize, I drafted obituaries for the movers and shakers in our community, much the way the New York Times and other major papers do it. During my early years as a reporter, I'd written the background for many of our local notables for the paper's morgue. In fact, that was my first taste of obit-writing.

"I'm thinking a Hungarian beef braise in the slow cooker. Maybe some homemade cornbread from Milillo Farms and one of those autumn salads with pear and walnuts . . ." Richard was warming to his menu and I put him on speaker so I could call up the calendar on my phone.

Aside from the urgent problem of getting my name removed from my client's obituary, my meeting with Carla, my marketing plans, and now, my prep for today's Village Voices event, I had research I needed to do before afternoon phone calls with a New York City CEO who was excited about the idea of having her obituary pre-written. In fact, much to Richard's dismay, I had one foot already in New York City with a number of contacts that could give my business a much-needed and dependable income boost.

The hour-plus I would give to Village Voices meant that something on my to-do list might get postponed.

"Any special reason for tonight's deck party?" I asked, absentmindedly.

Richard doesn't need an excuse for the food fests he started shortly after he moved us into the Lake Mamanasco cottage. Initially, his parties would be in celebration of some event, like my mom's acceptance into nursing school, or her graduation, or even getting my braces off. It was as if he studied the calendar and came up with every reason imaginable to invite friends and neighbors to share a meal while taking in the view of the beautiful lake. I suspected the events were less about culinary experimentation and more about making sure we had people we could depend on when he was away, especially during the early years when my uncle commuted back and forth to California.

"Just celebrating family and friends," said Richard, vaguely.

I guessed that it was my uncle's way of making sure I always knew in what direction I'd find home.

Chapter Five

Diva was now hoofing it back to the house, no doubt anticipating breakfast. When the Great Pyrenees pup came to me at three months old, I had every intention of finding her a permanent family better equipped than me to care for her. However, this little white pup, along with my Uncle Richard, my neighbor Horace, and a behemoth of a German Shepherd named Max, rescued Kip, Scoop, a young woman named Brittany, and me from a crazy woman who had murder on her mind. Richard, Horace, and I nurtured the adorable ball of fur after she was orphaned and none of us has made a move to find her any other "forever home."

The morning was crisp and the comforting scent of last night's fireplace lightings around the neighborhood filled the air. The brilliant sunshine emerging promised that this would be one of those days that made autumn so special. I was still marveling over the bear encounter and trotting to keep up with Diva when my cell phone sent a warning yet again, which at this point was about as welcoming as an incoming tornado.

I softened when I saw the caller ID.

"If you're calling for a favor, I've reached my quota for the day," I said by way of greeting.

If it weren't for Kip Michaels, I would already be splitting my time between Ridgefield and Manhattan, just an hour southwest, where there would be plenty more opportunities to expand my business. And while our relationship was slightly fragile due to what he called my fear of commitment, I wasn't ready to cut the Ridgefield cord completely.

"What? No, I was checking to see if you were still breathing," said Kip.

My voice sank. "You saw the obituary."

"How in the world did that happen?" he asked.

"I really don't know," I said.

And I didn't. My client had originally asked that I make all the submissions and I was just waiting for her to pull the trigger. What happened from there was still a mystery and I said as much.

"Winter, you aren't nosing around in anything that could make you a target, are you?"

"Stop thinking the worse. There are so many simpler ways if someone wanted to warn me off."

"You do have a tendency to . . . well, you know get overly curious about things," said Kip, and I noted his careful word choice.

"I cannot even fathom how it could have gone so wrong and I've got to call my client to find out, though I seriously don't think this is anything but a mistake. She must have submitted it incorrectly."

"Well then, she can't blame you for the error," he said.

I hoped Kip was right, although I had a sense of unease over this entire thing.

"Guess what?" I said, changing the subject. "I saw a bear."

I relived my walk with Diva and the bear sighting for Kip. Suddenly, I felt that prickly feeling you get when someone is watching you. I turned to look behind me and the large bear had stopped on the road as it travelled back toward the lake. It had paused to target wide inquisitive eyes on us.

"And now, Smokey is staring at me," I said, relieved that I was closer to my front door than to that massive beast.

"Wow, I can't beat that. I was only calling to ask if you wanted company on your walk this morning and maybe a tea afterward."

I explained about the Village Voices and my public speaking engagement.

"In about," I pulled my phone away and swiped to reveal the time ". . . oh geez, in like 45 minutes." Suddenly I was panicked that I wouldn't make it in time and as much as I wanted to hang up, dash home, and ready myself for a last words presentation, I thought of Scoop, pacing his apartment in wait of much needed answers. I also desperately needed more information on Chester.

"Listen, I do need to talk to you about a couple of things," I started, upping my pace to the house.

"I'm not talking to you about any ongoing investigations," said the guy who had an uncanny way of reading my mind.

"You can't seriously be looking at Scoop for these fires," I said. "He doesn't even believe in mouse traps!"

"Winter, I know you are more loyal than man's best friend when it comes to your buddy. *But . . .*" He emphasized the word so loud that I had to pull the phone from my ear. "Scoop knows something about the arsons that he isn't sharing with the police. Maybe you can pry it out of him, since right now, he is obstructing an investigation."

"He has a right to protect his source," I insisted.

Diva was already at the front door and looking at me like I needed some time at the gym.

"If he really has a source," said Kip. "And now that there is a fatality involved—and no I am not going to give you an ID until we notify next of kin—Scoop is on the radar of every cop in Ridgefield.

"I already know the dead person is Chester. Carla asked me to write an obituary for him."

Kip was quiet and I imagined him rubbing his hand across his brow which was his agitated tell.

Finally, he said, "I'll call you later—good luck with the Village Voices—those people will have some tough questions."

And then he was gone.

Between the rumors of my own demise and the bear stare-down, it was no wonder that I screeched when I pushed open the door of the cottage and bumped straight into another person. Before my fight or flight instinct could kick in, I realized with relief that it was only Carp. Appropriately nick-named because he could work magic when it came to anything construction, my carpenter was there to repair some of the damage Diva had inflicted in her efforts to escape the cottage when left alone. Before I learned that Diva was claustrophobic with destructive tendencies, she had chewed two windowsills and a bedroom door as she tried to find an exit.

During the few months that she had lived with me, Richard, and sometimes Horace, she added scratched doorframes and a gnawed-through staircase between the garage and the house to her list of victims. At Richard's bungalow, she destroyed the divided lights on his patio doors. The only safe haven from the torment she inflicted at the lake house was the back deck and the doors leading to it because she was also petrified of water.

Extensive repair and income as an obituary writer were not synonymous, so I convinced Carp to barter for his time. I created ads, social media posts, and press releases to help him grow his business. In exchange, he repaired canine catastrophe. Lately, we started doing reels. *Move over Babs!*

Grave Words

I doubted Carp would ever catch up to the popular social media phenomenon and "grandfluencer" Babs Costello, who once ran a nursery school in Ridgefield. It was during the pandemic that the seventy-something-year-old grandmother began doing reels. Ever the great cook, she translated her fifty years of accumulated recipes into culinary content and now *Brunch with Babs* has millions of followers. She expanded into life wisdom and now everyone's grandma offers advice on almost anything. Lately, Carp had been following her on Instagram because she posted reels on a renovation, she and Mr. Babs were doing on their future retirement home, an 1830's antique called the Basket House.

"I could do reels," Carp had insisted.

True to his word, he took to creating short videos like a kid to candy. His YouTube video on how to create a mitered corner had a thousand hits and he was becoming somewhat of a celebrity in his own right.

Initially, Carp had been skeptical about our arrangement and balked that my fees should mirror his. He was an artisan who could put the house back better than its original design. To prove my point, I pitted his eight-hour day against mine. In the end, while Carp was creating more sawdust as he beautified my house, I was putting him on the carpentry map. Two months in, with so many customers that he had a wait list, he and I came to an agreement that no longer required I prove my worth.

"We have to stop meeting like this," Carp flashed me his lopsided grin.

Anyone observing might think Carp has a crush on me. In truth, he only has eyes for Carla.

Carp's shoulder-length wheat-colored hair was pulled into a ponytail today. He normally wears a uniform of cargo pants and depending on the weather, a Grateful Dead tee shirt, or a flannel with probably the same tee underneath. Because he runs hot, today's sunshine left him bare-armed.

"I didn't realize you were coming . . ." I started to say and then stopped short. "What is that?"

Carp looked proudly down at the tattoo I was pointing to on his forearm.

"Just something I have been planning for a while." He smiled shyly.

"You didn't," I said, thinking about Carla's latest, a small hummingbird so artfully done that you'd swear it was hovering as it flapped its wings at hyper speed.

He shrugged and laughed.

"You don't think that's a bit . . . I don't know . . . invasive?" I asked.

Or creepy, I added to myself, because I was staring at a replica of Carla's tattoo.

"She'll never see it." His shoulders drooped. "She doesn't see me, why would she notice this?"

"Good grief, stop. Ask the girl on a date—and please keep that tattoo hidden when you do."

"Dead woman talking."

I shook my head. Not a conversation I wanted to have with Carp or anyone else today unless they were the person or persons who could make sure my client's obituary was corrected both online and in print.

Instead, I asked a favor and Carp agreed to keep Diva entertained until it was time for her to go next door to stay with Horace. My neighbor and his dog, Max, live in a ramshackle cottage that has seen more weather than repair. Carp was always looking for opportunities to give Horace a rundown of how much the cottage would be worth if improvements were made.

Grave Words

Horace would raise his bushy white brows and send a wink my way as he indulged him, feigning interest. In the end, Horace will live out his days surrounded by his ancient Formica countertops, linoleum floors, and peace-inducing views of the lake he loved.

"Where's Max?" asked Carp, suddenly wary. He was unnerved by the huge German Shepherd that was also rescued and now lived with Horace full-time. Max was a marshmallow, though we'd never convince Carp of that.

"He's with Horace, so maybe just stay over here today," I said, thinking how happy Horace would be not to have to tell Carp yet again that he liked things the way they were.

Chapter Six

The drive to Village Square is less than fifteen minutes from my house on the lake. Snaking through back roads until I landed at the intersection of Catoonah and Main wasn't the most direct route, though at this hour, it avoided some of the intersections that would be backed up with heavy traffic. If there was one thing that all Ridgefielders seemed to agree upon, it was the complaint that the traffic had gotten so bad that it now took longer to get from one end of town to the other than it did to travel to our neighboring city of Danbury. As I crossed onto Bailey Avenue, my gaze lingered on Tazza, where I longed for a cup of chamomile and a shortbread cookie. Not today. Despite his own tendency to be late, my uncle was the kind of guy who wanted everything in its place, including his speaker, well before the event.

Just as I reached the horseshoe-shaped complex with charming bungalows arcing around a clubhouse, my cell phone rang. My long-suffering Subaru was already a relic when hands-free became a vehicle staple, so I hurriedly slid into one of the vacant parking spaces and fished the offending sound from my bag.

"Hello?" I said in question because I hadn't looked at the caller ID.

"It's me, Amanda, on the obit desk—you called?"

Thank goodness. Now I could get this obituary error fixed and move on. I explained my problem, which apparently, she already knew about from my barrage of emails, phone calls, and texts.

I did a time check. 8:45. *Please make this a quick fix*, I thought, imagining Richard wearing down the hardwood floors of the clubhouse as he paced in wait.

"Listen, Winter, we've done business in the past," she started.

"Lots of business," I agreed.

"There won't be any charges for the changes and there's no problem fixing the digital copy. Just send me what you want it to say and I'll make sure it's corrected within the hour. The print copy for tomorrow's paper is another problem. Our deadline for these types of submissions is Tuesday at noon and quite frankly, I don't know that I can fix it—these days everything is electronically laid out and we don't have editing capability here."

"Hold on," I said, struggling to keep my voice neutral. "Are you saying that despite the fact that you've made an error, and the paper won't even come out until tomorrow, you can't make the correction?"

"We did send the proof to you and you didn't let us know there were errors." Her tone had turned icy.

"I didn't submit the obituary," I said. "Can you tell me who did?"

I heard some clicking, and then she said, "The form has your name on it."

I explained to Amanda that it must have been my client who submitted it.

"She obviously erred somehow but so did you. Who put my name in the obituary? And how in the world does that photo look like someone who is six years old, let alone a hundred and six? The copy doesn't even make sense. It's as if someone hit control-F and *replace all* instead of actually reading it."

I was guessing that the person who made all those errors was on the other end of the phone because her voice became a lecture, leaving no room for debate. "The time to make changes was when you or your client received the proof. It's too late now. Next time, you might consider giving your clients more information on how to submit properly."

Amanda had a point—but that was, well, beside the point.

"With a weekly paper circulating for another six days, I think my family and friends will have some very unsettling moments," I said. *Not to mention my potential clients who will disappear faster than socks in a dryer.*

"I'm sorry," she said, sounding anything but. "We could print the accurate obituary in our daily paper covering all neighboring towns because the readerships overlap. Of course, we'd make the correction the following Thursday in the local weekly."

"Unacceptable," I snapped.

"Next time, try to be more attentive to your job, Ms. Snow," said the suddenly very snooty Amanda. "I'll do what I can but you should not expect us to honor your request to bypass our very specific procedures."

And then, she hung up.

Unbelievable. I felt the steam rising, which always made my freckles erupt like a bad case of hives. With no more time to think about how this all happened, I hurried to the front door of the clubhouse which had already been flung open by my foot-tapping uncle.

"Hurry, everyone is already here." Richard grabbed my elbow and ushered me through an open common space where a number of residents sat in easy chairs reading newspapers, studying phones, or sipping from mugs in small groups.

Waving as he rushed me past his fellow Village Square neighbors, my uncle escorted me toward double doors opening to a meeting room beyond. There, about thirty members of the Village Voices sat chatting while they awaited my arrival. Trying to smile, I gripped the talking points I had hastily scrawled and practiced in the car on my way over.

As I waved to a couple of familiar residents, I inwardly groaned when I noticed that two seats were occupied by none other than the Nosy Parkers, the biggest gossips in the town of Ridgefield. If you want misinformation to spread faster than a runaway train, they were your vehicle. Their arms fluttered in aggressive waves, like students anxious to be called upon. I nodded at them as I followed Richard to the front of the room.

After Richard's introduction, there were a few grumbles from fortune-seekers who had hoped to be shown the money, so I kicked off my spiel by reading some funny obituaries I had found on the internet. That lightened the mood a bit and I spoke for twenty minutes about how obituaries have become a historical record and a source for genealogists. I talked about having fun with a loved one's tribute so that it represented the personality of the deceased.

"And by the way, it is *not okay* to lie about your age in your obit!" That got a few laughs.

I stressed the importance of accuracy, of making sure names are correctly spelled and facts are not just lore passed down over the years.

Suddenly, a bunch of hands flew up and I was sure I knew what was coming.

Abby Parker jumped from her seat, confirming my dread. "The obituary posted this morning with Winter Snow across the top didn't exactly have 'accuracy' written all over it."

Abby was a tiny woman, and even standing, barely a head taller than her seated neighbors, her size didn't stop the trumpet of her message.

Here we go, I thought. Abby and her sister, Gabby, were obviously looking for their next pot to stir. A murmur went through the room as cell phones and tablets materialized.

Winter Snow, predeceased by her own obituary, died of humiliation!

'Look here," said a gentleman, holding an iPad with the site called up. He showed it around the way a teacher might display a picture book to his class.

An unmerciful medley followed:

"God that's awful."

"So much fake news these days."

"Imagine how the family feels."

My presentation was spiraling out of control. When I glanced at Richard to see how he was taking it, he was hunched over a tablet his seatmate had thrust in front of him. My face felt on fire and I could only imagine the field day my freckles were having. Finally, I held up one hand for silence and reached out with the other hand for the iPad the man was sharing.

Stretching my fingers, I enlarged the photo and held it up for all to see.

"This is a perfect example of what can go wrong if you aren't careful." And I explained that I had written the obituary and I was guessing that my grief-worn client had accidentally submitted it incorrectly.

"Whatever happened with this submission, it's like the domino effect," I said. "Someone on the obituary desk was snoozing when they dropped in the headline and it was all downhill from there. One error created another and another until in the end, *this* was the outcome."

I enlarged the dates showing the years.

"Typos are easy mistakes to make," I said, going on to explain about the confusing online submission form. My theory was that where it asks for client name, my name had been added with the thought that I'd be the contact person.

"Whoever was checking the facts took my name and wove it into the copy. The photo is from my web site so I'm not even sure how that would have happened."

Mostly conjecture, of course, and I was anxious to reach my client to see what really occurred.

I called up Legacy.com on the tablet and showed the group how my name was now embodied on that site as well.

"Can't it be fixed?" asked the man whose tablet I had borrowed.

"Yes and no," I said, and told them how the online version would be corrected within an hour but tomorrow's print edition was more challenging due to the way the newspaper had simultaneously consolidated and outsourced.

We had a pretty lively discussion after that about the disheartening state of news media and all the things that can go wrong, even for the professionals. Maybe I should thank Amanda for providing enough conversation to fill the hour.

"For me, this was a learning experience," I said. "Going forward, I will insist that I do the submissions. A grieving family doesn't need the extra burden of navigating paperwork."

I then talked about writing your own obituary versus having one written for you or your loved one and was even able to work in the idea of writing a Living Legacy or life story.

We were about to wrap up when Abby sent the conversation in another uncomfortable direction.

"Aren't you worried that AI is going to put you out of business?" she asked.

Me and every other writer, I thought.

"I'm more worried there will be no one left to read obituaries, let alone write them," I replied. "Seriously though, AI can be a great organizing tool and can speed along the drafting process. It won't give you original ideas, though. It will only regurgitate what already exists. Writing an obituary isn't just about recording facts. It's also about connecting with people and using your creativity to capture the personality of the deceased. AI can't do that."

At least not yet.

A moment later, refreshments rescued me from having to defend my profession any longer. Everyone moved in the direction of the baskets of bagels, spreads, and fruit provided by Fletch's, a popular breakfast and lunch café in town. I planned to stay fifteen minutes and then slip away.

"My wife is insistent that we write her obituary together," said a tall silver-haired man who had pushed his way through the crowd to speak to me. His name tag read Hendrick Herman. "I'm just worried we won't be able to do it right."

Hendrick, who preferred to be called Henny, said that his wife was terminal and had been putting her affairs in order. This was the last thing on her to do list, he said, making air quotes.

"She sounds amazing," I said, thinking that few people would be so pragmatic when faced with their last days.

"She likes to be in control," he said, with a small laugh. "She wants everything to be perfect . . . we've got the flowers picked, the after-reception planned. She even wrote a farewell letter to all our friends. Thank goodness we don't have children. She would have written a novel to them if we had."

I smiled at Henny and pointed to the form he held which I had passed out to everyone.

"This will be a good springboard for any obituary." I tapped my finger on the bottom of the page. "It helps to note the next of kin when you have your head on straight—it's so easy to leave someone out when you are in the throes of grieving."

I thought about the snub a recent client had made when she left out the name of one of her relatives. Move over Hatfields and McCoys because intentional or not, that was the stuff that added fuel to the feud fire.

I also pointed out that choosing a charity ahead of time was something people often overlooked when planning for the end of life. However, it was important because the causes we choose to care about reflect who we are.

"Don't be surprised if we call you," said Henny. "Neither of us are good writers and we tried that AI thing. It was like you said, an emotional void."

I had finally reached the door and was about to leave when Gabby Parker grabbed my arm. Unlike her slight sister, she exuded grandmotherly warmth.

"You heard about Chester," she said, somewhere between statement and question.

"So sad," I replied.

"Your buddy Scoop is holding back information." Gabby glanced around to see who might be within earshot. Was she actually hoping someone might be close enough to pick up her accusation? "He was the last one to see Chester alive, you know."

Could this be true? And if so, why wouldn't Scoop have mentioned it? Was this the reason the police thought of him as a person of interest?

I tried to make my face a mask of indifference, though that was hard to do because I've been told that I wear my heart on my sleeve.

"Definitely guilty then," I said, my sarcasm surprising Gabby enough for me to push past with a farewell salute.

Fully conscious that the Nosy Parkers were assessing my every move, I fought the urge to run from the room. Instead, I waved to the Village Voices with a great big "thank you" and edged to the door. When I turned to take one last look, people were clustered together in conversation, enjoying a cup of joe and the spread of snacks. Village Square was the kind of place that gave off an energetic vibe and it wasn't the first time I felt grateful that my uncle had found such a community to call home.

And then, I noticed the downside of Village Square. Sitting aside from everyone else were Abby and Gabby, heads together in earnest conversation and I knew without a doubt the Nosy Parkers had some juicy tidbit they were chewing over. And they were getting ready to go viral.

Chapter Seven

Back outside, I shot Kip a text: *Still have time for a walk?* Three dancing dots materialized into a message saying he would meet me in front of the Lounsbury House in fifteen minutes. That gave me just enough time to leave my car at my uncle's bungalow and walk down to the stately Main Street mansion.

Built in 1896, the grand home was originally owned by Phineas C. Lounsbury, a former governor of Connecticut. The two-story classic revival, with its large wrap porch and imposing columns, was now owned by the Town of Ridgefield and operates as a non-profit venue for events. I recalled the wedding photo of my parents posing at the top of the grand center staircase. They looked so young and innocent, it made me sad to think that just sixteen years later, that world would shatter when my father's car crashed into a cement divider on Interstate 84.

Shaking off the memory, I headed to the Veterans Memorial Garden where Kip waited, slouched over his phone. I felt like a voyeur as I took him in. His wavy dark hair, in need of a trim by police standards, suited my taste. I liked the way his curls fringed around the collar of the fleece he wore which was as bold as Syracuse University orange. The color was fitting for the fall and looked great with his jeans—no police uniform today. And then, as if feeling my eyes on him, he lifted a steely gaze my way.

"Hey, is everything OK?" I asked, as I reached him.

Guessing from Kip's brow rub, he was wrestling with something.

"All this stuff about Chester—you said you heard, right?" He asked, doing a final swipe at his phone before pocketing it.

"The entire town has heard about Chester." At least that was my assumption given that the Nosy Parkers were already spreading their version of the news.

Kip blew out a breath and said, "Let's walk."

We headed up Main Street in silence. Over the past few months since we had been dating, we had developed a cadence and if the two of us were quiet, it was usually companionable. Not today.

"What's wrong?" I asked again.

Kip shrugged. "Just a lot going on and don't ask because—"

"I know, I know. You're not at liberty to say."

"Right—so tell me about the bear." He and Uncle Richard were masters of deflecting when there was something they didn't want to talk about.

I sighed and recounted the sighting. It used to be that seeing a bear in Ridgefield was unusual, though lately, as Kip explained, the black bear population seemed to have exploded—there are sightings everywhere. And apparently, people either posted on social media or called the police department.

"They really don't bother people, although they can be pests when it comes to bird feeders and garbage cans," he said. "Still, it's probably a good idea to carry bear spray. The dogs could make them nervous."

"Good to know." I was trying to feign interest when all I really wanted to do was to find a way to steer the conversation back to Chester and Scoop.

Grave Words

"I know you can't talk about the case," I finally said. "But can you at least give me Chester's last name?"

Kip stiffened, ready for the battle he was afraid I was about to wage.

"Why?" he asked.

"I already told you. I'm writing his obit and I need to find out a little more about him."

We had reached the Keeler Tavern where some sort of elaborate event preparation was underway. A large white tent with a divided light effect in the plastic windows made it look inviting, although I couldn't imagine enjoying an evening sharing my space with the noisy blower that I assumed was puffing warm air into the space.

Originally built in the late 18th century, the antique was rich with history—it was an inn during the Revolutionary War and bears the scar of a British cannonball embedded in its side. It was once home to architect Cass Gilbert who gave the town its iconic fountain that sits diagonally opposite the tavern. Now, it's a museum. Like the Lounsbury House, it is also listed on the National Register of Historic Places.

"Earth to Winter," said Kip, pulling me back from my musings. "Don't write anything yet."

It sounded like an order.

"Why not? Carla asked me to put something together—we even have a nice photo of him admiring the refurbished clock."

"It's nice to see that clock telling time more than twice a day," he said with a laugh.

That had been the social media joke when a viral SAVE THE TOWN CLOCK campaign had gotten enough traction to make fixing it a priority. Not that town fathers hadn't previously tried, though some residents thought of it as just an old and tired street clock and were unaware of its historical significance. Presented in 1958 by the American Women's Voluntary Service, it serves as a constant reminder of the wartime home-front efforts these women engaged in during World War II. Ultimately, someone knew someone who knew how to revive the ticker, and, for the moment at least, it told time.

"Nice try," I said, acknowledging Kip's stalling technique. "If you don't help me, I'll have to find out another way."

"You're going to have to trust me on this." Kip paused our walk to look directly into my eyes. "The obituary will have to wait."

"For how long?"

"I'm not sure."

We resumed our walk, taking in the beautiful houses past the fountain. We crossed to the other side of Main right before reaching the blinking light. We then reversed our direction. The canopy of trees left a layer of newly fallen leaves and we crunched along, stirring them so they caught in the light breeze.

"I have something else to ask you," I said. Noticing his body language I added, "You don't need armor—it's a simple question. Gabby Parker told me that Scoop was the last one to see Chester alive. Is that why he is a person of interest?"

Kip's scowl deepened. "Who told you he was a person of interest?"

"Scoop told me."

"You know, he is his own worst enemy."

"What does that mean?"

"I'm sorry Winter, I just can't talk about this."

I let the distance between us grow.

"Your eyes are like lasers when you're mad." He was being playful, though I knew it was his weak attempt to avoid the incoming missile.

I stared back into cloud-gray eyes that were pleading with me to understand.

Grave Words

"I am mad," I said, my fury and frustration balling my fists. "You are asking me not to do my job and yet you are not giving me any reasons why I shouldn't, besides that I should trust you. Why is it that you aren't trusting me?"

"I'm sorry. I want to tell you but—"

"If you tell me, you'll have to kill me, right?" I retorted.

"No Winter," he said. "If I tell you, someone else might kill you."

Chapter Eight

"What's to prevent anyone from thinking you haven't already told me?" I snapped back. "I mean here we are walking and talking."

Kip did a quick recognizance. The way his body went rigid and his head turned assessing, made me shiver. The expression *someone just walked over my grave* popped into my head.

The house we paused in front of was non-threatening with its round wrapped porch loaded with a garden of burgundy, orange, and yellow mums. Pumpkins were woven into the mix, reminding me that Halloween was just around the corner.

"Kip," I said, trying to get back on track. "The cops aren't really looking at Scoop as a suspect in these arsons, are they?"

Kip ignored my question.

"Do me a favor. Tell your buddy Scoop to start cooperating. This isn't a joke and he isn't some big city reporter sitting on the Watergate of his career."

I flinched. What had happened to the quiet, kind, albeit moody, Kip Michaels?

"It doesn't matter whether you are writing about national breaking news or local arsons, a reporter has a right to protect his sources," I said, trying to keep my voice calm.

Kip put his arms on my shoulders and as always, I mellowed at his touch. I reached out to gently slide my hand over the jaw he had clenched so tight, I thought he might crack a tooth.

A loud blast of a horn broke the moment and we both jumped apart as a car filled with teens blasted its way up Main Street.

"Get a room," shouted one of the kids.

"Shouldn't they be in school?" muttered Kip.

A heavy-set man and his King Charles Spaniel, also carrying a few extra pounds, smiled our way as they lumbered past.

"Kids," he laughed.

I nodded my agreement as Kip took my hand and we resumed walking.

"Winter," he said, softly. "Please listen to me when I tell you that there is a lot more to this story than you or Scoop know."

"I'm getting that. What I'm not getting is why you can't at least tell us the reasoning behind the secrecy. We're up to what, three arsons and one dead body? You have to have something to say to the public. Scoop can help."

Kip nodded. "I know that. But I can't tell you the whole story right now because this is an ongoing investigation and trust me when I say, even half a story might paint a target on his back. The same way writing Chester's obituary might place you in danger. Heck, when I saw your obituary online this morning, my first thought was that someone was already after you."

"Trust me, I have not been snooping around, if that's what you're getting at," I said, with an uneasy laugh.

Had someone intentionally been pranking me? It was close to Halloween. Maybe a ghoulish attempt at humor? More likely, it was my client's error.

"With most people, sharing a little info would be fine. Though I know you, Winter. You'll start digging and interfering and suddenly you'll be in the thick of it."

I couldn't argue there. I was heavily endowed with the curiosity gene and I was not going to apologize for it either.

We walked back to the town center and wove through inviting outdoor tables at the Lantern restaurant that were brimming with patrons. The unexpectedly warm autumn day brought sun-worshipers out in droves, no doubt soaking up as much vitamin D as possible before the long cold winter set in. Kip asked me if I wanted to stop to eat. When I said I had a lot of work, he suggested we get together later.

"Richard said something about cooking out at the cottage tonight. He wants to take advantage of these last gorgeous fall days. I'm not sure what he is making or who he is inviting . . ." I let that trail because now that I thought about it, Richard had been unusually vague about his plans.

Kip knew Richard's impromptu neighborhood gatherings well and said he'd check in with my uncle to see what he could bring.

"Winter," he called after me as we parted. "Promise me that you won't go digging."

I crossed my fingers on one hand and waved with the other.

* * *

The town clock said it was close to noon—a little earlier than I had planned to meet with Carla. I decided instead to walk back to Village Square, retrieve my satchel which I had left in Richard's bungalow for safekeeping, and then drive over. The day turned out to be much warmer than I expected and the black jeans and wool sweater I wore under my lightweight puff jacket, were making me sweat. I shed a layer and hoofed it back up the hill, past the old high school, as most of us townies still called the large brick Richard E. Venus Building, where Chefs' Warehouse has their headquarters, and down toward Village Square. Richard's car was gone and I suspected he was shopping for food, if not already cooking at my cottage on the lake.

The funeral home door was unlocked and feeling a little like a trespasser, I entered the cool quiet space. The large foyer, well designed to accommodate long lines of mourners when necessary, was empty. As always, when I was in this building, memories of my father's funeral sent a chill of longing and sadness through me. I shook it off and went in search of Carla.

My friend was in her office hunched over a pile of paperwork and oblivious to my arrival. The light from the window cast a ghoulish glare as it settled on her black polished nails. When I cleared my throat, she jumped and gasped.

"Oh my God, Winter, you scared me."

"Sorry," I said.

I wondered if maybe Carla got a little creeped out sharing her workspace with the ghosts of so many who had passed. I had no idea if the funeral home was reputed to be haunted, though one of the nearby buildings had an impressive number of reports of an old woman in her rocker over the years.

"I've got something for you," Carla said, with satisfaction, as she pushed the papers aside and pulled up a post-it note. "Arthur Willings, in his fifties, just passed. A woman I assume was his wife, asked for help with an obituary. I told her what we would do for her, and she wanted something more detailed, so I recommended you."

Thank goodness for Carla. I have the utmost respect for her almost daily dealings with the bereaved. Arranging services and picking caskets was not a job I could do with the kind of compassion

...arla, survivor of many things, did so well. And I understood recommending my services was something she did because she ...ieved I could offer some solace to the grieving. I was grateful that . lived up to her standards.

"Great news," I said, and then winced at the inappropriateness of my upbeat response.

"Death and taxes." Carla repeated the same mantra whenever either of us felt guilty about being happy for more business. While neither of us wished for more people to die, she liked to remind me regularly that it was an inevitable part of life. If we weren't the ones doing the job, our services would be performed by someone else, possibly someone less sympathetic.

When my dad died, I remember how caring and respectful the people at the funeral home had been. While there is little comfort to a ten-year-old girl who is suddenly fatherless, they made sure every detail was attended to with a sensitivity I will never forget.

As for writing about a loved one, I tried to approach it with the same respect and compassion that I was shown. According to my uncle, my own losses made me more empathetic, though I could recall from a very young age trying to look at the world through other people's eyes. And it never ceased to surprise me how important the final words affected a family. Gallows humor was fine as a private coping mechanism, but never on the job.

Carla cleared her throat and interrupted my thoughts. "Mrs. Willings is expecting your call. I'm hoping you can get back to her today."

I slipped the paper into my satchel and asked if there was anything new on Chester.

"I was about to ask you the same thing."

I recounted my conversation with Kip, emphasizing his warning that it would be dangerous for me to know any more details at this point.

"Strange," she said with a frown. "Listen, the obit can wait a few days—Chester still has to spend time in Farmington to confirm his cause of death."

Carla was referring to the state's Office of the Chief Medical Examiner which occupies a 30,000 square-foot mortuary, laboratory, and administrative facility at the University of Connecticut Health Center Campus about an hour away. It was protocol for all violent, suspicious, and sudden unexpected deaths to be certified there. Chester certainly fell into that category.

Carla reached for a pack of sugarless gum on the desk and held it out like an offering.

"No thanks," I said, as she unpeeled a stick. "What happened to your bubble gum?"

She groaned and popped a piece of gum into her mouth. "Trying to cut back on sugar. I'm getting a bit too curvy." She chewed and snapped her gum before adding, "Let's give Chester a day or two before you write it up. Maybe by then, we'll have info on the services. And, if we still don't have anything, maybe you could just do a nice little thing with his first name and the photo."

I mentally debated the pros and cons of writing an obituary without a last name and came up with mostly negatives. Even the hermitess cave dweller, Sarah Bishop, had a surname. Not for the first time, I thought about the unpredictability of life—so many stories swirled around the woman. Regardless of whether she had been widowed by her captain lost at sea or kidnapped and escaped British privateers, she lived on West Mountain until she died.

While most lore falls victim to exaggeration, and stories morph into elaborate variations of the truth over time, there is actually documentation that Sarah Bishop had existed. Townsfolk would want to know what happened to Chester, who he was, and how he got here. If I didn't write it, there would be no accurate record for the future, and that bothered me. As I told everyone at Village Voices, obituaries are no longer just death notices. They are historical documents living on the internet in perpetuity. They are the stuff genealogy buffs depend upon.

"Any luck at getting me off Legacy.com?" I asked.

"No prob—just got it done a short time ago," said Carla, snapping away at her gum. "It will take a little time before the history gets buried in Google. No worries about the obituary itself though. On another note, I had to resort to calling PD to see if I could get more on Chester and no luck there. You'd think Chester was the spy that came in from the cold."

"What if it wasn't Chester and someone just assumed it was, because the guy was crashing in one of the offices above Pop's Place?" That question gave Carla pause.

"I suppose that could happen," she said slowly. "Though my brother said they were sure it was him."

"Any cause of death?" I asked. "Because if Pop's Place had minimal damage, what would he have died from?"

I guessed that Chester had been somewhere in his fifties. He looked fit, never had that lingering stale after-stench of a drinker or pothead, and despite his lack of home, he was always clean. In fact, if you met him on the street, you'd think he was just one of the many other Ridgefielders who were either stay-at-home dads or working remotely.

"Good question," said Carla. "I guess the autopsy will tell."

* * *

Back at the cottage, the kitchen looked like a restaurant prep station with cutting boards laid out and pots and pans lined at the ready. Richard and Horace sat at the kitchen table with their heads together, plotting some scheme I probably didn't want to know about. Diva and Max carried their rawhide bones to me with happily wagging tails. I gave them each a pet and they retreated to their corners to chew.

"What's up?" I asked as I headed to the cooktop and turned the kettle on to boil water for tea.

I opened my well-stocked tea caddy and selected my favorite—chamomile with lavender. I then pulled a mug from the cabinet—this one with photos of my twin nieces—a gift for my birthday last April. Recent photos on social media showed the tweens looking more mature than the little girls on the mug and I didn't think their upcoming Christmas visit could come soon enough.

The whistle on the kettle blew and as I turned to remove it from the burner, I realized that both Richard and Horace had stopped talking and were staring at me. The dogs paused in their bone ecstasy to do the same.

"What?" I asked, eyeing them suspiciously as I poured.

"Nothing," said Richard. "We were just talking about Scoop's problem."

I slid into the seat next to my uncle and gazed out at the lake. This was one of the many unusually warm "pinch me" days in October—so vibrant with color it made me want to sit on the deck and bask in the sunshine. Despite today's warm temperature tease, by five o'clock, we were headed for what I called fireplace nights announcing that the days were getting shorter and colder.

It was still early afternoon and the lake rippled in the light breeze. It was hard to believe the bucolic scene could ever spell trouble, though I could think of a lot of mischief that kids had gotten into over the years, starting with the leap into the lake we all made from the Cliffs, a thirty-foot wall of rock on the opposite shore that has tempted teens for generations. How I made it to the age of 29 is still sometimes a mystery.

"Scoop's problem . . ." I began, as I dunked my tea bag, "is that he hasn't found a way to give the police the information they need without revealing how he got it."

"You know dipping that tea bag up and down like a bobbing Texas oil drill won't make the tea steep any faster," Horace observed. "I'll bet you're one of those who hits the elevator button repeatedly, as if that would make it get there sooner."

I inwardly smiled. My octogenarian neighbor was keenly observant.

"Guilty," I said, as I continued my ritual. "This giving up a source problem is age-old. Damned if you do and damned if you don't."

"Did you talk to Kip at all?" asked Richard.

"He said he couldn't tell me anything because it might get me killed."

"What?" Richard scraped back his chair and both Diva and Max left their spots to hover closer.

I signaled *stop*. "I'm sure he was kidding. All I asked for was Chester's last name so I could do a decent job with his obituary."

Richard ran a hand through the silver streaks of his once blonde hair and looked at me skeptically. Nicknames like Slugger had long ago stopped sticking, as he hung up his sports equipment to pursue a scientific career, first for the government and now at Western Connecticut State University in neighboring Danbury.

"And I asked why they were coming down so hard on Scoop," I admitted.

You couldn't get much by Richard, that I learned as a teen when my sister and I pretended we were going to a friend's house rather than to the alcohol infused party being held at the Cliffs. We were gleeful in our subterfuge until, to our horror, Richard showed up. I glanced across the lake at the steep rock face as the memory surfaced. Richard had sat down next to my sister Summer, dangled his legs over the rock ledge, and told us that if we were going to jump, so was he. None of us took the leap, at least not that night.

"Are you sure Kip was kidding?" asked Richard. "Because there's something sinister surrounding Chester's death."

"Well, of course there's something sinister. Someone started a fire and the poor man died," I replied.

Horace and Richard exchanged glances.

"Spill," I said.

"You know your uncle has connections with folks all over town, right?" asked Horace.

I nodded and sipped. Richard played bridge with the Fire Chief. He was part of the Community Emergency Response Team, always helping with damage assessment and distributions when there were extended power outages or other town emergencies. And, he was recently elected to serve on the Police Commission. When he wasn't teaching classes at Westconn or experimenting with recipes, my uncle was a busy and well-connected man.

"Chester was murdered," Richard interrupted before Horace could get to the punchline.

"Why do you say that?"

I had already surmised that it wasn't the fire that killed Chester because very little had been burned. I thought it might possibly be smoke inhalation, though more likely, he might have had a stroke or heart attack.

"My source says that he took a very heavy-duty whack to the back of the head," Richard replied.

I didn't bother to ask who his source was. Richard and Scoop were cut from the same cloth when it came to keeping people in confidence.

"Who would want to kill Chester?" I asked.

Maybe, Kip hadn't been kidding when he said, if he told me what he knew, someone else might try to kill me. My stomach lurched.

What would keep someone from killing Kip if they found out what he knew.

"That's the question, isn't it?" asked Horace.

The dogs had finally returned to their corners. Oddly, I noted that they had changed places and each was now chewing on the other's bone.

"The grass always looks greener somewhere else," Horace said, chuckling. Richard stole a look at me. Was that another one of their not-so-subtle suggestions that moving even part-time to New York City was a bad idea?

"Could we get back to Chester?" I asked.

Richard got up from the table and went to the countertop where a slow-cooker meal of Hungarian beef braise simmered.

"I thought I'd serve this until I realized we have too many people for a sit-down—we're going to need a different kind of meal."

"What about pizza?" asked Horace. "Everyone loves pizza."

"Homemade?" asked Richard, striding over to yank open the refrigerator to take stock. With Richard around, the refrigerator always bulged with fresh fruits, vegetables, cheeses, and anything else he thought I might grab to eat, even if on the run. Same was true with the wine cooler. No-one on my budget could routinely enjoy the offerings he provided me—Matanzas Creek, Rombauer, Flowers. He'd pretty much spoiled me for a night out at one of the local bars.

"I'll run downtown and get some of those premade crusts—we'll have some choices—margherita, vegetable, pepperoni . . ."

"We can do halves—half mushroom, half veggies—I'll chop," said Horace, warming to the menu. "Pepperoni doesn't agree with this old constitution, but the young folks like it—just keep it away from the margherita."

I slammed the palm of my hand down on the table so loudly the dogs immediately leapt to their feet and studied me in anticipation.

"Enough about the food. What about the murder?"

Richard shook his head. "That's all I know."

Why did I not believe that?

"I'll buy the dessert," said Horace, as if he hadn't heard anything I'd just said. "Maybe the mini cupcakes from The Cake Box? Those gluten free ones taste fabulous—not to mention the brownies."

The two of them could be so exasperating at times.

"Who's coming tonight?" I sighed, giving up the fight.

"A few of your neighbors and a few of mine," said Richard.

I stared at both suspiciously and suddenly, they were retreating, eyes averted toward the lake as if it held the answer to everything.

"Tell me you did not invite the Nosy Parkers." I wasn't in the mood to deal with them twice in one day.

"Gabby and Abby Parker know more about what is going on in this town than the First Selectperson," Richard said, finally meeting my eyes. "Do not underestimate the gossip queens."

And then, I got it. Inviting the Nosy Parkers was for me, probably Scoop, and Kip. While the gossip ladies might embellish the stories they told, their narrative usually held a kernel of truth. And it was that truth, if you were able to find it, that could lead you to your next steps.

"Is that what this food fest is all about? A fact-finding mission? You think maybe someone knows something about Chester or the arsons?" I asked.

"If anyone knows anything, it will be Gabby and Abby," said Richard.

I stared at my uncle. His bright blue eyes, the same eyes that my mother, his sister had, shone with . . . was that pride?

Horace laughed. "I told you Richard, she doesn't miss much."

Richard laughed too. "It took ten full minutes for her to figure it out."

"Hey guys, I'm right here. You mean you were timing me? For what?"

"To see how long it would take you to put two and two together," said Horace.

"There was no two and two—just a lot of nonsense," I said shaking my head and yet I had to smile.

This entire impromptu foody event was to help Scoop get out of his bind and now me, to get my work done.

"You two work in mischievous ways," I said, getting up to go to the small study at the front of the house to make my phone calls.

"You mean mysterious," said my uncle.

"No, I mean mischievous!"

Chapter Nine

Richard and Horace had gone all out for their fall fest. Soft white lights were strung from makeshift poles around the deck, reflecting festively off the water. It felt like that party you always wanted to be invited to. We lucked out because the unusually warm week meant less evening chill. Just in case, warming towers had been placed strategically around the deck. The massive doors that folded into each other from the living room were wide open and the gas fireplace was set on high. Aside from the downstairs powder room, the rest of the house was closed to guests, thereby containing the party and keeping the indoor space limited enough to stay warm despite the open doors.

I always say I'd like to attend my own party without all the work. In this case, I had done none of the preparation because I spent the afternoon lining up appointments and beginning a draft of Chester's obituary. I also checked back in with the newspaper for any updates on tomorrow's printed edition. I was still holding out hope that somehow, I would not be listed as dead for a week until a correction could be printed. Amanda's voice mail promised a call back tomorrow.

Putting my worries aside, I felt like a teen getting ready for the prom, as I slipped into a royal blue sweater that was a favorite of Kip's because he liked how it brought out the color in my eyes. I had invested in a new pair of black jeans with flared bottoms, something my mother might have worn when bell bottoms made a resurgence in the eighties and nineties. I added ankle boots, fitting for the season. I even broke down and put on eyeliner, mascara, and lipstick. I shrugged off the thought that I was going to an awful lot of trouble for a guy who kept disappointing me.

The sound of water lapping at the deck was becoming drowned out by the murmur of guests and Richard's playlist—the Beatles wanting to hold my hand. Richard was a huge fan of the group, especially their earlier songs, because he claimed they influenced the music and culture that shaped his life.

"Just get your work over with and then have some fun," instructed Horace, who was leaning in the open doorway and scanning the crowd when I arrived. "They're in the far-left corner talking to your uncle."

The spoiler for the night would be trying to figure out if Abby and Gabby Parker had anything useful to offer. It would be a complicated dance, with me hoping for snippets of truth while they tried to elicit something useful for the rumor mill.

My uncle's neighbors were drama junkies and since they lived rather sedate lives, they stirred the pot by embellishing the stories they heard. Campaign season was a harvest ripe for the pickings for those two.

Horace was right, though. If I wanted to enjoy what was no doubt our last outdoor gathering until spring, talking with them sooner rather than later would be best.

I hesitated a moment as I watched Abby's long fingers waving in a wild attempt to explain something. Gabby enthusiastically observed, her head nodding in agreement like a bobblehead doll. Every now and then, she rescued her sister's hand from waving too close to Richard's face. I squeezed by my lake neighbors with a hello, and wove my way toward the comical scene.

"We were just talking about you," said Gabby, standing in shadow, her whisper striking a sinister tone.

Here we go, I thought. "Good or bad?"

I spotted Carp across the deck helping himself to pizza while talking to a young couple who had recently moved down the street. No doubt he was trying to convince them that their new purchase needed updates. From where I stood, there was no sight of Kip or Scoop, both who said they'd be here. Despite Carp's regular attendance just in case, Carla was usually a no show.

"We wondered if you were able to get the obituary stopped in tomorrow's paper," said Gabby.

"Probably not," I said. "Though it was not for a lack of trying."

"You should sue them," declared her sister, her pointed finger coming dangerously close to my eye and instead diving to brush my chest.

Dressed in a bright yellow sweater and a pair of flowered pants that looked like they came straight out of an attic box marked 1970, Abby's tiny frame was overwhelmed by the busyness of her outfit. The string of lights blew in the gentle breeze, bringing her face in and out of shadow.

"Shame on you. Two wrongs don't make a right," said Gabby, often the counterbalance to her sister. She saved my chest from another jab as she slapped her sister's hand away.

Gabby wore one of her favored flowing caftans, also covered in bright flowers. The two of them looked like they belonged in the deck pots we filled every spring.

"You have to be angry at the paper for getting it so wrong. They should compensate you," said Abby, ignoring the rebuke.

"Someone at the paper made a mistake, but I made the bigger one," I said. "I should have insisted on approving the final submission and sent it in myself."

And, I never should have entrusted the job to a jet-setting relative who left on a cruise the morning after she submitted the obituary.

"Well, that's a business buster, isn't it?" asked Gabby, and it was depressing to think that even if the obit didn't make it to print, the Nosy Parkers would be sure that people knew about the error.

Richard, whose eyes had been darting around, was ready for escape and gave my arm a reassuring squeeze before waving to someone across the deck.

Abby again jabbed at me and said, "Have they arrested your reporter friend yet?"

The sudden change in topic caught me off guard and I took a step backward. As if choreographed, the Nosy Parkers moved with me, landing directly under the string of lights.

I did a double-take. Abby had a streak running down the center of her short-cropped pixie cut and looked very much like a skunk painted purple. Gabby had bright pink locks framing both sides of her chubby face. Between the outfits and the strange dye jobs, they looked like they belonged in a psychedelic garden.

Noticing my gaping mouth, they giggled. "We got it done for the party. It's the rage," said Gabby. "You should try it."

Closing in again, Abby reached for a handful of my hair which I had recently begun streaking with blond highlights. "This is so yesterday," she agreed.

By now, Richard had disappeared in the crowd and I felt like a cornered animal. Where was that bear spray when you needed it?

Satisfied with the shock she had created, Gabby returned to the conversation. "Scoop was the last person to see Chester alive and we all know that he has inside information on the arsons." As she spoke, her sister sipped her drink and listened in smug silence. "Did you know that Scoop sometimes had Chester spend the night at his place? And they had drinks at Pop's Place the night Chester bit the dust?"

Gabby sounded like she was imitating her sister's habit of using catch-phrase lingo.

"I'm guessing there was an altercation," interjected Abby. "Chester probably had proof that Scoop was the arsonist. You know how that man was always snooping around."

"Chester did have his nose in everything," agreed Gabby.

I thought it odd coming from two women whose narrative was always at someone else's expense. Still, was this finally the kernel of truth I had been hoping for?

"How do you mean?" I looked around the deck, feigning disinterest. When you were talking to the Nosy Parkers, you had to constantly remind yourself that they too were fishing.

"He was a watcher," she continued. "He'd be helping you load your paint cans in the car when you were at Ridgefield Hardware but he'd always be looking at something or someone else."

Gabby jumped in. "Remember that time we were walking and we saw him just hovering around? He looked like a hawk circling for prey. And by the way, don't you think he would have made more in tips if he had planted himself at Stop & Shop?"

"Too far from town center," replied Abby. "You know how he depended on being able to crash in one of the places in the village."

"Well, look where that got him!" Gabby said.

Between the two of them, they might be very good at writing murder mysteries because there were more red herrings in their commentary than I could figure out what to do with.

"Was he watching anyone in particular?" I asked.

The two sisters looked at each other as if one or the other might have the answer. They shook their heads no in unison, a synchronized move that had plenty of practice.

"I did see him checking Scoop out one day," said Gabby. "Scoop was parking that scooter thing he rides."

"And, I saw him watching the bank," added Abby. "It was around lunch time and there were a lot of people coming and going."

"His eyes were always glued on the bank," agreed Gabby.

"Which bank?" I asked.

There are two banks right next door to each other in the village center: one, a red brick structure anchoring Main and Governor Streets; the other, a prominent Neo-classical style stone structure with Art Deco features with the name of the original owner, Ridgefield Savings Bank 1871–1930, etched across the façade. Though it has since changed names, leaving the original is a nod to the town's history and has become an iconic commercial landmark. This was where Richard had taken me to open my first savings account.

"Why? Do you think this is important?" asked Abby, suddenly rounding her eyes, a cat ready to pounce.

I shrugged as if it was nothing and tucked the piece of information away, hoping that this conversation might finally be paying off.

"Do either of you know Chester's last name?" I asked. "Or anything else about him for his obituary?"

"I heard he was a billionaire who periodically wanted to see how the other half lives so he would know where to send his contributions," said Gabby.

Abby let out a *tsk tsk* and looked at her sister as if she had just littered on Main Street. "If he wanted to see how the other half lives, he wouldn't come to Ridgefield, Connecticut. He'd go where there were lots of homeless people, like New York City or even San Francisco. I hear they have entire homeless sections in that city."

I had to agree with her there. Ridgefield had a proactive social services department and when there was someone down on their luck, people came to the rescue. As far as I knew, Chester was the only person who lived on the streets in town at the moment. That reminded me that I might just visit that social services department to see if Chester had ever asked for help.

"Let's get some pizza before it's gone," said Gabby, glancing anxiously at the buffet table where the food was disappearing fast.

"Nice talking to you," I said, as the two women moved in the direction of the food. And then Gabby looked back over her shoulder and tossed out a final tidbit. "Arthur Willings and Chester were chummy."

Not to be outdone, Abby added, "Chester did odd jobs for him."

And then, they shouldered through the crowd.

Were they missing a beat on keeping up on the gossip, or did they already know that Arthur died earlier this morning and they were hoping I might do some digging?

"What was that about?" asked Kip, materializing at my side.

He was dressed in blue jeans and a charcoal half-zip pullover that made his gray eyes look even more steely. His hair still had the remnants of his shower clinging to the wisps at the back of his neck, and I could smell the scent of his aftershave.

"They have interesting theories," I said, tamping down my urge to curl into his arms right there and then. "Do you ever pay attention to what they are saying?"

Kip contemplated for a moment. "I try to deal in facts. Sometimes, though, I wonder if the Nosy Parkers stumble on critical information because people probably ignore them when they're around, not realizing they are snooping."

"So, do you listen to them?"

"Let's just say, I keep my antennae up." He handed me a glass of wine and added, "I noticed that you were empty-handed."

I sipped the chilled Chardonnay and thought back on the day.

"You could save me the agony of having to pry things out of them," I said. "It's like doing a complicated dance. You have to concentrate so hard so they don't trip you up."

Kip's normally brooding features took on thunder clouds.

"I thought you promised not to go digging," he said.

"I didn't promise," I said. "I only waved."

Kip shook his head and rolled his eyes.

"What did the ladies have to say?" he asked in resignation. "You seemed very engrossed."

"If I tell you, I'd have to . . ." I started.

"Don't kid around about this, Winter." Kip did a quick scan of the room, took my elbow, and escorted me from the deck and through the living room into the empty kitchen.

He pulled me into his arms and gave me a full-on kiss—the kind that could buckle my knees and make me abandon all practical thinking. Before I could succumb, I took a quick glance at the kitchen window where I had a full view of the partiers.

And to my horror, all eyes on the deck were watching us. Some clapping, some laughing, and the Nosy Parkers were lasering in as if assessing our every move.

I felt Kip's hands begin to roam and I stopped him. He looked surprised and maybe even a little hurt when I pulled away.

"I think if we want privacy, we should go to the study," I said.

Kip looked out toward the window with flaming cheeks that mirrored mine. While most of the party people had turned their attention in another direction, I could still feel the focus of Abby and Gabby's watchful eyes. I waved with a smile I didn't feel. Kip and I then went back through the living room toward the front of the house where we had closed the study door to guests. I turned the knob, pushed it open, and was about to step inside when I stopped.

Silhouetted in the window light stood a person by my desk. I reached for the light switch and snapped it on.

"What are you doing in here?" I demanded.

"Sorry," said Scoop, stepping away from the desk where my computer sat. "I know this looks bad."

Bad is not the word I would have used to describe finding my best friend invading my privacy. My stomach twisted and I felt like my heart had just split in two. Before I could say another word, Kip pushed past me and towered over Scoop, making sure to fill his personal space. It was a threatening gesture, even more so when he shut the laptop and then folded his arms across his chest. Scoop looked totally beaten.

"I can explain." As he took a step away from Kip, his hand brushed the desk and the cup filled with pens tipped over with a clatter. Before he could grab the implement-filled cup, pens and pencils rolled to the floor.

Scoop was already bending to pick them up when Kip snapped, "Leave them."

An uncomfortable silence shrouded us as Scoop stared at the fallen pens.

"I realized that the party probably wasn't a good idea, especially with Kip here so I was going to leave you a note," he stammered, making sure to avoid my boyfriend's eyes. "I didn't hear back from you this morning and I thought maybe you just didn't have a chance to let me know what was going on. So, I was going to ask you to call after the party."

"You're here at the house. Why didn't you just ask her?" Kip said, not giving up an inch of space. Scoop was now trapped between the desk and Kip. "And, I don't see that you are leaving a note. It looks more like you're snooping on Winter's computer."

Scoop leaned around Kip to look me in the eye.

"I got your text and decided a deck party would be a good distraction from everything else. When I got here, I could see that you . . ." and here he pointed to Kip "were here. Like I said, I was going to leave a note."

"So, you broke into Winter's office instead and started searching her computer?" asked Kip.

I stared at the laptop Scoop had been hunched over. Next to it lay the jacket he had shed. Apparently, he had been planning on staying a while.

"I didn't break in. The door was unlocked." Scoop sounded indignant. "And, it's not like I haven't been here, looking over Winter's shoulder as she works, hundreds of times."

True, though maybe more like two or three times when we had been collaborating on something. What was my friend doing in here?

"The computer was here so on impulse I wondered if maybe she had left some notes," he continued, warming up to his bravado.

Kip was about to say something else when I pushed forward.

"This is not right," I told Scoop, swiping tears of disappointment and waving my hands around my study. "This is my personal space—it's as bad as reading someone's diary without their permission. You really crossed a line."

I rarely lose my temper, yet I was so incensed that I couldn't stop the tears dripping over my cheeks and I was sure my freckles were front and center.

Scoop looked like he had just lost his best friend, which he might have.

"Winter, I'm sorry." I softened slightly when Scoop mumbled something that sounded like "I'm not myself."

Kip stepped aside and the second he did so, Scoop, continuing to mutter about making it up to me, hurried from the room, leaving his jacket behind.

"Something's up with that guy," said Kip.

I nodded with a sinking heart as I watched my friend disappear into the hallway. A few seconds later, I heard the front door open and close.

"He's just pounding those nails into his coffin," said Kip, shaking his head. "What was he thinking?"

"We have to help him," I said in a voice barely above a whisper. "He's not thinking clearly."

"Help him? Geez, the guy broke into your study and tried to access your laptop," he said. "I would think you'd be furious."

"I am furious. I also know Scoop. He must be desperate to pull a stunt like this. I have to try to help him."

Kip covered the ground between us and pulled me in close. All my defenses surrendered in that second and I wanted to bury myself in the security of his body.

"Stop digging," said Kip.

Good grief, why did I have to have a boyfriend who needed a course in Romance 101?

"How about, 'yes Winter, we'll find a way to help your friend' or at the very least 'try not to worry,'" I said, as I pushed out of his arm wrap.

Kip looked at the ceiling, shook his head, and said, "What would be the point? You'd see right through those platitudes. The truth is, Scoop's unsettling behavior and your . . . your interference into police business is putting both of you in danger."

"How am I interfering with police business? All I'm asking for is Chester's last name. The same thing the funeral home is asking for. And, what is it you know about Chester that might endanger me or Scoop? Don't you think we have a right to know?" I was trying to be calm though I bristled—*interference*—that was really an insult.

"Chester was murdered and the more involved you get, the more you place you and your friends in danger," he blurted out.

I could see the pain it cost him to tell me something he wasn't supposed to. He was shaking his head and rubbing his hand over his mouth, as if he regretted every word that had sprung.

"Richard already told me about the murder," I said.

Kip looked resigned. "How do Richard, Horace, and all your other cronies know these things before they are released?"

I almost felt sorry for him.

"Reliable sources," I said. "And no, I can't reveal them."

Chapter Ten

Morning broke into a dismal day, which mirrored my mood. Cloudy, chilly, with a prediction of rain and I imagined that the best of October was behind us. There was no evidence of the bear this morning as Diva and I traipsed down Mamanasco Road, though I patted my pocket where my bear spray container was at the ready. We had stopped at Horace's cottage next door to pick up Max and the three of us trekked up to Richardson Park and back. When I returned, Horace stepped to the side of the doorway, making way for the dogs to bound inside. Then, with a gentlemanly swoop of his hand, he ushered me inside where a tea kettle whistled.

"What did you learn last night?" He asked, as we headed to the kitchen.

"I'm not sure," I said honestly. "You know how Gabby and Abby always seem to have a thread of truth in their stories. It's hard to pick that thread out."

"I think the two of them could write fiction," he said, with a laugh.

"Exactly! Anyway, they mentioned a couple of interesting things."

Although my heart was heavy after last night, I was doing everything possible to focus on the problem in front of me. I told Horace about Abby's theory that Chester had been a billionaire pretending to be homeless so he could learn about their challenges.

"That definitely sounds like fiction," he said, removing two mugs from knotty pine cabinets. "He wouldn't learn much about the needs of the homeless by being the only person in town who was sleeping rough."

I let my eyes wander over the familiar trappings of Horace's ancient cabin. The dogs had spent last evening here, so as to stay out of the way of the neighbors on the deck, and yet there was no evidence of Diva's escape attempts. Why was it that she nibbled—no take that back—devoured my doors and windows, yet treated Horace's tired cabin like a palace? It was almost as if she knew it wouldn't make a bit of difference to Horace if she massacred a door or two.

The worn floors, pink-swirled Formica countertops, and wood-paneled walls felt so much a part of Horace that the lone attempt made to update with avocado appliances somewhere back in the 1970s felt like an insult. To me, the house was right where it belonged, stuck in the 1940s when it was built and loaded with warm memories. Summer and I had shared many hours with Horace and his late wife while we were kids, playing Go Fish, eating chocolate chip cookies, and talking about our day. To me, it was like a second home.

I slid into a chair by the large picture window. It wasn't that long ago that Horace replaced it, following a pane-shattering microburst that hit the Lake Mamanasco area hard.

"I should have done this a long time ago," he said, nodding at the window, an update I did approve of. Even on a gray day, Horace enjoyed his beautiful view and peaceful vibe.

"Any thoughts about selling and joining Richard at Village Square?" I asked.

Horace chuckled. "Despite humoring your uncle, I'm not going anywhere anytime soon. And, when I get to that great big lake in the sky, I'm leaving instructions that the house be torn down, with the property left to the town for open space. These old cottages were never intended to be year-round, and all the run-off from waste and fertilizer is strangling this poor lake."

Horace filled two cups with hot water, dropped a tea bag into each, and carried both to the table. I knew from experience that this was his favorite spot, the place where he did his best thinking. I was lucky because I was often the beneficiary of his philosophical musings and this wasn't the first time I had heard his concerns.

"What else is happening in your case?" he asked.

I hadn't thought of my interest in the murder and the arsons as a case and I said as much.

"Ha," said Horace. "Keep telling yourself that. Now again, what's going on?"

Horace was all ears as I gave him the overview from Chester's surprising death to Arthur Willings' unfortunate passing.

Steamy lavender chamomile drifted into my senses, reminding me of the few visits to a spa I've had over the years.

"Anything else?" he asked.

"Well, there was this little thing, but I feel like I'm grasping at straws. You know, trying to make it fit into my already befuddled theory."

Horace waited.

"It's probably nothing," I added.

Horace's shaggy white brows went sky-high in question.

"Since when do you not trust your instincts?" he asked, letting his shoulders rise and fall. "It might be nothing, it might be something."

"OK, here goes," I said. "The Nosy Parkers said that Chester was always watching."

Horace nodded slightly. "As in noticing what others were doing?"

"Exactly what I was thinking," I said. "They said he would be helping them with packages but watching, say, the bank, and who was coming and going."

Horace stroked his chin in thought.

"Anything else?"

He rose to fill two dog bowls with fresh water. He also filled two matching metal bowls with dried food.

I shook my head no, and then laughed. "You have matching China."

Horace's house was a mismatch whether it was in the attic-vintage furnishings in his living space, or the cups and saucers in which he served his tea.

He laughed. "Yep, I finally have matching dishes in this old house."

We watched in silence as two hungry dogs wolfed down the contents of the bowls.

"I thought it odd that Scoop wasn't at the party last night," Horace said finally.

Kip and I had discussed Scoop's transgression well into the night. After he left, I fell into a troubled sleep, struggling to understand how desperate my friend must have been to do what he did. I had decided not to tell Horace or Richard about it.

"I'm guessing he thought it might be awkward knowing that Kip would be there," I mumbled.

Horace let out a dubious *hmm* and then said, "Any news on the print edition of today's paper?"

I did a mental refresh with a sip of tea. The online obituary, with me listed as dead, was still findable this morning, though not as easily as it had been yesterday. My plan was to run downtown right after dropping Diva and pick up a hard copy of the newspaper.

"It's a wait and see," I said. "Although, if the obituary lands in the printed edition, my timeline for expanding my business to New York City might be escalated because my credentials here might need a rest."

Horace smiled and toasted with his teacup. "Things have a way of working out," he said. "Who knows, maybe people will think it was just a marketing ploy to call attention to your business."

"You don't really believe that, do you?" I asked.

"No, I just said it to make you feel better."

* * *

Back at home, the rich aroma of chocolate transported me to Deborah Ann's. Our local chocolatier on Main Street houses two floors of sensory overload—penny candies in jars, cases of homemade chocolates, homemade ice cream and fudge so thick and creamy it probably adds pounds just by inhaling. Which is how the house smelled now.

My uncle's presence at the cottage had a lot of pluses, including the good food I was consistently enjoying. He and Horace could sip their favorite Maker's Mark nightcap without the worry of driving home, and I didn't have to think about him being alone all the time, something I found myself doing more as he got older.

Knowing my uncle as I did, however, the time he was spending at the cottage also suggested that he had something on his mind. For Richard, the kitchen was synonymous with therapy and while his was being renovated, mine had become the psychiatrist's couch. I made a mental note to confront him sometime in the very near future about his new habit because if he was having second thoughts about deeding the house to me, he needn't. To say I had been surprised by the unexpected birthday gift was an understatement, and I had been thrilled. Truthfully though, it was a big and empty house when he wasn't around.

After a shower, I pulled on black jeans and a sweater, and stopped in the small study where we had found Scoop last night. My laptop was still on the desk and the pens were still on the floor where he'd knocked them. Nearby was the open door to the train room where Kip and I had ended the evening.

I ducked my head in now, and admired the tiny room that had been Richard's answer to two grieving little girls way back when my dad died. With my mom in nursing school, Richard's distraction had been a big empty table, save for two plaster mountains with tunnels and a train track.

My sister, Summer, had immediately taken to the empty canvas and began creating a small neighborhood house from a kit my uncle had us choose from the model railroad magazine he subscribed to. Hers came with picket fences and happy families waving at the caboose as it disappeared into the tunnels. Her roads were straight with purposeful destinations, like the post office or grocery store. It was idyllic and probably should have been our first clue that she would quit college and marry young.

My roads wound unpredictably, very much like the back roads of Ridgefield. The kits I bought for houses and businesses, were eclectic, and definitely not shaped from the same cookie cutter that Summer used. Richard did his best at filling in the gaps with landscape that seemed to make it all work.

I rarely shared my special space with anyone, though lately, Kip and I had been dusting and cleaning in hopes that my sister's ten-year-old twin daughters would enjoy it when they visited at Christmas. No surprise that Kip wanted to add a police station.

Turning back to the study, I retrieved my laptop and noticed the jacket Scoop had left last night. Grabbing it, I proceeded to follow the beckoning aroma of chocolate.

"Smells good," I said as I entered the state-of-the-art kitchen my uncle had added when he renovated the cottage. It had stood the test of time, with stainless steel appliances and plenty of good workspace. A table for four sat in front of the window and took in the view.

I stopped short. *What the heck?*

Richard, dressed in jeans and his Rensselaer sweatshirt, the uniform he kept at my house, was frantically bouncing between two pots and stirring like a madman. The rising steam flushed his cheeks as he wielded two wooden spoons, and his frantic efforts made him look like the father of twins—not knowing which crying baby to attend to first.

"Is that fudge I smell?" I asked.

"Quick," he said, thrusting a chocolate-coated spoon toward me. "I had this idea that I could do two batches at once and I forgot about all the last-minute stirring."

Reluctantly, I put down my things and began the tedious task of swirling the fudge in its pot until it thickened. The trick, as Richard had taught me over the years, was not letting it get so thick that it wouldn't pour onto the greased wax paper already laid out on the counter, and yet not pouring too soon because then it would remain too soft to eat. His technique, handed down from his own father, was to keep a glass of ice water handy, drop a dollop into it and if it formed a ball, it was ready.

Not for the first time, I wondered why we didn't own a candy thermometer.

"Now," cried Richard, as he began pouring.

"I don't think mine is quite . . ." I started. And then, I realized my near fatal error. Mine had gone from glistening to dull, which meant it was almost too ready.

Richard scraped as I poured, and we both watched the batch that had been in my charge plop onto the butter-greased wax paper.

"Still edible, though not the best. I'd call this batch rock fudge," he said as he stroked his chin.

"My mom's favorite," I said.

"It's shocking that my sister still has teeth after eating this stuff," he reflected.

I knew that for this level of cooking spree, my uncle must be feeling especially troubled about something. I opened the oven door.

"Lasagna?" I asked.

"I thought we should have some in the freezer—you know just in case," he said.

I definitely needed to have that conversation with my uncle soon.

Chapter Eleven

The rain spitting at my windshield as I drove downtown, reminded me that Halloween was just a few days away. For some reason, my most vivid memories of the celebration were on cold rainy nights with me tagging along after Summer and friends. Summer was the Taylor Swift of her group and the gaggle of friends who followed her barely took notice of the younger sister trailing behind. Back home, Summer became my buddy again, helping me into warm PJs while Richard and my mom heated hot chocolate. Together, we'd examine our haul, Summer always taking charge of the swapping.

"Call the twins," I said aloud, reminding myself that two little girls needed me to remember all these small details about their mom.

Scoop's Vespa was parked behind the funeral home in his designated spot. I climbed to the second floor, entered a small vestibule, and shook the rain off the bag I carried. I had stopped at Tazza for a tomato and mozzarella on French bread for Scoop—my way of saying we could mend our fences. I tapped on the door. No response. I tried his cell. Still no answer.

While my friend probably didn't want to face me, there was no way I would let this sandwich go to waste. And then suddenly, I felt the grip of my overactive imagination, as visions of dead Chester and dead Arthur Willings made my tapping turn to pounding.

"I know you're in there," I yelled.

As I lifted my fist to beat the door again, it flew open and I just managed to stop short before hitting Scoop in the face.

"Geez, Winter, you'll wake the dead," he said, ushering me inside and quickly shutting the door behind us. "I had to secure the cats so they didn't get out."

"I thought Heady and Topper never tried to escape?" I looked around for his two friendly Tabbies.

"Not them, we have two new rescues that I'm fostering and all they try to do is get out—especially Frankie," he said. "He and Becky sit at the windows all day and meow. I'm wondering if placing them with someone who wants indoor cats is the wrong thing."

"Maybe one of the horse farms would take them," I offered.

"Good luck with that. People seem to want easy care items these days. Outdoor cats bring things home like mice, rats, bats, and birds. It's a pride thing with the felines. Anyway, I'll check the farms in Ridgebury and even those in North Salem."

No cats for me. I was having enough trouble with my windowsill-chewing charge.

"So, what's up?" Scoop asked, accepting the jacket I thrust at him.

"What's *up*? That's all you have to say?"

Scoop, AKA Kevin Blake, is several years younger than me and about an era smarter. With a mom in memory care and no other close relatives besides some cousins he rarely sees, Richard, Horace, and I are like family. Because he spends a lot of time alone, he doesn't always cue into the social skill department.

I tapped my foot to make a point.

"Really, Winter, there's not much left to say," he said, as I followed him through his apartment. "I screwed up."

Scoop is a vegetarian neat nick who lives in a minimalist space. It works for him and, despite the cool landscape of the room, it is always comfortable. I took one step in and stopped. The pillows were tossed on his leather sectional, books were strewn from the shelves that flanked a good-sized TV, and drawers gaped from his desk as if mid-scream. In fact, his entire apartment looked like someone had turned it upside down and shaken it. The ever-squawking emergency radio he had running 24/7, was the only thing that didn't appear out of place.

"You've had a break-in," I said.

"I was looking for something," he replied.

"Did you find it?"

"Yeah, one of the kittens got loose," he murmured. "It was a tense moment."

Looking for a kitten behind books or in desk drawers? I frowned at the less than satisfactory explanation, however, Scoop's mouth stayed sealed shut.

I handed him the bag with the sandwich. "Have you eaten lately?"

The open floor plan revealed a kitchen without a crumb on the counter, though cabinets had been opened and things removed.

"What's really going on here?" I asked.

Ignoring my question, my friend opened the bag cautiously, as if he thought I had planned some sort of revenge by hiding a snake inside but a twitch of a smile reached his mouth when he recognized his favorite sandwich. He led me to the island counter that separated the kitchen and the living room. I declined his offer for something to drink and climbed onto one of the surrounding stools.

Scoop placed the unwrapped sandwich in front of him.

"Eat," I said, and when he slid it between us to share, I pushed it back. "I already had breakfast."

Scoop wolfed tomato and mozzarella and took a long draft of water from his Yeti. He was a camel when it came to water, sucking down several refills of his thermos daily.

"Now that you are sustained, do you want to tell me what happened here and why you were snooping last night?"

He shrugged and sipped again, more slowly this time.

I was sure he could hear the frustration in my voice when I pleaded, "Speak."

He finally looked up and said, "I am sorry. I was wrong to invade your space. It's just that I was feeling cornered and then, when I realized Kip was at the party last night, I knew I wouldn't get to talk to you. I had hoped you made some notes or something that might help me."

None of this was ringing true so I just stared at him.

"Your laptop was already open," he said. "I swiped and all the password protections stopped me from going any further."

Had I left my laptop open? Maybe in my haste to get ready for the party? And, it was true, I didn't think Scoop had my password so what did he hope to gain?

As if in answer, he said, "I was about to leave you a note and I was looking for pen and paper when you and Kip walked in."

"And this?" I asked, waving my hand around the apartment.

"I don't want to talk about it."

"I might be able to help."

Scoop shook his head. "It's all tangled up with these arsons and I cannot . . . *will not* involve you. It's bad enough that I'm a person of interest. I don't want people pointing the finger at you."

"Why would anyone do that?"

"Because whoever trashed my place was looking for something and since they didn't find it here, they might look in the next logical place—a place where I spend a lot of time, my best friend's cottage on Lake Mamanasco."

One of his cats sauntered into the kitchen with a meow and Scoop got up to refill the cat bowl.

Subject closed.

For the moment, I had decided I would let everything go, though I wondered how long I would feel the sting of his betrayal.

"Any more news on the arsons?" I asked.

Scoop sucked in a breath and looked toward the window facing Catoonah Street. It framed the outline of the fire department.

"The police talked to me again, this time about Chester. They want to know why I didn't write the same details about the fire at Pop's Place that I did about the others."

"What did you tell them?"

"The truth. My source has run dry," said Scoop.

We talked some more, both picking each other's brains to no avail. Whatever secrets Scoop had, he was keeping them locked up tight.

Scoop's eyes roamed the room and landed on Heady or Topper who were both now crowded around the cat dish. I could never tell the twin Tabbies apart. "You'll make sure the cats are safe, won't you? I mean if anything happens to me."

"Nothing is going to happen to you," I said.

"I'm being serious here. I'll text you the code to the lock on my door. I'm getting new locks today."

Scoop's eyes reminded me of Diva's when a clap of thunder sent her shaking at my side.

Chapter Twelve

The only thing my visit to Scoop had done was confirm that he was in serious trouble and didn't want my help. For some reason, both Kip and Scoop seemed to think that the less I knew about Chester and the fires in town, the safer I'd be. In my experience, though, the less information a person has, the more likely they are to make a mistake. You can't stay out of the line of fire if you don't know where the line is drawn.

My next stop was the bank. I snagged a parking space right in front, which was lucky because at that moment, the misty drizzle turned to serious rain. The wind kicked up and Ridgefield Alerts showed up in my text to say heavy gusts might cause power outages.

Ridgefield's tree-lined streets, with their stunning medley of brilliant golds and reds at the height of the fall season, were a source of pride for townsfolk. That is, until one of the increasingly frequent storms turned them into destructive hazards, knocking down wires and making streets impassable. With the uptick in torrential storms, there were more trees uprooting even days later. It only took one extended outage to convince us that lugging buckets of water from the lake in order to flush toilets, wasn't the way to go. Richard, who preferred preparedness, had invested in a generator and listening for the whining of its weekly test had become as important as brushing my teeth.

I opened the door cautiously and looked to the sky. Some of the town's most damaging storms had happened on Halloween and thousands of unhappy families complained when weather-induced curfews were necessary. I hoped that this year the trick or treaters would win out.

The bank was library quiet and when I entered, a number of heads looked up from behind their glass-walled offices. It looked like they were working in conjoined fishbowls, though I'm sure it was a lot better than having no walls at all. The lack of privacy, however, made me feel on display, as I made my way to the young woman who looked to be in her mid-thirties, with pixie cut dark hair, working behind the teller's window.

"How can I help you?" she asked, with a big toothy smile.

"I have an odd question."

She looked at me encouragingly.

I glanced behind me and was relieved to see there was no-one breathing down my neck and noticed that all the fishbowl workers had resumed what they had been doing.

"Do you, by chance, know this man?" I held up my phone to show the photo of Chester that Carla had sent.

She leaned forward and squinted through the glass partition, so I slid my phone through the window opening, accidentally knocking over a sign advertising home loans.

"Sorry," I said, righting the sign, as she enlarged the photo with large fingers that dwarfed the tiny screen. Even the ring on her finger looked too small for such large hands.

"Oh," she said, her mouth rounding like a goldfish. After a quick survey of the people around her, she slid the phone back to me. "That's Chester. So terrible what happened to him."

"Would you by chance know his last name?" I explained that I was to write his obituary and that I had very little information on him.

"I don't know anything about him."

She looked around the room again. I looked too, though no-one even glanced in my direction.

"Did he do business here?" I asked, though I couldn't imagine what kind of bank business a homeless man might have.

She shrugged her shoulders and lowered her voice to a near whisper. "Sorry, I can't help you. Privacy considerations and all that."

"Is there someone else I could talk to? Someone with authority? I'm only looking for his last name."

The woman's wide smile had disappeared as she shook her head no.

I turned. Behind me stood a man who looked to be in his mid-forties, with flecks of silver woven through his trim brown hair.

"Is there a problem here?" he asked.

His warm hazel eyes were enhanced by thick lashes and his smile had customer service written all over it. I took him for one of the managers.

I was about to ask him about Chester when the young teller interjected. "This woman was just inquiring about interest rates. I was about to direct her to one of the loan officers."

The man asked what kind of loan I was interested in. I looked down at the Home Equity Loans advertisement and tapped at it.

He took in my jeans, sweater, dripping jacket and boots, no doubt adding in my age, as he considered whether I had home-borrowing clout, then waved to one of the glass cage folks.

"Lana will help you," he said, as a matronly woman with emerald, green cat's-eye glasses began to make her way over. "Miss. . . . um. . . . Sorry, I didn't catch your name."

"Snow, Winter Snow," I said, holding out my hand to shake.

"Winfred Thomas the third," he said, reaching a well-manicured hand toward me. His shake bordered on limp, no doubt to avoid injury with the large signet ring he wore. "And, this is Lana, one of our loan officers. She'll take care of you." Lana apparently didn't rate a last name, never mind a number. I shook her hand as well.

With a "thank you" nod to the teller, I was escorted by Lana back to her glass cubicle where for the next twenty minutes, I learned all about the pros and cons of borrowing against my Lake Mamanasco cottage. Lana stored my contact information in her computer and promised that when I was ready to "pull the trigger," she would put things in motion. I wasn't able to catch the teller's eye on my way out because she had left her cage and followed Winfred somewhere into the bowels of the bank.

Back outside, I darted through rain drops and hopped into my car, all the while wondering what a homeless guy might be doing in a bank and why the teller didn't want me to ask my question of Winfred Thomas III.

Chapter Thirteen

My cell rang the moment I got back into my Subaru—Kip's face flashed on caller ID.

"What are you up to today?"

Kip's comment about interfering still stung so I was pretty sure he wouldn't approve of my questioning the bank teller about Chester. For the moment, I'd keep my ongoing search for the man's identity a secret.

Chester watching the bank might be explained as something as simple as a deep pocket tipper doing his business there on a regular basis, and wanting to be available to wash a windshield or carry a package. However, the teller had insinuated that she couldn't give out customer information when I asked about Chester doing business with the bank. What kind of banking would a homeless man be doing?

"Winter? Did I lose you." Kip's voice jolted me to the present.

"Oh, sorry, just thinking about what I have to do today," I said.

"Which is?"

"I will be visiting Mrs. Willings because I am writing Arthur's obituary," I said.

Kip was quiet for a moment before asking, "How did you get that job?"

"Carla, who else?" Kip knew that the manager of the local funeral home was also a good friend.

"Right, Carla," he said it with a sigh, as if he was relieved I hadn't come across the job from someone else. My boyfriend was acting weird, though now was not the time to confront him.

"Can we get together later?" he finally asked. "Maybe meet at the Mariner for a bite to eat?"

I hated to pass a chance for a burger at the local pub which has been a townie favorite for over forty years. Kip was now joining the many newer implants to Ridgefield who flocked to the Ancient Mariner for the food, comradery, and casual ship-like interior.

"After I meet with Mrs. Willings, I'm going to draft Arthur's obituary," I said. "Let's talk later."

I still had some time before my appointment with Mrs. Willings. I didn't want to show up at her house looking like I had just dunked for apples, so I skipped my walk. Richard had waved me off this morning saying he would care for Diva until Carp arrived; however, I knew I needed to check on things at home.

After being passed off to Carp who had first-hand experience with the havoc the little pup could wreak, she would then go to Horace. Diva, whose fear of storms was only second to her fear of being trapped, would need a walk and I doubted Horace would be able to coax her outside by himself. The responsibilities the dog presented made my chest constrict. After being orphaned twice, would she feel abandoned when I moved part-time to the city or would all the people who routinely cared for her be enough?

Before heading home, I ran into CVS to pick up the newspaper. When I got there, no papers were to be had. Ever since our local press had been bought out and the offices relocated to Danbury so as to share resources, I'd lost track of where else I could buy it. I could check the mini marts, supermarket, and other drug stores, but boosted by the lack of phone calls, texts, and emails asking me if I was still alive, I decided the paper could wait until after my visit to Mrs. Willings.

Carp was intent on a "gentle sand" of the windowsill when I arrived. I knew better than to interrupt a genius at work so I donned my rain gear, grabbed Diva's leash, the bear spray, and herded her out the door.

Fortunately, there was no rumble of thunder and the steady drizzle didn't seem to set off any of the dog's alarm bells. Our walk was short, punctuated by its purpose and with the poop scoop bag now filled, we trotted back to the cottage. Despite the light rain, Diva smelled like wet dog so I toweled her off and then gave her a blow dry until her fur was restored to down comforter soft.

* * *

My street on Mamanasco butted into North Salem Road and looked directly across at Ridgefield High School. I cursed myself for not planning better because a flood of traffic showed no hint of letting up until every car from the parking lot was gone. It seemed like every one of the nearly 1,500 RHS students either drove to school or had someone drop them off.

Fortunately, the guard who risked life and limb by standing in the middle of the street, waved his arms at the student drivers to pause so I could turn right onto North Salem. Bus after nearly empty bus passed me as I made a left onto Ridgebury Road. I can remember my sister protesting that no-way was she ever riding in that "big yellow banana." After that statement, despite the heavy traffic cutting across Mamanasco Road, Summer and I were sentenced by our mom to walk to school.

Grave Words

As I passed Tiger Hollow, the high school's impressive track and field stadium, nostalgia poked its head. I remembered so many events that took place there. Tiger Hollow holds up to a whopping 5,000 spectators so along with high school sporting events and RHS graduation, the stadium is booked during spring, summer, and fall for other events including the July 4th fireworks.

I slowed, remembering my school days. I hadn't been the popular one—that had been Summer. And yet, I had my group of friends, and what I've learned from Richard and my mom is that over time, cliques fade, until all you're left with are friendships forged by a mutual experience. It doesn't matter if you were the cool kid back then. When you're facing your fiftieth class reunion, the only thing you are cheering for is that everyone is still alive.

The school must have been getting ready for something because even in the drizzle, there was activity beyond the normal football practice. And then, it hit me. Homecoming must be happening soon.

I hadn't been back to the event since my sister died. Summer had been a high school cheerleader and her constant practice had been enough to drive me out of the house sometimes, as she used the reflection of the large windows to practice her jumps. Lately though, she was gradually disappearing from my memory, just the way Marty's sibs faded in the family photo in *Back to the Future*—one of the old movies I often feasted on. *Could I push past the hollow in my heart by returning for RHS homecoming to revive her memory?* I wasn't sure.

Discarding the thoughts that always left me feeling empty, I took the dangerously sharp switchback at Pope's corner a little too fast. Thank goodness no one was coming from the other direction as I steered the car back to my side of the narrow road. The notorious corner got its name because it was where famed musician, conductor and teacher, Charles Pope, once resided. He had a long history in music, but the story that always stuck with me was that he was an arranger of choruses and English hand-bell groups. While there was no connection, the peeling of the bells on Christmas eve at the Congregational Church was high among my favorite holiday memories.

Pope's house has since been replaced by a massive concrete and steel, 16,000-square-foot hilltop residence designed by world renowned architect, Rafael Viñoly. I'd been to several fundraisers at the unique house and was impressed by the sharp edges, abundance of glass, and stunning vistas.

I slowed a bit after my near miss and took in the changing vibe of Ridgebury, an entirely different side of Ridgefield. Vast fence-hemmed fields hinted at the horse farms dotting the countryside. Open space from the protected land once known as McKeon's Farm, is rented by Henny Penny Farm, and I always slow to search for the llama peacefully meandering among the grazing sheep.

According to my GPS, the Willings home was about a half a mile past the Meetinghouse, a gathering place located in the Ridgebury Congregational Church's Martinson Barn, aptly named, because it was dropped purposefully amid the rural landscape of private homes and estates, where the closest stores were either six miles away downtown or over the line in Danbury. I passed the Ridgebury Cemetery and resisted the urge to press harder on the gas pedal because a quick glance at the clock told me I was already a few minutes late. Finally, beyond a string of houses and neighborhoods, I came to a driveway almost hidden by shrubbery.

Gravel crunched under my wheels as I wondered what I would be facing. I had no advance information on Arthur. There was a Mrs. Willings, I knew from Carla. Would there be children? I hoped not. A man in his fifties might have a youngish family, and in my experience, meeting the sad confusion of children who had lost a parent was a stab to the heart I remembered well.

When the bright red door to the charming white Cape Cod swung open, I was met by a woman who could have been my grandmother. I put her at Horace's age or older.

"Mrs. Willings?" I asked tentatively. "I'm Winter Snow."

She cocked her head at my name and nodded. "You are the obituary writer that the young woman at the funeral home sent? Come in, come in."

"I'm so sorry for the loss of your husband," I said.

Mrs. Willings raised grey-streaked brows and smiled sadly. "Son, dear. Artie was my son."

I followed her through a surprisingly open and airy space, obviously redone because most houses of this style had small rooms. This one probably once had a kitchen, dinette, and living room clustered together on the first floor along with a bathroom and one or two bedrooms. Now, it embraced open space living with kitchen, eating area, and great room, all in one. A small hallway, off to the right side of the house, probably led to the sleeping area.

She steered me to an island where a pitcher of water and two glasses awaited. A pad of paper, with notes she had written, sat next to it. I glanced around at the neat airy room. An out-of-sync bulletin board, with paper upon paper pinned to it, was the only unruly thing in the space. The papers fluttered from the breeze sneaking through an open window, reminding me of the flipbook animations Summer and I used to create. A bright red logo danced in the puffs of air, then settled, until the next gust set them in motion.

The great room/kitchen overlooked a back yard smothered in leaves. When Mrs. Willings saw me glance in that direction, she said, "I've lost my Artie, who took care of things, and my yard help—all within hours of each other." She shook her head as if still in disbelief.

She looked so small and lost, I thought I might take up the rake myself.

"Was Chester your yard help?" I asked.

"Yes," she said in surprise. "Did you know him?"

"Only from a distance," I replied.

"Nice fellow. He and my Artie were friends. I never thought he did much around here until I started noticing the leaves. He was reliable, I'll give him that, but then why not. Artie paid him pretty well."

"Do you by chance know his last name?" I asked.

Mrs. Willings put her fist to her mouth in thought and then shook her head.

"I'm sure it'll come to me," she said. "Right now, this old mind is cluttered with other things."

I wanted to ask a bunch of questions about Chester and Artie's arrangement, though now didn't seem the time. I was here to do an obituary for Arthur Willings, and that's what I would do.

According to his mother, Arthur Willings made his career in collections. *Ugh*, I thought. *Was he a thug who went around repossessing vehicles when people fell behind on payments?*

Mrs. Willings smiled. "You should see your face," she said. "I get that a lot when I describe my son's career."

Chapter Fourteen

By the time I left the Willings home, the sun had outwitted the clouds. Oddly, there was that post-summer-rain smell in the air, reminding me that the weather these days was out of sync with my expectation of the seasons. Climate change and all those worries aside, today's reprieve from autumn's bite was uplifting.

As I drove back, I thought about my time with Betty Willings. Like other people in their eighties that I had come to respect, the woman was articulate, observant and had the calming effect of someone who understood the ebb and flow of life. She was clearly distraught over her son's death and yet, she accepted it in a way that only someone who was living her last chapter might understand.

I had been trying to figure out a positive way to describe his career when she asked me to accompany her out back. She led me to a small cottage built on their property, then went through an elaborate process of opening locks and entering alarm passcodes.

"Remember I told you that Artie was into collections?" she asked, as she held out her arm in an *after you* motion. "Well, this is what he collected."

Mrs. Willings clearly enjoyed the look of surprise on my face as I took in the rows of shelving, all packed with games, action figures, toys, coins, stamps, vinyl—you name it, Arthur collected it.

"My son was born with a fragile heart and couldn't join the other kids on the Tiger Hollow field. Instead, he poured his energy into collecting everything he could."

Mrs. Willings' weathered face flushed and her eyes shone as she talked about Arthur, a good reminder of how important an in-person visit was, when it came to writing obituaries. *Take that AI . . . no way could AI capture the look of pride on Betty Willings' face.*

"It's OK dear, go ahead and touch things. Artie loved showing them off and he always said, 'they are meant to be appreciated.'"

I ran my fingers gently over comic books, all stacked and labeled by year and category. *Superman, Captain America* . . . an entire set of Marvel.

"Happy Meal Toys? Really?" I asked, staring at a shelf of Hot Wheels.

"These are fun, but not as valuable as the things in the warehouse," she said. "I think we have two full sets of those Dukes of Hazard vehicles."

It was nice to see the crinkle around Mrs. Willings' eyes and hear the tinkle of her bell-like laughter as she talked about her son's collections. "Arthur started doing this when he was old enough to think. I always thought it odd that he seemed more enamored with the packaging on his gifts than the gifts themselves."

We were walking by a Barbie Doll dressed up like a princess when Betty tapped her finger lightly on the protective box. "Millennium Princess Barbie from 2000. Never opened. Worth somewhere around $15,000. My Artie always knew whether it was trash or treasure."

We continued strolling as Mrs. Willings pointed to various collectibles and identified values that sent my mind whirling. *One Teddy Roosevelt Panama Penny and I could buy a New York City apartment.*

"Granted, he made some mistakes, but mostly he had a gift for anticipating what he should save. When he was fifteen, he paid $500 for a discontinued version of a board game. I was furious—all that money he earned from helping people with their electronic devices, down the drain. Or so I thought, until a year later he sold the darn thing for $2,000."

As we walked by shelf after shelf of collectibles, I paused in front of a stack of slim booklets neatly arranged and categorized.

"Show me the money," I said aloud, as I fingered a stack of coin collections.

Mrs. Willings faced me in surprise. "You know about the talk Artie was supposed to give?"

I explained how I had replaced Artie at the last minute when the Village Voices found themselves without a speaker. Mrs. Willings laughed. "No offense, dear, but you must have been a Debbie Downer."

I laughed too, as the air of sadness lifted like an early morning fog. "I was. They were looking for a get-rich-quick talk and instead got to look mortality in the face."

And then, as I looked around in awe, I had a suddenly overwhelming heartsink. *If I wrote about his passion the way Artie deserved, it would be like painting a target on Mrs. Willings' back.*

"I want you to highlight this," she said, as if she knew my thoughts. "Tell everyone how accomplished he was. Do you know he is worth millions? A boy who couldn't even go to a damn football game because the excitement might send him into a heart episode, deserves some recognition."

"Mrs. Willings," I had started.

"Betty, dear," she said.

"Betty. I wouldn't want to share all this with the world at large until you moved it to a secure location."

"I've got plenty of alarms," she said.

"It's not only the potential robberies, which might be scary enough, but there are so many people who might try to swindle you," I said.

You had to be so careful what you put into obituaries these days. For instance, when you listed the service times and locations, there was always the worry of someone robbing the family home while they were saying their final goodbyes. Many people hired someone to watch their properties when they memorialized their loved ones. A friend of mine even gave a house watch as a gift, in lieu of flowers. Part of what my clients paid me for was to assess what I should and shouldn't put into the death notice.

"You think people will try to take advantage because I'm old and in mourning."

I was glad she said it, and not me.

"The original Darth Vader," said Betty Willings, holding an unopened package for me to see. "My Artie loved *Star Wars*—he's got multiples of everything—action figures, the Death Star, even the Ewok Village. His latest passion is Dune. I can't quite see it with all that sand, but my son loves it."

Mrs. Willings was bouncing back and forth between past and present tense, and the picture she painted, made me feel like Arthur might be cataloging his collections in the next room over. Finally, she slumped back into reality.

"I guess the advantage of knowing you are living on death row, is that you have time to plan," said Mrs. Willings. And then, she did a slow turn, taking in the vault of collectibles. "By the way, this is just a sampling of my boy's giant warehouse. Now, that, is something to see. This was only his 'calling card.'"

Grave Words

I spent the ride home doing a mental draft of Arthur's obituary. Betty Willings had been insistent that I write about his unusual career choice and promised that Artie had put a plan into place so there would be no scamming his mother. Arthur's sister would arrive tomorrow from Los Angeles. The two had been close and, according to Betty, Artie and Mandy had worked out detailed succession plans, which her daughter would set in motion the moment she arrived.

I was glad that Betty Willings had turned out to be a pragmatic woman who wanted an upbeat sendoff for her son. She didn't ask for phrases like *died peacefully* or *was called home*. While I envied those with strong beliefs, I couldn't help wondering, *if all those folks were in heaven, who was keeping the hell fires burning?*

Despite the fact that I avoided certain clichés, my job was to write a tribute deserving of the individual and one that would bring their families comfort. Fortunately, I'd only had one person who said "good riddance" to an annoying relative. I convinced that woman, that including that phrase in the obituary would reflect more on her than on her dearly departed Aunt Gertrude.

For the most part, I included what my client wanted, unless it was totally inaccurate—like changing someone's age. I also avoided anything that might place those left behind in jeopardy. I would find a way to talk about Artie's amazing career as a collector without subjecting his family to scammers whose only interest was to separate them from their money.

"One more thing," said Betty Willings, when we had reached my car. "This is going to sound odd."

"Odd in what way?"

Whatever debate Mrs. Willings was having took a moment before she decided to continue. "I don't want to sound like someone who wants to blame Artie's death on something besides the very thing he inherited from his unlucky gene pool—his heart condition."

Sometimes, the only comment required is silence.

"Artie just had his check up, you see, and the doctors told him nothing had changed. Even for a man in his fifties, his heart condition hadn't worsened. An attack could still be dangerous but in this day and age of modern medicine, Artie and I were beginning to hope that maybe he could start thinking about the future instead of just living day to day."

"So, he hadn't been unwell?" I asked.

"Just the opposite. And, he was so happy. He had a nice group of friends at Pop's Place and while he was a short-hitter and never had more than one glass of wine—he would go there two-three times a week. I used to kid him saying if I didn't know better, I would have thought that he had a special friend there."

"And, did he?" I asked.

"No, Artie was in love with being part of something for the first time in his life. Remember, he never had a group of friends because he couldn't really go anywhere or do anything with the rest of the kids. He kept to himself. But this group at Pop's Place—they made him part of it."

I made a mental note to ask Scoop if he knew Arthur. Scoop spent a fair amount of time there, though he rarely talked about the guys he hung out with.

"Artie was even mentoring one young man—can't recall his name, although every time Artie said it, I thought of those Japanese noodles. Anyway, Artie said the guy never had an opportunity to graduate from high school, never mind go to college. Artie tutored him so he could get his GED. Just last week, he told me the young man was applying to Westconn to study criminal justice."

"Your son certainly made a difference," I said, and noted to track down the noodle kid if I could. "You sure you don't remember the guy's name?"

"Sorry, it's like I said. I don't have much of a mind for names these days—they usually pop into my head when I least expect it," she said. "But that's what was going on in my son's life, so to suddenly just up and die with no warning—and then when you mentioned Chester today, it kind of triggered something. Chester Halliday—that was his name." Mrs. Willing's clapped her hands in delight. "I knew I'd remember eventually. Anyway, he was one of Artie's close friends and I know that Chester also hung out at Pop's Place. Both dying just hours apart seems too much of a coincidence."

Chester Halliday. Finally!

"Do you know anything else about Chester?" I asked.

"Everyone said he was homeless. Granted, Artie said the guy never had to pay for his own drinks and Artie helped him out by hiring him for odd jobs. Artie never said, but I had the impression that Chester wasn't who people thought he was, and maybe a select few—like the Pop's Place group—knew that."

"Why do you say that?" I asked.

"You'd have to be blind not to notice the way he held himself. And his clothes—sure they looked well worn, but they didn't totally work on his body. He was gym-toned fit and it was as if he was dressing up for Halloween."

Betty had an eye for detail, that was for sure.

"Besides," she continued, "I seriously doubt Artie was paying him all that money just to rake leaves."

Maybe, the Nosy Parkers were spot-on when they said Chester was only pretending to be homeless.

"Miss Snow, I heard that you and your friends recently solved a mystery. I wonder if you would consider looking into Artie's death a little bit and maybe Chester's too, because the more I think about it, the more I wonder if Artie and Chester were digging around in a place where they shouldn't have."

Chapter Fifteen

There was a lot of commotion when I walked through the door separating the garage from the kitchen. The dogs greeted me like a long lost relative, and neither Richard nor Horace were anywhere in sight. I followed the muffled voices coming from the living room, with the dogs trailing behind me, and stopped short.

"What's everyone doing here?" I asked.

Richard, Horace, and Scoop were sitting in the chairs that flanked the gas fireplace. The flames flickered over expressions that suggested they had just been talking about me. Only then did I remember that I hadn't stopped for the newspaper.

"The paper came out, right? And, my name is still listed as the deceased, isn't it?"

I sunk into the love seat that completed the u-shaped sitting area and shivered despite the warmth of the fire.

"No, not that," Richard reassured. "In fact, I forgot all about it. I don't even have the paper."

"Me either," said Horace, pointing to Scoop. "I was more interested in this."

Scoop cleared his throat and twisted his computer for me to see the latest online post. "There's been another fire."

I stared at a late-breaking news article. A garage on New Street, with an apartment above it, was engulfed in flames. From the picture, the damage was excessive.

I pulled the computer closer. Sure enough, the online story had Scoop's byline.

"My source reemerged," said Scoop.

"Why? I thought they were ghosting you."

Presumably, Scoop's source had clammed up because he or she thought the police were too hot on their tail. If Scoop's source turned out to be one of the firefighters, they'd be in a boatload of trouble. They might even lose their jobs.

"My source says it is important that the other fires are not linked with the two earlier ones," said Scoop. "This story doesn't have the same detail as the first two because my source had no more information than what was in the official statement."

We stared at each other as I let my mind catch up to what he was trying to tell me. Sensing the tension, Diva and Max left the corner of the room where they had companionably rested and filled our space with wagging tails and attention-craving head nudges. I gave each a generous pet before they moved on to Richard and Scoop. Horace settled them back into Max's favorite spot where the two pups retrieved half-gnawed rawhide bones. Both seemed intent on their prize, though I noted their quick glances my way. Diva panted a bit as she tried to settle and I suspect the proximity of the room to the water made her edgy. Not for the first time, I wondered what had occurred in her puppyhood that had instilled her with so many phobias.

"Does that mean what I think it means?" I asked, forming the question I didn't want to voice.

Scoop hung his head and nodded. "At first, I thought my source had the inside track on information and that's why they knew so much."

"But you now think otherwise?" Richard concluded.

"I think that either my source is protecting someone, namely the arsonist, or my source started the first two fires and is now afraid that, if caught, they'll be blamed for everything including Chester's death. In retrospect, I can see why the PD thinks I'm the bad guy. The kind of information I printed—it usually takes a few days to flesh that stuff out—not the few hours that my source or I had. It won't be long before they realize that. I'd like to preempt them. I just don't know how."

As Scoop maintained his pronoun charade, I shook my head.

"Scoop, why would you of all people ever fall for something like that? And why would you continue to protect this . . . this so-called reliable source? I hardly think this person is worth the risk."

"My source is someone I knew would have the kind of information I was printing," said Scoop. "I just got so excited about it that I didn't pay enough attention to the timing. Now, I'm stuck—reveal the source and my credibility is ruined; protect the source and my writing career might be from a remote location behind bars."

Horace shifted. "Now, Winter," he said. "I don't have to tell you what a thrill it must have been for Scoop to 'scoop' those other reporters and papers. He had a source he thought legit. He was reporting accurate information and he got the by-line to boot. And, he got there first. Any reporter could be blinded by that."

"Thanks, Horace, but this is on me," Scoop mumbled, and I could see his admission had turned his cheeks red and if his hair hadn't covered his ears, my guess was that they too were scarlet. "I let my ego overrule my sensibility."

My friend looked lost in the oversized chair he had melded into and appeared as dejected as I've ever seen him. His normally boyish good looks had a hollowed-out edge and I realized he had lost enough weight for it to show in the jeans that now bordered on baggy. Despite my efforts to let things go, his breach of trust had left the air between us still chilly and he had trouble meeting my eyes.

"There's more," said Richard. "Scoop received a death threat."

"From who?" I asked, still trying to wrap my head around everything that was happening in our small New England town which was always winning awards as one of the safest places to live in the United States.

"Death threats don't usually come with a signature," said Scoop. "Which is why I'm here. I don't know what to do and I thought you guys might have an idea."

"Well to start with, you should call the police," I said.

"Would that be the same police who think that I'm the local arsonist?"

"What exactly did the threat say?" I asked, ignoring his sarcasm.

"It's weird," said Scoop, as he reached into his jacket pocket. He pulled a piece of folded printer paper and spread it over the ottoman that doubled as a coffee table. I had to look twice before realizing the black squared print had been written, not typed:

Death comes to those who speak out of turn.

The message itself seemed more like something designated for the Nosy Parkers rather than for Scoop.

"What do you think that means, *speak out of turn*?" asked Richard.

"Well," I said. "If they are threatening Scoop for revealing the truth, they don't know their English language very well. *Speaking out of turn* means you've said something you didn't have the right to say. In other words, it wasn't your story to tell."

"Scoop is a newspaper reporter. He has the responsibility to report on truths that he finds," said Horace, stating the obvious.

"There's more," said Scoop, pointing to another line a few spaces below:

Be careful that the cat you let out of the bag isn't the cat that gets the sack.

"I guess they were trying to be clever," I said. "What secrets are you keeping? Something to do with Pop's Place maybe, because I doubt your source would be threatening you?"

"It's not from my source. I already confronted them."

"Scoop does have cats—maybe, it was a reference to them," said Horace.

"Or a threat to them—you tell and the cats die," said Richard.

It was then that Scoop jumped from his seat and raced to the hallway bathroom, slamming the door behind him. The distinct sound of retching made me gag.

Chapter Sixteen

The familiar sounds and smells in the kitchen, as Richard "rustled up some dinner," restored some of the balance often missing from the house since he'd moved out. Scoop had recovered from his bathroom episode enough to disappear into the fireside chair again. After delivering a glass of water to him, Horace and the dogs joined my uncle.

"Are you OK?" I asked, studying Scoop's bleached-flour pallor.

"Not really," he said.

"Do you want to talk about this? Because I don't know what 'this' is, though I'm beginning to realize it can't be about a couple of insurance scamming arsonists. You need to tell me what the heck is going on at Pop's Place."

Scoop had no reaction at my mention of Pop's Place and I suspected that the threatening letters and his subsequent violent reaction had to do with Chester's murder. I had originally discounted the Nosy Parkers' claim that he had been the last one to see the man alive, although now, I wondered.

Scoop stared out at the lake, the place everyone seeks unrequited refuge, when in difficult conversation. I looked too, a habit honed from years of practice. What was that saying—insanity is doing the same thing over and over again and expecting a different result?

My friend was almost ashen now as he reached for the glass of water with shaky hands.

"I heard that the guy who lived in that New Street apartment just managed to get out in time. If someone did that to me—I don't have another exit and if I wasn't home, Heady, Topper, and the other little guys would be killed."

"You also have very good smoke, heat, and CO_2 detection. Not to mention the firehouse is still right across the street. Plus, cats have a way of self-preserving. They would hide in the most smoke-free space available and wouldn't reemerge until the fire was out and the firefighters were gone."

Scoop was clearly eager for some relief to his anxiety because he had such hope in his voice when he asked, "You think so?"

"I think you know who lives in the apartment that was recently burned, don't you?" I said it more as a statement because Scoop knew way too much about the guy's escape to have gotten it from official statements. "Was it your source, by chance?"

"Let it go, Winter," he said.

* * *

Afternoon had slipped into shadow. I hadn't received any texts from anyone asking about an obituary in the print edition, though I had several from Kip asking me to call when I had a chance. Richard served a meat sauce over corkscrew pasta, salad, and ciabatta.

"What happened to the lasagna?" I asked, as Scoop pushed food around his plate, only taking a nibble here and there.

"Already in the freezer," he said. "I cobbled this together from the leftover sauce."

We fell into a quiet that was the opposite of our normal dinner conversations. Maybe, this was as good a time as any to ask the question that had been bothering me. Before I could, however, Horace piped up.

"Your uncle appears to be planning for an invasion," he said. "Richard, you might as well tell Winter what's going on."

I put my fork down and even Scoop appeared to come out of his stupor.

"Tell me what?" I asked.

Richard sent Horace a look that said, *you're speaking out of turn!*

"Don't get huffy, Richard. The girl has a right to know," said Horace, and then he reached for another slice of bread. "Pass that butter, will you?"

Scoop slid the butter dish toward Horace before turning to Richard.

"I'm sure this is private," he said. "In fact, I think I need to get going anyway."

"It's not," said Richard, who then turned to me. "Look, I have a few things going on. I just feel like it's a good idea for me to hang out here for a little while. I mean, if that's OK."

"What kind of things?" I asked, trying to keep the alarm out of my voice.

Before Richard could answer, Scoop slid his chair noisily from the table. "I'm going to take off. Winter, I'll pick up a copy of the paper on my way home and I'll give you a call to let you know if you're dead or alive."

It was a relief to hear some of Scoop's humor return, though he hadn't put much energy behind the comment. He stooped to give the dogs a pet and with a wave, trudged to the living room to retrieve his computer bag. A minute later, I heard the front door close and the noisy rattle of his scooter starting.

"I'm leaving too. Can you two do the dog walk?" Horace didn't wait for an answer. He stacked his and Scoop's plates next to the sink and hurried from the kitchen.

"Well, that was . . . unexpected. Sounds like those two already know what you're about to say and definitely did not want to be here for my reaction."

"Nah, it's nothing like that. I think they thought we should have some privacy is all," said my uncle.

"OK, we have it. What is going on? You usually cook when you have something on your mind and I suspect we have enough food to take us through the winter. Are you having second thoughts about living at Village Square? Because I can tell you right now, I have no problem reversing the deal and giving you the cottage back. It's more yours than mine anyway."

Richard winced at that and I realized that it made me sound ungrateful that he had turned over his pride and joy to me, his niece.

"I could have some of this stuff removed," he said, waving his hand at the kitchen table and chairs. "It was never a stipulation that you keep the cottage as is. I should have considered that you'd like to do your own thing here."

Richard looked as if he just realized that the birthday gift he had so carefully chosen last April, was meant for someone half the age.

"That isn't what I meant at all," I assured him. "This cottage is its own being, in a way, and I couldn't imagine it without all these things. What I meant is that if you want to come home, I'm OK with that. You do seem to be spending more time here than not, so I figured . . ."

Richard smiled and reached over to pat my hand.

"You're a good one," he said, and rose.

"Hey, wait, you aren't leaving until I know what is going on," I said. I must've sounded like the school principal because Richard immediately sat back down and cleared his throat.

"I met someone," he blurted out.

The breath I had been holding escaped like the air from a punctured tire. I had been gearing up for rounds of chemotherapy, a fatal diagnosis, or at the very least, trips to the doctor. I was so relieved, I giggled.

Richard frowned. "What's so funny? You think I'm too old?"

"Too old? Not at all. I'm just surprised that all this is just about you meeting someone. You know how my imagination works. I had you on death row."

Richard smiled. "News isn't always bad, you know."

That other shoe had a habit of dropping more often than I liked, though I didn't tell Richard that.

"I would think that if you met someone, you'd rather spend more time with her than me!"

"It's complicated," he said.

"It always is." I said with a smile in my voice. These were words my uncle had voiced many times over the years.

The familiar phrase went right over Richard's head as he explained that the two had met at Westconn, an awkward situation at best.

I looked at him suspiciously. Richard was an adjunct professor at the university in next-door Danbury where my mom had gotten her nursing degree all those years ago. I broke out in a cold bead of panic and said a silent prayer that Richard hadn't gotten involved with one of his students because that cliché never seemed to turn out well.

Richard stood and walked to the built-in wine cooler that he kept well-stocked.

"I have some Rombauer if you'd like a glass," he offered, as he went about pouring himself a full-bodied Barbaresco. "I didn't want to waste this on corkscrew pasta—it deserves a really nice Italian gourmet menu." Richard smacked his lips with the flavor. "Intense. As the saying goes, *Life's too short to drink cheap wine.*"

I glanced at my ever-present phone. More texts from Kip. By now, he would be finished with his Mariner burger and hoping to head over. I texted back. Nothing from Scoop yet. Right about now, I'd welcome a glass of wine.

Richard returned to the table and placed a generous pour of the pricey California Chardonnay in front of me.

"You do know you are spoiling me with these nice wines, right?" I asked, as I savored the full buttery flavor.

"We're moving in together," he said.

I almost doubled over as the wine caught in my throat and debated whether to exit through nose or mouth.

Richard was on his feet, patting my back, racing to the sink for a glass of water, pulling Kleenex from the tissue box to help dab my flooded eyes.

"I knew it," he said. "I was right to think you'd be upset at the thought of me moving in with someone."

When I finally stopped coughing and caught my breath, I shook my head the way Diva did when she had nosed into something unpleasant.

"It's not that," I rasped out. "You just took me by surprise."

Finally, I stopped choking enough to ask who his lady friend might be.

"She's a professor and it's funny that we only just met last spring because she's been there over twenty years and I've been there for how long?"

Richard started an unnecessary finger tick. It was ten years ago that he semi-retired from his job in Silicon Valley—the same year my sister died—as if the date was ever far from our minds.

The relief at finding out that his lady friend had been there at least two decades made me giddy. What had I been thinking? Richard would never have gotten involved with one of his students. And then, I wondered about this woman. *What if she was a gold-digging opportunist after my uncle's sizeable bank account?*

Richard was babbling between sips as he told the story of spilled coffee, a messy cleanup, and all the six degrees of separation stuff that happened as the two started to meet occasionally between classes.

What a niece! I could kick myself for not picking up on the clues; for one, Richard's recent efforts to get in better shape by upping his daily walk routine and adding chair yoga.

"I just didn't know how to tell you that we were moving in together," Richard continued. He went on to say that it would be more practical if he spent more time here at the Lake Mamanasco cottage while his bungalow was being renovated. The idea had been for his girlfriend, whose name was Mary, to purchase the attached unit next door and combine both for more space. Several folks had already done that, though as Richard explained, there was a lot of red tape. Village Square wanted to make sure a certain percentage of the units remained small enough for people who came in as singles, so he had to petition for this and there would soon be a vote by board.

Richard explained that with two others already combined, it would come down to whether the assisted care units and the health center would be included in the percentage count.

Meanwhile, Mary was on a sabbatical and wouldn't be back until next semester.

"Do Gabby and Abby have a double unit?" I asked because a successful vote might be influenced by the gossip campaign I was sure they would wage.

"No, theirs is a two bedroom. But, they really like Mary."

"What will you do if you are voted down?" I asked.

Richard frowned. "I'm not sure, although we think the owners are looking at this very favorably. They even applied for two bedrooms when they went for permits to add units."

"I'm not kidding about transferring the cottage back to you," I said. "And why in the world were you worried about telling me you were seeing someone? Don't you know that if you're happy, I'm happy?"

Richard didn't answer and looked out toward the lake. We stayed quiet as we took in the eerie glow created by the homes surrounding Mamanasco. Most had been transformed from small, cramped cottages to luxurious houses designed to take advantage of the peaceful view. A few, like Horace's, still clung to an earlier era when this was one of several Ridgefield lake communities that had been a refuge for New Yorkers escaping the hot city in the summer.

"Did you hear me, Richard? If you are happy, then I am happy."

He smiled. "I know that."

Richard avoided my eyes as he hurriedly rose to begin the cleanup. That simple evasion told me there would be a lot more cooking in my kitchen, because my uncle still had more on his mind.

Chapter Seventeen

If daytime was uncertain about what time of year it was, nighttime had no such confusion. I pulled my fleece closer to my body and picked up my pace, as Richard and I walked the dogs.

"Makes you feel alive," said my uncle, though I noted that he too zipped his coat up higher and wrapped his scarf, so it covered his neck rather than just hung down over his shoulders as was his habit. As we walked, I tried to pry out more information about Mary but Richard had shut the door on that conversation. Instead, he began a slow steady interrogation about everything I had found out related to Chester's murder. I explained about Betty Willings' strange question about her son's death being related to Chester's and how, like the Nosy Parkers, she suspected that Chester wasn't who people thought he was. I left out the information about Scoop's increasingly odd behavior, his tossed apartment, and his invasion of my study. I saw no reason to cast a cloud over Scoop or to give my uncle any additional reasons to worry.

By unspoken agreement, the garage apartment was Richard's domain where he kept some of his belongings so he could crash when he needed a "lake fix." Now that he and this Mary were moving in together, I wondered if he would take all of that with him, or if Mary would suddenly be adding her clothes to the closet.

Richard announced that despite his need to stay at the Lake Mamanasco cottage while the renovations were underway, he would go home tonight because he had early morning meetings with the kitchen contractors.

"Just remember what I told you about the cottage—you and Mary are always welcome and if Village Square doesn't allow you to combine your units into one, you can come back here to live. I can get an apartment—heck, I'm already planning that part time move to Manhattan."

Richard has one of those faces that no matter how poker he tries to play it, his expressions are a dead giveaway. I was sorry that I mentioned my move.

As if grasping for a lifeline, he asked, "All good with Kip?"

My boyfriend's harsh words, earlier in the day, still rankled.

"It would be better if he would tell me what is going on with Chester, Scoop, the fires, and everything else that's happening in town."

We were just steps from Horace's cottage when he opened the door, and Max bounded ahead, taking the three steps as if they were one, his tail wagging like a flag in a gale. Back home, Richard waved goodnight, and while Diva plopped down contentedly with her chew toy, I returned Kip's calls.

"I was worried about you," he said, and those simple words made me smile.

"Sorry, long day. Any chance you picked up the newspaper?" I asked more hopeful than I wanted to be. I had forgotten to stop on my way home from visiting Betty Willings and then, after Scoop's threatening notes and Richard's big reveal, I didn't even know what would still be open.

"Geez, I'm sorry, I forgot. Are you still written into the obituary?" he asked.

"I don't know. I haven't seen the print version and Amanda from the paper hasn't called me back," I said.

Kip offered to do a town run and I told him that I could ask Carla or just wait until tomorrow. Wouldn't I have had a barrage of texts, calls, or emails, if the obit hadn't been fixed?

I told Kip about Richard's girlfriend, Mary, which is why I hadn't called him back earlier.

"And?"

"I hope she isn't some gold digger and is worthy of him," I said.

Kip chuckled and asked what I had done today. I didn't have it in me to explain the entire Arthur Willings connection to Chester Halliday, and from the yawn I heard Kip stifling on the other end, he didn't have it in him to listen.

"Winter, are you sure you're OK? I can still come over."

"I'm tucked in with Diva and there was no sign of the bear on our walk tonight," I assured him.

"I wasn't worried about the bear," said Kip.

"What then?"

Kip took a deep breath. "You're writing an obituary for a guy who was murdered. What if the murderer thinks you knew the guy and decides to tie up loose ends just in case . . ."

"In case what? I don't see how writing a person's obituary makes me privy to their deep dark secrets."

"I suppose you're right," said Kip. "I was just remembering how we all almost lost our lives because people thought you knew more than you did."

It would be hard to forget my crazed client who had no problem murdering for money.

"I'm only writing tributes to a person I didn't know. It's no different than what I do almost every day of the week."

We wandered into other things and I was careful not to let it slip that I was more curious than ever now that I knew Arthur Willings had hired Chester to do odd jobs. And, they were both dead within hours of each other. What would Arthur's autopsy reveal? Maybe Mrs. Willings' question had merit.

"Scoop is really in a bucket of it." Kip startled me by dropping the statement as if we had been discussing it all along.

When I asked what he meant, Kip explained that Scoop had printed information about the first two arsons that had not yet been released. He could only have gotten that info if his source was the arsonist or if he had started the fires himself.

"Not necessarily," I said. "His source might know someone who is feeding him."

"Fine," said Kip with finality. "Either way, unless he comes clean, I can't protect him any longer."

Interesting. Kip trying to protect Scoop surprised me.

"Look, you could know almost anything about the fire if you were there watching or had some insight into the place and the people," I said.

"You wouldn't know what accelerant was used to start the fires before the RFD found out. For that, you'd have to have information directly or indirectly from the arsonist himself. Oh, and by the way, even if that information was available, they did not intend to release it to the public."

"Because they wanted to have a detail only the arsonist would know?"

"You got it."

Grave Words

I could almost hear the pounding of the nails in Scoop's coffin.

* * *

After ending my call with Kip, I carried a cup of lemon ginger tea onto the deck, hoping that the chill in the air would clear my brain. The tea was part of Richard's collection that he kept in a tea caddy on the counter. I had to admit, as much as I loved the lavender chamomile I usually favored, this had a soothing effect.

The warm liquid did little against the temperature drop and I shivered, not sure if it was against the chill or the gut-wrenching fear that my friend really could have something to do with the arsons. Maybe he did want more award-winning stories and had resorted to making up a source to cover his involvement. Every instinct about Scoop screamed no, impossible. And yet, his strange behavior of late and this new piece of information planted the seed of doubt.

Diva hovered near the wide expanse of doors and windows that opened on to the deck. I gave her a beckoning pat against my leg, though the puppy stayed put. The dog hadn't gotten over her intense fear of water and if I wanted her on the deck, I'd have to drag her out there.

Back inside with doors locked against the chill, I fired up the gas fireplace, snuggled into one of the chairs that Richard, Horace, and Scoop had been in just a few hours earlier, and opened my laptop. Scoop's problems aside, I had an obituary for Chester to write and to do it well, I had to find his next of kin.

Employing a technique that I had found successful in the past, I went straight to Legacy.com and typed in Halliday. A list appeared and I began a scroll, reading every obituary. Laura Halliday McGown, David Donald Halliday, Mark Halliday, and on and on it went. Some with one *L*, some with two. There were tributes and often there were repeats, the obituaries showing up in multiple places. I searched everything Halliday. Last name alone. Then first and last name in case Chester had been named after his dad and would be listed that way. No such luck.

A number of women popped up, though none would fit the time frame for Wandering Chester if he had a sister. I then followed through with all the women where Halliday emerged often as a maiden name.

I had to read through every obituary because what I was really searching for was next of kin with the same name as Chester. I finally zeroed in on an obituary for a Howard (Hal) John Halliday of Nyack, New York, who had died six months earlier. I liked this one because the town wasn't far away from Ridgefield. I was a bit uncertain because this Hal was quite a bit older than the estimated fiftyish Chester. The clincher was when I saw listed in the next of kin, a brother named Chesterfield Halliday.

I made a note of the man's wife, an Anne Halliday. After doing a search and finding both her address and, then paying for, her cell phone number, I inhaled deeply. I let my shoulders rise and fall before making a cold call.

Anne Halliday's *hello* had a question mark at the end of it and made me check the clock to make sure I wasn't calling at what I called the *nerve-wracking bad news on the horizon* hour—the times when it was too early or too late for social conversations.

Once I introduced myself and asked about Chester, however, I was surprised at how open and willing the woman was. We made a plan for me to visit tomorrow and I hung up, relieved that I had finally found our homeless man's family.

Diva and I had settled in my room, window cracked, because there is nothing like fresh air for a good sleep. Diva looked hopefully at my bed. She was getting bigger now and while I had initially allowed her to snuggle with me, I could see the writing on the wall. She was no longer the size of a large cat and had already outgrown two collars. The sooner she learned to sleep on her bed in the corner of the room, the better. I had been trying to train her to do that.

Interestingly, though, her bed would move closer and closer to me in the night.

"Ok, how about we make a change," I said to the pup, and dragged her dog bed so that I could flop an arm over and touch her furry head. If I needed a clear exit, I'd have to scooch over to the other side of the queen bed. Oblivious to the inconvenience, my dog curled onto her bed and closed her eyes.

Lights out, window open, pup in place—of course that was when Scoop's caller ID flashed on my cell phone.

"Sorry, CVS was still out of the paper, and I didn't have the energy to run all over town looking for one," said Scoop. Then he shifted gears, asking if anyone had called me about the arsons—no doubt the real reason for this conversation.

I wasn't sure if I was the one who should confront Scoop about his knowledge of the fires—especially the fact that he knew which accelerant had been used before it had been confirmed.

Or was I? Maybe that's why Kip broke his cardinal rule of never discussing his cases with me. I thought back to our conversation during our walk yesterday, about trust. I also recalled the discussion the night of the deck party, when I insisted that we help Scoop. Did he sense the growing wedge between us? Was this his way of showing me that he could be trusted, and he would try to help?

And, what was I supposed to do with that information? Did he want me to warn Scoop? And if I did, what good would it do? It's not like Scoop could disappear. He had a mother in memory care and an apartment full of cats depending on him.

"I thought maybe when you talked to Kip, you would have told him about my threats," he continued. "That might convince him that I didn't have anything to do with this.'

"Or he might say you wrote the notes yourself," I pointed out.

Scoop let an exasperated groan. "Why do you always have to have a plausible alternative to all my reasoning?"

I didn't really think Scoop would have penned the notes, although he was playing his cards close to the vest, and his lack of cooperation with the police wouldn't earn him any sympathy points.

"You need to figure something out with this source of yours because he or she gave you information that even the fire department hadn't yet confirmed. In other words, information that only the arsonist would know. Do you get what I'm telling you?" I asked.

Scoop was silent as he processed. Finally, he asked, "When did you figure it out?"

"You could be charged, end up in jail, lose everything you've been working toward, and that's your question?"

"It's my question because if you told me this earlier tonight when I hinted at it, I would have handled things differently. Now, I'm on the defensive." Scoop's anger leaked through the phone.

"You've been on the defensive all along and for your information, I only just found out but I suspect you've known all along that you screwed up. Am I right?" If people could bark, I'd be doing it. Even Diva perked up at the sound of my angry voice.

"Thanks for the heads up," he said, and then, he clicked off.

Chapter Eighteen

For Diva, riding in a car is akin to the way I feel about sliding into an MRI tube. She starts panting so hard that the fur beneath her face and down her chest becomes so drenched, you'd think she'd just had a shower. By the time we reach our destination, the Subaru looks like it's gone through a carwash with the windows open. In short, I only take her in the car when necessary.

Richard was waiting with an old towel when we arrived at his Village Square bungalow, and when I opened the door to let Diva out, she bounded at him as if he were her savior. She didn't even complain as he wiped her down.

"Wow! She's getting big. What are you and Horace feeding her over there?" he asked as he put two fingers between her neck and the collar she wore. I had already replaced it twice since we first acquired the little ball of fur, and even sitting, she already reached close to my hip.

"Don't tell me she needs another collar." I peered at Diva like a mother who is suddenly aware that her child's shoes are two sizes too small.

"She's OK for the moment," he said, giving her a pat which she leaned into. Diva thought that everyone was put on earth for her alone, and she was happiest when that notion was confirmed by pets, walks, or any other kind of attention she was given. Whether she was aptly named or she grew into it, who knew. Either way, she was definitely a Diva.

The drive to Nyack should take only forty-five minutes, unless there was a lot of Friday traffic. When I told Richard I wasn't sure exactly how long I'd be gone, he let me know that Diva could stay with him as long as I needed.

"As for you," he said, giving Diva a pet, "we'll do a nice long Main Street walk, how does that sound?"

* * *

I left uncle and dog to their walk and climbed into my car. My first destination was to get the newspaper to see how my client's obit read. I ran into CVS—still no papers, and the helpful salesperson told me they'd sold out yesterday. I let out a frustrated sigh as I contemplated where else to try. With no physical presence of the newspaper in town, I decided on our only supermarket. No papers there either. I had a sneaking suspicion that there had been an uptick in paper sales due to the ongoing fire investigations. Still, this was beyond frustrating. Even a call to Amanda sent me to voicemail.

With no more time to spare, I headed up West Mountain Road and into South Salem, where Bouton Road would take me to Route 35. I had already loaded an audio book in my phone, something I rarely climbed into my Subaru without. I was well into the trials and travails of life in Three Pines with Inspector Gamache, when the car in front of me hit the brakes hard. I was quick to flip on my blinker and check my sideview mirror as I squeezed into the lane to my right just in time to avoid hitting the vehicle coming up beside me. The tinted windows didn't allow me to see the driver of the black SUV, so I waved my thanks grateful that he or she didn't blast a horn. As I passed the car that had caused the near miss, I was about to give the driver a *bad move* shake of the head, when I could see that he had stopped to avoid hitting a confused baby deer. The deer waivered a bit before turning back toward the woods from where it had originally emerged. That had been one quick reacting driver to avoid the demise of Bambi, a frequent occurrence on these country roads.

I slowed my speed, wove back into the other lane, and decided to leave more car lengths between me and the guy in front. The black SUV was now beside me and I slowed even more to give it a chance to pull ahead and into my lane. Despite the left blinker going, it dropped back and fell in line a few vehicles behind. I guessed that I wasn't the only one shaken by the close call.

I wove my way onto the Saw Mill River Parkway, keeping close to the speed limit. It's a scenic road, though narrow, with winding hair pin turns and sudden stop lights in the middle of the highway. Cars whizzed by like they were competing for a NASCAR trophy, and definitely too fast for this ancient New England relic. I settled into what my uncle calls a Sunday drive—slow and easy.

My cell rang. I was reluctant to leave my audio mystery, though I glanced at the phone, now propped into a holder attached to the heating grill. Caller ID said it was Scoop. The gulf between us had been growing and it upset me to think that I might lose my best friend.

Phone calls with Scoop had always been our way to keep in touch. Long nights discussing the pros and cons of staying with the newspaper, or trying to help each other out on a story, is how we had become such good friends in the first place. Maybe that's how our fences would mend.

"Hey," I said.

"Where are you? Driving, I presume, and definitely breaking the law because I know you don't have hands-free."

"I got this device that attaches to my visor. The good news is that it connects to my phone by Bluetooth. The bad news is that you sound like you are talking from the bottom of a well."

"You sound a little distant, though I can hear you, at least for the moment," he said. "Where exactly are you, somewhere easy to talk?"

"Crossing the Tappan Zee... I mean the Mario M. Cuomo Bridge." Why in the world did New York take perfectly good bridge names and turn them into something political? What was wrong with the Triborough Bridge? It connected three boroughs, for God's sake! Now, it's the Robert F. Kennedy Bridge. Talk about something that described nothing!

I had landed in the middle lane of the three-mile-long expanse over the widest part of the Hudson River, which connects Westchester and Rockland counties. On any given day, the shared bike/footpath is crowded with people, and I had a sudden urge to ride my bike across the spectacular twin span that replaced the old Tappan Zee in 2018.

"Hold on," I said as I turned my blinker to move into the slower lane again.

I checked my sideview mirror and did the awkward over the shoulder look, feeling envy for those with the three lighted safety indicators on their mirrors, that let you know if someone was too close to change lanes. As I moved over, I was surprised to see that there was an SUV, black with tinted windows, looking very much like the one that I had cut off earlier. It was a couple of car lengths back. A shiver ran through me. The car hadn't honked in annoyance earlier when I cut it off; however, what if some road rage infested driver was just biding his time.

"I can talk now," I said, keeping an eye in my rearview on the SUV.

"I called to apologize," he said.

"For which transgression—your rude comments, your unjustified anger, or for just plain being a lousy friend for not telling me what's going on, and oh, don't forget, for breaking into my study."

Traffic was light, so I did a calculated lane change, making sure the cars behind me closed the gap before I switched. That earned me a honk. The SUV lagged back and waited for a large traffic gap, and then, followed me into my lane.

"Geez, Winter, you really know how to lay the guilt on."

I said nothing.

"OK, I get it. I really have been a jerk and I'm apologizing for all of the above. How can I make it up . . ."

"Scoop," I interrupted. "I think there might be someone following me."

I expected to hear the deep telltale sigh that always followed when I made such comments. Next, I'd hear, *You're an alarmist. You can make a mountain out of a molehill. I've never met anyone as paranoid as you.*

Instead, Scoop's voice took on an urgent tone. "Where are you headed?"

"To Nyack, to see Mrs. Halliday, Chester's sister-in-law, and the exit is coming right up. My GPS won't work while I'm on the phone, so I'll have to call you back."

I was about to disconnect when Scoop's intake of breath rattled through the receiver. "Wait, so you found out his last name? How did you find the sister-in-law?"

I recapped how Betty Willings had given me Chester's last name and how that led to a search for his family. I was talking fast now, watching as the SUV followed me into the slow lane again. I watched as it dropped back, putting a little distance between us. Did they know I was onto them?

Keeping an eye on the stalking vehicle, I stayed in the right-hand lane because my exit was just a mile away.

"I came across Chester's name as next of kin to a Howard Halliday when I searched for online obituaries," I continued telling Scoop. "Howard's wife was listed as Anne. From there, it was just a matter of getting her contact info."

"You'd make a good investigative reporter," said Scoop.

I laughed because we both knew that had once been my dream. That was before I realized that I was better suited for writing features than trying to separate fact from fiction when it came to writing the news.

"I'll leave that job to you. Listen, let's talk later—my exit is coming up."

"*Wait*," Scoop hollered into the phone so loud that the hands-free device squealed in protest like a mic turned too loud. "Are you still being followed?"

I looked in the rear-view mirror and the black car was still with me.

"Still there."

"Don't hang up and don't get off the exit." Had my paranoia finally rubbed off on my poor friend? "Keep going for about fifteen more minutes and get off at the Garden State Parkway—then, take the exit for Ridgewood. I can walk you through it if you stay on the line."

"Why am I doing all of that?"

"In case someone really is following you. The Ridgewood exit is tricky and if you do as I say, you can lose the tail."

I listened as Scoop guided me to the Garden State, traveling in the far-left of the three lanes to see if the black SUV stayed with me. It did.

"When you see where it says, you can go straight through with the EZ pass or go to the full-service lanes on the right; you're going to take the full service at the last minute. Don't use your blinker—just change lanes at the very last second," instructed Scoop. "Anyone caught in the two left lanes has to keep going and the next exit is quite a way down."

Another near miss in the making. Keeping an eye on the black SUV, I stayed in the far-left lane as if I intended to bypass the exit. The car followed. I timed the break in traffic just right and at the last minute crossed two lanes to the far right, bringing an eruption of horns from angry drivers.

Winter Snow, 29, died trying to escape from a road rage stalker . . .

"How do you know all this?" I asked, as I squeaked in front of a driver who slowed to let me in. I waved my thanks and he blasted his horn in response. I guess my Connecticut tags weren't enough to elicit forgiveness.

"My cousins live in Ridgewood, and we used to visit them all the time. I could find my way there with my eyes closed. Did you lose the tail?"

My execution had been perfect, save for the horn blows. I was ready for triumph when I sailed through the toll lane, EZ pass at the ready. Once cleared, I finally was able to check my rear view.

"Oh my God, the guy is still there. What do I do?"

Scoop had a backup plan. "Turn right after the toll booth, then turn left toward downtown Ridgewood."

When I asked what I was to do there, Scoop instructed that I would be in a very busy part of town and that I'd park, enter a nice coffee shop, and inform Mrs. Halliday that I'd be late.

"That car can wait me out."

"Just stay put when you get to the coffee shop. I'm on it."

I cruised up Linwood Avenue until I reached a stoplight. A large, man-made pond and recreation area, drained for the season, bordered one side. Ballfields and municipal buildings lay on the other. I crossed the intersection and made a left at the next light onto Oak Street, which brought me into the charming Village of Ridgewood. I made a right on Franklin, passing a cluster of restaurants and day spas. My shadow was with me at every turn, but the traffic and pedestrians gave me comfort. I doubted anyone would attack me in broad daylight with so many witnesses. Turning onto Chestnut, however, cooled that comfort. Scoop had been wrong about it being busy.

It was being readied for a repaving project and "no parking" notices were posted up and down the street. Rey Sol sat toward the middle of the block, between a mediterranean restaurant and a place called Cozy Nails. There was some foot traffic but no cars, giving the place a desolate feel. After lapping the block twice, I settled for a public lot diagonally across the street from the coffee shop. As I pulled into a spot in the emptier half of the lot near the street, I watched the black SUV slow at the lot entrance then pull into one of the empty "no parking" spaces along Chestnut. The tinted windows hid the driver, though he had a clear view of my Subaru. I was pondering my next move when another car, a gray Audi, parked in a spot nearby. A woman emerged from the driver's side and walked to a standalone machine near the entrance. I climbed out of my car and followed, feeling like I was in someone's crosshairs. After the woman punched in her plate number and dipped her credit card, I asked if she'd show me how to operate the meter. It was help I didn't need, but I figured staying near her would deter any action from the person following me.

"Sure thing," she said in the gracious way of people who like to help. She was maybe mid-forties, her jeans crisp and blue, beige flannel stylishly rumpled. She glanced over at my car. It sat alone, surrounded by empty spaces. "Connecticut, huh? Whereabouts?"

At the mention of Ridgefield, she lit up. "My brother and his family live off West Lane," she said. "We'll be there again for Thanksgiving this year."

Our small-world conversation continued as she coached me through the parking payment process. She noted the similarities of our two towns—population size, demographics, small-town vibe, strong community. "It's a tale of two Ridges," she quipped. "What brings you here?"

"A friend," I said, which was technically true. "I'm going to wait at Rey Sol."

"Oh, they are so sweet in there," she said. "I highly recommend the spinach empanadas."

We finished with the machine and started walking up the sidewalk together. The carabiner that attached my keys to my purse jingled loudly as we walked, and my new friend named Kathy laughed, saying I was a bit early for Santa. I explained that I was one of those people who could lose their car keys in a pocket, so I always used the handy clip.

Kathy was heading to Cozy Nails for a manicure. In my peripheral vision, I could see the black SUV idling.

Near the middle of the block, we crossed the street. Outdoor dining tables were set along the sidewalk, though there were few patrons willing to brave the autumn chill. I gave Kathy my card and told her to drop a line if she ever needed anything in the "other Ridge." Then she was on her way, and I stepped into the coffee shop.

Rey Sol, with its wood floors, tables, and millwork, had a barn-like décor, punctuated by a mural of mountains amid pale green fronds on one wall and a brick façade behind the counter on the other. An antique industrial-size coffee grinder anchored the front of the shop next to a large window with panoramic views of the street. There was only one entrance, so it was easy to keep track of who was coming and going. And most people weren't going. It was the kind of place that encouraged you to stay, whether to socialize or scroll a screen. Clearly, they were a victim of their own success because a sign on the counter asked patrons to limit their stay to one hour. I hoped I wouldn't need that long.

I ordered a chamomile tea to calm my nerves, then perched on one of the barstools at the front window. People inside were engrossed in their laptops or phones and the only customers coming in after me were three teen girls, complete with giggles, who appeared to be skipping school to drink designer coffees. As Scoop had suggested, I called Mrs. Halliday and explained my delay, then called Scoop.

"Is the guy still on you?" he asked.

"Not sure," I said, scanning the street for the umpteenth time.

Outside, a woman clearly in a battle with one of her two young children was clinging to the other so the tot wouldn't escape. A pensive young man lurking in a doorway caught my attention until he suddenly brightened at the sight of a girl walking down the sidewalk toward him. When she fell into his arms, the joy on their faces made me wonder about their story. Two bundled-up moms with strollers shrouded in blankets were sitting outside, soaking up the last vestiges of autumn. The only other faces on the street were a ghost, a witch, and a jack-o-lantern, staring out from a window-painting on one of the opposite storefronts.

"Now what?" I asked.

"Stay put and leave it to me," Scoop said. "Though you're going to be a little late for your appointment."

Chapter Nineteen

One chamomile tea and a chocolate chip brownie later, I was back on the road—this time in Scoop's cousin's truck—while another of his cousins named Nat orchestrated Subaru subterfuge.

I had followed Scoop's instructions by exiting Rey Sol and heading to my car, which I had climbed into and started. I then pulled my phone and hunched over it, as if reading important texts. A red pickup sat next to my car, its engine idling.

A moment later, Nat leapt from the driver's side, leaving the door open on the sheltered side of the truck. She hurried around to the passenger side, where in full view of the SUV, a man had jumped out and slammed the door. She began to yell at him and wave her arms, and soon they were both gesturing aggressively as they argued.

Per instructions, I slid across my seat and opened the passenger side door. Keeping low, I scooted out of my car and ducked into the driver's seat of the idling red pickup. I stayed out of sight as I pulled on a Yankees baseball cap and sunglasses, duplicates of those worn by the arm-waving woman. A moment later, she jabbed her finger at the man's chest and pointed to the passenger door. He made a show of looking cowed and climbed back in.

"Once I'm in your car, count to three, you pop up, and slam your door," she whispered.

I did as she instructed, and a minute later, she was behind the wheel of my car, wearing my sunglasses, her hair pulled back in a ponytail, and hunched over her phone. Anyone watching would assume that she had been sitting there the entire time and that the arguing couple were now back in their truck.

What a waste of time if my stalker was no longer nearby, because their acting was Broadway-worthy.

"Peel out of the parking lot like you're angry," my co-passenger had said.

That wasn't hard because I wasn't used to the clutch on standard shift of the old truck. One buck, a screech, and I was tearing out of the parking lot. In my rearview, I watched as my Subaru eased out onto the street, heading in the opposite direction.

"Hit the corner, turn into the bank parking lot, and inch out enough for us to see if anyone follows." My passenger, a man I approximated to be in his thirties, wore a collared ecru shirt tucked into his well-cut jeans. His black leather jacket hung open loosely.

"I'm Scoop's cousin, Ben, by the way," he said, his eyes following the retreating Subaru. "What we are going to do here is trail after your car to see who might be tailing you. Once we're sure the mark hasn't figured out what we're doing, you can take my truck to your destination. We'll rendezvous later."

"What about you?" I asked pretty confused because I didn't know the end game.

"You'll see," he said.

* * *

The black SUV materialized behind my car by the time the driver reached the corner. It kept with her as she drove in circles, in and out of neighborhoods. Ben bypassed some of the wanderings to stay out of sight, and because he knew the roads well, he was able to reconnect on the busier streets. We passed charming houses, adorable neighborhoods, neighbors walking, conversing, and heading to destinations I would never know. Ben repeatedly attempted to snap a shot of the stalker's license plate.

"OK, we're good," said Ben. "Let's head toward the highway. You can drop me at that corner up there. In about fifteen minutes, Nat will pick me up. She'll make a big show of getting out the car, so the guy following will realize he's been duped. By then, you should be in Nyack."

"What if he's a bad guy and tries to coerce you into telling where I've gone?"

"Didn't Scoop tell you? We help folks out with messy things all the time. Nat is wearing a cop uniform under all that bulky clothing. She'll take the fleece off before she gets to the rendezvous. Once he sees the uniform, it should discourage him from approaching."

I hoped Ben was right and that I hadn't inadvertently put Scoop's cousins in jeopardy.

And your truck?" I asked.

"Call when your visit is over. We'll meet you on the other side of the bridge. That way, even if we haven't convinced the tail that his efforts were useless, we can switch cars without him ever knowing where you went . . . unless you're afraid of him, in which case, I'll arrange with Scoop on getting the car back. Gosh, it was good to hear from my cousin. Life is so busy that we haven't gotten together much."

When I thanked Ben for the help, he grinned widely, and said he hadn't had that much fun since he and Scoop used to play cops and robbers.

Once I dropped Ben at the designated rendezvous point and got on the highway headed back to Nyack, I reported back to Scoop.

"Thank you for believing that there really was a tail," I said.

"I know you have a tendency to exaggerate, but there's too much going on to ignore the possibility."

"Why would someone be after me?" I asked.

"You ask a lot of questions," said Scoop. "The guy tailing you might think you know something."

"Does someone think you have information that they don't want shared? Is that why your apartment got trashed?" I asked.

Scoop was quiet for a moment and I imagined him calculating how much to tell me. Finally, he said, "That's as good a reason as any I can think of."

"Well, thank you, you saved me," I said.

"We were lucky that my cousins were free. The moment I told them the problem, they came up with a solution."

"What's their story?"

"Their dad and my mom were siblings, until he passed a number of years back. Ben's a fixer—fixes anything including problems like this one. You might say, he troubleshoots. Nat helps him out. They do a pretty good business."

"Sounds illegal," I said.

"Nah, more like private eyes with exemplary problem-solving skills," said Scoop.

"Maybe they can help solve your problem," I offered.

"I wish. Anyway, I meant to ask you, did you by chance pick up all the pencils I dropped the other night?"

"Good grief, now you're checking on my housekeeping skills?"

"Never mind, just wondering."

"Were you calling for any other reason besides your apology, which I accepted, before we got sidetracked with my stalker?" I still had a few minutes before I had to turn on the GPS that would guide me to Mrs. Halliday's house, close to the village of Nyack.

"I wanted to warn you to be careful," he said. "Guess it's too late for that."

I felt my body go rigid and instinctively glanced in my rear-view mirror. No black SUV in sight.

"What do you mean *warn* me?"

"There's a lot of stuff going on and you might be ruffling some feathers with all the questions you've been asking. I don't think that trip to the bank was wise."

"Carla told you, right?"

Scoop didn't answer but it had to be her, unless he knew the young teller I had spoken with. Scoop had sources everywhere in Ridgefield. Still, it was unnerving.

"Why wasn't it wise? All I did was ask if anyone knew Chester. What was the harm in that?"

"I'm not sure," he said, thoughtfully. "It's just that something about Chester never rang true. Like him being homeless and then disappearing for a week. When he came back, he looked pretty well rested, and he never had that haunted lost look that so many people without homes adopt. I'm just wondering if something he was up to, got him killed. If you start digging around, then it might put you in danger."

"Aren't you digging around?" I asked.

"Yes," said Scoop. "Which is why I'm getting threatening letters."

Chapter Twenty

Nyack turned out to be a charming town right over the Mario M. Cuomo Bridge. Its downtown center reminded me a little of my hometown, though when I googled it, I found that the village itself only has about 7,300 people, a lot less than our 25,000.

When I phoned that I had been held up, Mrs. Halliday suggested a later time because she had a few errands, which gave me time to kill. I stopped in town at a small coffee shop called the Art Café. It's the kind of place where locals gather for good food and drink. Worn wood floors, a robust atmosphere featuring local artists on the walls, an alcove overlooking South Broadway, and just a stone's throw from the park and the Hudson River beyond. It had the kind of vibe that made it feel like coming home. I settled at one of the alcove tables and sipped chamomile tea while I studied the unique menu. I was tempted to try the avocado toast or one of the toastinis described as a panini pressed Israeli bagel that can be loaded with fresh cheeses, spices, veggies, and no doubt, calories. Unfortunately, I had only enough time for a quick cup of tea while I reviewed the questions I had for Mrs. Halliday.

I took out my notebook and added additional questions that Scoop's comments had prompted.

Where did Chester go when he left Ridgefield?

How did Chester support himself?

The Nosy Parkers thought he was a billionaire trying to decide where to send his next dollar. Like everything with the gossipers, there was a kernel to be found. Mrs. Willings also had her doubts. What if Chester had come to Ridgefield for a different reason and had hidden under his cloak of being homeless? What better way to get information than to pretend that you were someone who most people thought of as invisible?

Had Chester learned something that had gotten him killed? And, what did Scoop know, that he was afraid to share with me? With all his snooping, he managed to get a target painted on his back. Were the threats for real or just notes designed to warn him off?

* * *

Mrs. Halliday met me at the door with a warm welcoming expression on her face. She looked to be somewhere in her sixties, and had inquisitive brown eyes etched with lines that matched the curve of her smile. She was comfortably dressed in jeans and a navy sweater, making me feel right at home. The house was a charmer—something she described as a Tudor Revival, with inviting lines, and I thought it suited the woman well.

"Kitchen OK?" she asked over her shoulder, as she led me to a cozy table, scarred by years of use and dwarfed by a large window overlooking the backyard gardens. It was not unlike my table at the cottage or Horace's either. Autumn was in full bloom in her backyard and the colors framed in the window made me feel like I was painted into an impressionist masterpiece.

"I am so sorry for your loss . . . I should say losses," I said, feeling a bit awkward about grilling a woman whose husband and brother-in-law had died within months of each other.

She smiled, an incredibly warm light-up-the-room kind of smile designed to put me at ease. I had a fleeting wish that Richard hadn't met someone because maybe, Mrs. Halliday would be a nice partner. *Really, Winter? This is what you are thinking about when you've come to upend her day by talking about her dead brother-in-law?*

"I didn't know Chester well and while his death was shocking . . . well more than shocking, I won't be disingenuous. I'm sad that he met an untimely and unfortunate end, but I'm still missing my husband and that's where I put my mourning energy. The rest of the time, I'm focused on living life to its fullest because I have no intention of wasting a second of the time I have left on this earth," she said.

I squirmed.

"I promise to be quick," I said.

Mrs. Halliday laughed. "I didn't mean to insinuate that you were wasting my time. I'm glad you're here."

I smiled back, immensely relieved, and explained what I needed.

"Chester, or I should say Chesterfield—strange name I always thought, but then Hal, that's my husband—he said his parents were odd. Chester was named for the cigarette, if you can believe that. Their mother was addicted to them. Hal said she called them her 'precious.'"

"As in *Lord of the Rings*?"

"Exactly. By the way, you can call me Anne," she added.

Anne Halliday was a great storyteller. She talked about her husband, his quirky parents, and his much younger brother, Chester. She gave me the details about where they grew up and how she and Hal chose Nyack, because of its small-town charm and for its close proximity to New York City.

"Granted the 37-mile commute sounds a lot closer than it is, because of the city traffic, but still it has been a great place to live and raise our family.

"Listen to me going on and on. You'd think I never had guests. It's just that with the kids and grandkids, I never get to tell my stories," she said, and again came the smile crinkle that made me feel so welcome.

"No worries," I said. "I really do get it. Although, I'm the guilty one—my uncle would probably love to get a word in edgewise about something else besides me."

Maybe that wasn't entirely true. My uncle and Horace did most of the talking. However, the conversation was usually focused on my life challenges. As is evidenced by me not realizing that Richard was dating someone.

I did a mental scan of the women at Village Square and really couldn't come up with anyone likely. He said he met her at Westconn while teaching there. I wondered if the college had an online directory.

I snapped out of my musings when Anne cleared her throat, realizing that she didn't have my full attention.

"Like I said, I didn't know Chester well and it's so sad to think that now, I'll never know him," said Anne.

She went on to tell me how Chester stayed in an apartment over the Halliday's free-standing garage. Anne only returned a month ago, after being with her children on the West Coast for the last six months.

"After Hal died, I just didn't want to be here for a while. Now, I can't imagine being anywhere else," she said. "Chester moved in while Hal was sick and gave me breaks in the caregiving. He was a very kind person and he and Hal became the friends they never were as kids, growing up. I like to think both of them were at peace with their relationship by the time Hal passed."

I had a million questions, starting with where Chester was before he moved in, and did he work at any kind of job before he became homeless.

"Goodness," said Anne, with a laugh. "What makes you think Chester was homeless? He's a private investigator and very much in demand, I might add."

"He pretended to be homeless in Ridgefield. He bummed free lodging from local property owners and helped people carry packages to their vehicles for tips," I said.

Anne smiled sadly. "It was part of his undercover, I suppose."

It made more sense to think of Chester as a private eye than the mystery man without a permanent residence. It occurred to me that the Nosy Parkers had been right about one thing. He wasn't who he pretended to be.

"Chester's expertise was tracking down scams—he did a lot of work for insurance companies. You'd have to ask Chester about the details . . . Oh my," she said, holding her hand over her mouth in horror. "No-one can ask Chester about anything." With that, her upbeat demeanor crumbled, and I saw the face of true grief.

Chapter Twenty-One

By the time I said goodbye to Mrs. Halliday, I was armed with enough information to write a reasonable obituary for Chester. And, I now knew why Kip wanted me to stay in the dark. I shivered to think that someone might suspect I knew what the private investigator had been chasing down. While both Chester and Arthur had taken that information with them to the grave, someone driving a black SUV might think otherwise.

Fortunately, I could see no one stalking me on my way over the bridge.

The vehicle exchange was with Nat only. Ben had gotten called to "fix" something. Nat reported that the second she stepped out of the car in her bogus police uniform, the SUV had sped off. She and Ben drove around for over an hour before determining that the SUV wasn't following.

"We checked your car for tracking devices and didn't find any, so you should be good to go," said Nat, handing me my keys.

"I don't know how to thank you," I said.

"Are you kidding me? Ben and I had a real ball today. Most of the things we fix are pretty boring, but this was downright exciting."

Grave Words

Nat had pulled her Yankee's ball cap over her copper shoulder length curls but lifted her sunglasses to reveal bright green eyes. She had full lips and a wide smile which she bestowed like a gift.

We exchanged keys and as she climbed into her bright red truck, she hollered back, "Tell that cousin of mine to start saying yes to our invitations."

* * *

Ridgefield on a Friday night feels like Times Square. It used to be that you could walk into your favorite restaurant without a reservation. Not anymore. With the exception of Uncle Richard, I didn't think anyone in the 10,000 households in town still cooked. Even those on tight budgets found acceptable alternatives to kitchen duty, often doing take out from one of the many Italian restaurants highlighting pizza on the menu. When Kip suggested dinner at Della Francesca in Danbury, I knew it was a good alternative to trying to squeeze into one of the town's hot spots.

Della Francesca is like an oasis in the midst of many strip malls lining Mill Plain Road. It is wedged between a no nonsense building with large red garage doors called Mill Plain Independent Hose Company 12, and a group of businesses boasting other eateries along with something called burn boot camp.

Kip had gotten a ride from a fellow cop who lived not too far away in the 55-and-over community called Rivington, just over the Ridgefield line in Danbury. As retired boomers shed their large houses in favor of condos with active communities, they chose these residences, for their proximity to Ridgefield, their convenience to Danbury, and their ample space and amenities. The complex sits high on a whopping 250 wooded acres, with a nice horizon, and has everything from luxury townhomes to condo-style living. Kip's buddy says, "It's like dying and going to heaven."

Since his co-worker suggested we try Della Francesca for its food and service, Kip and I have become regulars. We met outside, where a spattering of tables were partially protected from parking lot view by some plants and gray metal fencing. Given the close proximity of the parking spaces, which practically butted up to the divider, I was glad Kip had opted for an inside table. Yet, it was really no different than the coveted dining spots in all those New York City outdoor makeshift add-ons that had sprung up during COVID.

The waiter led us past an expansive bar into an interior dining area you might expect to find in the heart of Italy. We passed a few patrons and into another room, where we finally reached a cozy table, tucked privately in a far corner. Small table lamps that have replaced candles in so many places, gave off a warm glow. Overhead, embedded in the tall ceiling, lights twinkled to emulate a night sky. The building must have once been a warehouse, because it had exposed piping in some sections, though barely visible, because everything above was painted black and low lit. A vibrant buzz could be heard from an adjoining porch area, that was a bright contrast to the rest of the space.

"I asked for the most private table possible, hope that's OK by you," said Kip, as the waiter materialized with a pitcher of water.

I eyed Kip suspiciously. He could be shy when it came to things like holding hands or other public displays of affection—unless you can count the hug on Main Street, when he thought no-one was paying attention. His request for an out-of-the-way spot meant that he might be planning something romantic.

Suddenly, I felt my breath catch, and my heartbeat began heading into a full gallop. *He wouldn't be proposing, would he?* We'd only been dating a few months, though it was clear that our relationship was more than a passing flirtation.

The overwhelming cold clamminess, and the desire to climb out of my skin, signaled that I was headed straight into a panic attack. The tension hadn't fully disappeared after my wild ride to New Jersey, and I wasn't fully equipped to ward off the attack with thoughts of lapping waves and warm beaches.

Kip quickly shoved a glass of water in front of me. He was wide-eyed with concern and his face said 911.

"Are you OK?" he asked, as his eyes darted around the room, maybe hoping for someone who might take the emergency decision out of his hands. "Should I call for help? Do you need air?"

I shook my head no and kept sipping the water with hands that shook like an addict's. The water helped as I tried to imagine myself in another place. For some reason, heaven came to mind, though I was pretty sure that had to do with the still unresolved problem of my client's obituary. Distracting thoughts, I've found, are key to overriding an incoming attack.

I fanned my face with my napkin, letting the cool air wash over me until finally my galloping heartbeat slowed.

"Do you want to leave?" asked Kip. Buoyed by the tamp down of my symptoms, he too began fanning me with his napkin. "Or go somewhere else?"

I took a few more yoga breaths, breathe in deep, breathe out. I felt like Diva during a thunderstorm.

"I'm OK," I finally gasped and finished my glass of water, only to have a waiter materialize by my side to refill.

I had escaped the worst of it, though I was tentative about my reprieve.

"Sorry, I'm prone to panic attacks." My voice sounded froglike and I cleared my throat.

"Is that what that was? Geez, what sets them off? If I did something, I need to know what it is, so I don't do it again. You looked downright scary."

Situations where I felt out of control usually were the springboard. I shrugged in answer. I wondered if panic attacks would send Kip running, though too late now—the cat was out of the bag.

"Let's change the subject," I said. My heartbeat had returned to its normal lub dub pace, though I felt like a wrung-out dishrag.

"Should we go to the emergency room to get you checked out?" Kip asked.

"No, I'm good—or at least I will be. The ER docs don't do much for a panic attack except reassure that you aren't dying—even if that's how you feel." First-hand experience had taught me that.

The waiter placed a plate with a tasting of bruschetta in front of us, and took our drink order. That, and the water, revived me enough to get Kip talking, though his earlier enthusiasm had deflated like a popped balloon.

"This case." He rubbed a hand across his eyes and frowned.

"Hold on." I held my hands up to stop him. "I don't want to be responsible for you telling me stuff and then feeling like you're trudging to the gallows because it's against your cop rules."

We'd been down this road before and on those rare occasions when Kip did let something slip, he'd spent the next few days pummeling himself. His dark mood was almost more than I could take.

"My friend who dropped me off—he said he tells his wife almost everything and it's like a big weight off his shoulders at the end of every day," he said. "He doesn't think he could be a cop without his wife."

Breathe, breathe, water, no—*Kip was not going to ask me to marry him, was he? What would I say besides I am definitely not ready for that.*

"And so, I thought, well, you and I are close . . ." He continued, oblivious to my discomfort.

I tried to make my face passive but I could feel the moisture forming along my temple. *Do not panic, Winter. Just tell him that you aren't ready and that you hope that doesn't change things.* I nodded at Kip to continue, anxious to get this proposal over with.

Just then, the waiter showed up and placed our wine orders in front of us, and with still shaky hands, I took a welcoming sip.

"All I'm saying . . ." said the guy who usually said little, "is that we should hash out all the stuff that's going on. I'm really sorry that I can't share everything, but I will tell as much as I can. I just don't want this coming between us anymore."

"And anything else?"

"As a matter of fact . . ."

Kip leaned over and unzipped the backpack he carried. I had assumed he had grabbed some toiletries, and maybe a change of clothes, because we had planned for him to stay at the lake tonight. Whatever was in that bag was making him look like the cat who swallowed the canary.

Please, please, please don't let it be a ring.

And then, he pulled a piece of paper from his bag, and carefully unfolded it.

I stared.

And then, I grabbed it and held it gratefully to my chest. Kip had brought the obituary page from yesterday's newspaper and on it was the beautiful photo of my client's mother with a headline that read her name only. I scanned and sure enough, Amanda at the obit desk had found a way to correct the obituary.

Kip grinned. "It's good to see that you are still alive and kicking."

The overwhelming release of tension bubbled into a laugh and I could feel tears stinging my eyes, which I hurriedly swiped with my napkin.

Still holding the clipping to my chest like a treasured photograph, I asked where in town he had tracked this down, because it appeared to be sold out everywhere.

"Turns out the PD subscribes to the paper," he said. "This is my peace offering. I know I've been a jerk. I never wanted you to feel like you couldn't trust me."

And then, damn if he didn't lean over and press his lips on mine. Okay then, idiot for thinking he was about to propose aside, this was progress. The waiter cleared his throat, and when we pulled away, he smiled and handed us backlit menus.

Kip ordered oysters, followed by Bolognese with penne pasta. My stomach was still in protest mode, a leftover symptom of my panic attack, so I settled for the Eggplant Rollatini appetizer. The by-the-glass Chardonnay offerings hadn't been up to Richard's standards, though I contentedly nursed a nicely flavored Kendall Jackson, all the while willing hands that felt overcaffeinated, to quiet. Kip, not in the town where he worked and not tonight's designated driver, was ready to let his hair down. He enjoyed two glasses of Montepulciano red which he declared to be very good.

"You said you wanted to tell me some things," I said, feeling a little like a vulture come to pick the bones clean.

Kip laughed. "That's one of the things I love about you, Winter. You always keep the prize in sight."

Though I winced, he said it in merriment, and I thought Kip's night off was doing him wonders.

"Sorry, always on the case," I admitted.

Kip leaned into the table. The waiter had taken our empty dishes away, and in turn left dessert menus for our perusal. Kip reached across and took my hands in his.

"What did you find out today?" he asked.

"You first," I said. I still wasn't sure I would even tell him about my visit to Mrs. Halliday. I didn't want him warning me off writing the obituary, as he had done earlier. And I certainly didn't want to ruin his good mood.

He studied me for a minute, took a huge breath, and said, "I told you about the accelerants. That's a finger point at Scoop, because he wrote about them in the paper before the fire marshal even released his report. Not to mention, it's a fact that we planned to hold back."

I stayed quiet.

"I told you the other night. Any dragging of my feet that I've done, is over." Kip slid a little lower in his seat, as if he could hide from the awful truth.

With the change of topic, Kip's jovial mood slipped, and I recognized the yo yo of feelings he was trying to manage.

"Thank you for your attempts to help him," I murmured, feeling like a jerk for being so accusatory the night we found Scoop in my study.

The thought of that night still gave me pause. It had been such an odd confrontation and still made no sense to me. Scoop had to know he couldn't access my computer, so *what had he been doing in there*?

"What if I told you that we don't think the first two arsons have anything to do with the recent fire at Pop's Place?" Kip said, shaking me out of my musings.

I get my poker face from Richard, and Kip didn't miss it.

"You're kidding me," he said. "You already know this?"

Poor Kip. He was probably trying to share some things he thought would ease the trust gap between us. Instead, he was finding out that I was two steps ahead.

"Do you know who started those two fires?" I asked.

"No, *do you*?"

I shook my head. "And, before you ask, no, Scoop hasn't shared his source with me."

Kip looked resigned. "What else do you have?"

I told Kip about how the Nosy Parkers kept pressing that Scoop should be arrested for the fires and how they really seemed to believe he was the arsonist.

"I'm not sure where that is coming from," I said, almost to myself.

"What else did the Nosy Parkers have to say?" asked Kip.

I told him how they thought that Chester was always watching who was coming and going at the bank. My admission about my unusual encounter with the teller brought out an audible sigh. Aside from that, he listened intently as I went through everything I had learned. I omitted the black SUV tail to New Jersey, and Scoop's cousins who had come to the rescue.

"You might want to consider a career change," he said. "You have a knack for detecting."

"Is that a compliment?" I asked with a grin.

Kip's smile oozed onto his face as if he was uncertain about whether or not it should be there. He took a sip of wine, watching me for any abrupt change that might signal that he hadn't read my flirtation correctly. Finally, he relaxed and grinned back. This time, when he reached for my hand, I didn't break out into a sweat.

When the waiter came back asking if we wanted dessert, Kip said we'd skip it. He then turned to me and said, "We can have dessert at home."

Chapter Twenty-Two

Chesterfield Halliday, 55, of Nyack, New York, and a frequent visitor to Ridgefield, died under suspicious circumstances while working undercover as a private investigator. The cause of his death is still under investigation.

Affectionately known as Wandering Chester because he presented as a person experiencing homelessness, he ran a private detective agency called Eyes See, a company he formed after retiring from his job as a New York City detective.

Anne Halliday had gone to great lengths to share Chester's accolades, and I was able to get them all into his tribute without explaining the specifics of why he was in Ridgefield.

Of course, the obit begged the question—why would a private eye be posing as a guy with no known address?

What were you investigating, Chester? And what was so interesting about the bank?

I thought the obituary worked nicely and despite Anne Halliday's insistence that she would pay for my work, I was reluctant. Capitalizing on Chester's death didn't feel right. However, an empty wallet didn't feel so good either. I would put off the decision as I let my need for preservation war with my conscience until billing time.

Anne wanted Chester's obituary listed in the *Rockland County Newspaper*, *The Ridgefield Press*, the *New York Times,* and a number of online publications because apparently, Chester knew a lot of people in a lot of places. We agreed that Anne would reimburse me for the submissions, and pay for the time it took to tailor each to suit the guidelines.

After dropping Kip at his apartment on Saturday morning, I hit the pavement sans Diva who was still with Richard for a power walk around the village loop. While I love having the Great Pyrenees puppy on my walks, it was surprising how much time it took for her to sniff every tree and greet every passerby. I ended my walk on Main Street, sitting on one of the tribute benches placed strategically around town. This one read *Remembering George Hanlon who warmed the hearts of all he met.*

The family's plaque ended with *We miss you!* and those three words twisted my heart in a way that only someone who has suffered a devastating loss can understand. *I miss you Summer,* I whispered silently to my sister.

Turning my head away from the bench, I looked toward bustling Main Street, which I always found to be a spirit lifter. Saturday mornings felt a little like Disney World at spring break, with families scurrying from one activity to another, vehicles vying for precious parking spaces, and a line a mile long at the coffee shops. Despite it still technically being morning, even Chez Lenard had a line growing, as he readied his free-standing hot dog cart.

Ridgefield's popular staple has been on Main Street since 1978, when a Madison Avenue executive decided to retire from the rat race and open a charming umbrella covered cart with a chalk board menu, featuring hot dogs with a French flair. The business has changed hands a number of times since then, however, all owners seem to have been like-minded, as they donned billowy chef hats and welcoming smiles.

* * *

I wandered up Main Street toward the Fairfield County Bank. Passing through the outdoor eating space of the Lantern, I wasn't surprised that even with the biting chill that had begun to invade New England, there were still diehards who soaked in the remaining vestiges of autumn sunshine. With Halloween just around the corner, the place was packed, and I wanted to smack my head in realization.

It was the Halloween Walk where all businesses inhaled and sucked up the cost of giving out treats to the thousands who wandered Main Street for the popular annual event. Children from tots to teens dressed in everything from traditional ghosts and goblins to elaborate superheroes. Downtown was blocked to traffic and the kids had free reign to collect treats.

It's an expensive output for the businesses and I can remember one store owner, no longer around, who hired young tweens to go around and collect candy. The kids would return to the shop periodically with their stash, and the store owner would then offer it out to the trick or treaters. It was a lot cheaper to hire the tweens than to shell out thousands of dollars for candy to participate, while all the while knowing the effort wouldn't bring in customers. Add to that, many of the kids wandering our streets were not even from town, so I kind of got it. Though to me, it did feel like cheating. Maybe we needed a better support program for these stores, who gave so much back to the community. Halloween aside, they were tapped for every local fundraiser imaginable.

Undeniably, however, the lively atmosphere is an uplifting reprieve from the steady stream of gloom and doom permeating the media these days.

I didn't think I had a destination in mind as I strolled along observing the festivities, although I suddenly found myself standing in front of the bank, where my subconscious was obviously urging me to talk to the teller who had warned me off Chester. I hoped to confront her without having to have another crash course in refinancing my house. I pulled at the door. Locked. A sign said this branch was closed on Saturdays.

Disappointed, I turned away, and began meandering back through the outdoor Lantern tables that leaked onto the sidewalk. As I maneuvered along the walkway, narrowly avoiding one of the waiters who balanced a tray of drinks, my eyes landed on none other than Winfred Thomas III. He was sitting at one of the tables closer to the street, and facing the bank, as if he couldn't leave the building unattended.

Watching his workplace on his day off? I couldn't for the life of me imagine why everyone was so interested in that bank.

Suddenly, I thought his eyes locked on mine.

I was about to nod an acknowledgement when he shifted his gaze and picked up what looked to be a Mimosa and sipped. Maybe, he didn't recognize me. We'd only met that short time at the bank.

The waiter was hovering but Mr. Thomas waved him off dismissively.

Curious, I quickly ducked down the alley to the parking lot behind the Main Street buildings. I entered Ursula's, the abutting shop to the restaurant, from the rear, wandered through their design area, and admired some nice fabric before reaching the front of the shop. Under the pretense of window shopping, I perused the early holiday displays of glittering Christmas trees ideal for a mantel, stunning handmade ornaments, and an assortment of Thanksgiving decor, all the while keeping my eye out the front window at Winfred Thomas III. He was fidgeting with his phone one minute, scanning the crowd the next, and I assumed he was waiting for someone who was late.

It wasn't long before a tall brunette slid into the seat opposite him, and moments later the waiter placed a Mimosa in front of her. She had a big toothy smile and when she dropped the Jackie O sunglasses, it was none other than the teller who had warned me off my request to learn more about Chester.

Odd. My original reaction was that she had been afraid of her boss. It didn't appear that way now. They both fell into animated conversation which surprisingly ended before Teller Girl took more than two sips from her Mimosa. She stood, gave an odd salute as if she were reporting for duty, and then strode off purposefully. Winfred shook his head as in disbelief, downed both drinks, and called for his check.

I was about to hurry out of the store to follow Teller Girl when the salesperson asked if she could help me. I murmured "just looking," however, the distraction was enough for the woman to disappear into the throng of costumes. I hurried outside anyway and scanned the street, all the while avoiding being in the line of sight of Winfred.

Teller Girl had vanished.

Back on George's bench a few minutes later, this time with a cup of chamomile to go from Tazza, I called Carla.

"You sound, how do I say this . . . chill," said Carla.

"I finally had a good night's sleep."

She snorted. "Ha, Kip must have spent the night," she said, before turning all business.

"We don't have any arrangements yet, because Chester's still up with the State Medical Examiner in Farmington. Sorry, but I think it's going to take a few more days. He got bumped when they got backed up with an ongoing multiple murder investigation. Do you want to hold the obit a little longer?" she asked.

Already, those foxy newspaper reporters were putting out information on the murder, although they also said that the deceased man had not yet been identified. Maybe, if we delayed, the public wouldn't be so hungry for the gruesome details, and instead might want to know more about the man.

We agreed to hold the obituary until I heard from Anne Halliday. Anne had told me that she would do a simple memorial in Nyack and bury Chester next to his brother, Hal. It might not matter to her that we printed the obituary locally without service notifications. It wasn't as if Chester had a lot of friends in Ridgefield, though I was pretty sure Scoop would attend. I said as much to Carla.

"I'll also be going," she said. "Chester and I were friends of sorts."

If she was going for shock with her admission, she achieved it.

"Don't get all righteous on me," she continued, reading the silence and imagining the look on my face. "I would have mentioned it sooner but I didn't think it was relevant until you said someone followed you when you visited Chester's family home. Then, when I read the copy of the obituary, I started to think it might be important, and I've been trying to figure out how to tell you."

"You could have just used your words," I said.

"I knew you'd be annoyed that I didn't tell you sooner, and I couldn't conjure up a time when I wanted to risk your wrath." Carla must have popped in a piece of gum, because her next words sounded muffled like she was rolling marbles around in her mouth. "Besides, I might be just creeping myself out, but I've had the feeling lately that someone is watching me."

"Say again." Had I heard her correctly?

Carla repeated herself, and the frustration I felt over being kept in the dark was tamped down by the fear I felt for my friend.

"Tell me," I said.

"Nothing specific," she said. "Just like when you know someone is staring at you but you can't pinpoint it. Could be something, could be nothing."

I had an uneasy feeling that my carpenter was taking his crush too far.

"It's probably some secret admirer," I offered.

Carla considered that for a few seconds before saying, "*Right*."

Remembering my race to ditch the black SUV and Scoop's messed up apartment, I uttered my next words with *stop the presses* urgency.

"Where are you and who is watching your back?"

"Don't worry, I'm safe. I'm waiting for a delivery at the funeral home. My boss is here with me."

I relaxed a little as I surveyed the chaos around me. This portion of Main Street was closed to through traffic. A stalker could easily blend in with the hundreds of trick or treaters. Carla was probably safer where she was than I was where I sat.

"This might be a good time to tell me why you lied about Chester," I said. "Why did you make me go through all those orchestrations to get his last name when you knew about him all along?"

"Really, Winter? Do you think I'd do that to a friend?" Carla took on a self-righteous attitude. "I thought he was just some guy down on his luck, who'd stop by the funeral home for a cup of coffee, work some odd jobs. I'd always find something for him—you know, just to give him some pocket change."

"Out of your own pocket?" Carla would give someone her last dime if she thought they needed it.

I imagined her lifting her shoulders in a shrug as she replied, "No biggie. The thing is, I'm telling you now, because he'd always be asking me stuff about how the system works, and the more I think about it, the more I wonder if maybe his visits were less about us being friends and more about sniffing around here."

Her voice dropped, and as I chewed on what she said, I suspected that Carla had had feelings for Chester.

"He liked knowing the inner workings of everything, from how to buy a plot to who oversaw the burial. Once he even asked me how we could be sure the right body got into the right hole in the ground! Like we'd ever make a mistake like that."

"I wonder why he was asking about that kind of stuff?"

"And, it wasn't just that—he wanted to know all sorts of things, like how the death certificates were issued and. . . ."

A large clamor stopped Carla midstream.

"Some kind of commotion going on—gotta go—talk later," and she clicked off.

I immediately texted for her to meet me at Queen B in an hour, and she sent back a thumbs up emoji.

My next call was to Anne Halliday, who surprised me when she asked to have Chester's online obituary held.

"Just do the print edition on Thursday, before all those Ridgefield folks think Chester was some kind of transient guy cooling his heels until he travelled to the next town for handouts. Chester had a pretty amazing career. He should be remembered for that," she said.

"I could get that out online right away," I said.

"I don't want anyone searching the web to find it without all the arrangements listed, and we're not there yet. Ridgefield folks probably aren't the ones coming to the memorial."

We settled on the print version for Thursday, and I promised to follow up with all the other places, both online and print, when she was ready with her arrangements.

"And, the fact that he was murdered?" No way to say that gently.

"It was the cause of death. You might say what the detectives said to me . . . *died under suspicious circumstances and still under investigation.*" Her matter-of-fact comment told me that Anne Halliday wasn't kidding when she said her mourning time was for Hal only. Still, the lady was doing all the right things for her brother-in-law, and who was I to suggest that she should act any differently.

We agreed that I would make the submissions tomorrow, once she had time to review the final. After that, Anne Halliday wanted this over.

* * *

I got a whiff of the beckoning aroma of the offerings from Planet Pizza just two doors down, as I made my way to the Main Street entrance of Queen B. Inching my way past a couple of tiny tables with a family of *Star Wars* characters crowded around, I headed to the counter where patrons placed their orders. Queen B's main floor was a sliver of a place that made Tazza look roomy. Downstairs was another story. Wide open and bright, the place was packed.

I balanced a Busy B Midnight Light for Carla, a water for me, and a coffee cake to share, as I navigated the stairs and snagged one of the last tables. Carla breezed through the back door, a few minutes later.

"Whew," she said, shielding her eyes as if she had gotten stuck in a patch of sun. "I always forget how bright and cheerful this place is."

I laughed, thinking how the lively space with its apple green walls, bold contemporary art, and lights strung around the room and on every post, contrasted so drastically from the cool sanctuary of the funeral home.

I looked around at the patrons, some gathered in groups and others alone, many slumped over their computers or phones. Even on weekends, the rage of taking your work to the local coffee hangout was prevalent. How long before Ridgefield shops would follow in the footsteps of that charming Rey Sol in Ridgewood, New Jersey? What had the sign read? *One hour only, please?*

"They must be going for *garden*," Carla said, as she plopped into one of the chairs.

"The owners are bee lovers and I think this is supposed to represent something akin to a pollinator garden."

"Ah ha," said my friend, as she took in her surroundings.

"All OK?" I asked, remembering the clamor that caused her to disconnect from our earlier conversation.

"Ugh. Fine. I ran in to the funeral home to accept a special-order casket delivery. I thought the guys dropped it, which would have been a disaster, as the funeral date depends on having that casket. You know how they tell you on airplanes to be careful when you open the overhead bins, in case things shift in flight?"

I waited.

"Fortunately, the one that came crashing out wasn't ours." Carla took a sip of the coffee I had placed in front of her. "They do a nice brew here."

"Hungry?" I pushed the coffee cake into the middle for sharing.

Carla had an appetite that would do Richard's meals justice. She didn't hesitate to reach for the goody and break off a sizeable bite.

"Not good for my girlish figure. You could use a little of this, by the way," she said, and patted an ample hip. "Now, tell me why we're here."

We were there because I wanted to look Carla in the face when I asked her just how close she and Chester had been. I was getting so tired of people not being straight with me. Richard had some sort of secret he was keeping, and it wasn't just that he had a new girlfriend. Scoop's secrets ran deeper than the ocean, and now, I find out that Carla had known Chester well enough for him to come by a couple of times a week for odd jobs and coffee. Why in the world would she not have mentioned that she knew Chester, on the morning of her first phone call? Remembering the crack in her voice when she told me he had died, I probably should have guessed.

Grave Words

"You're overthinking," said my friend, as she dusted a crumb from the front of her blouse.

I sighed. "I wanted to ask you more about what kind of things you and Chester talked about."

Carla looked at the ceiling in thought.

"The first time he showed up, he came into the office to ask what happened to indigent people when they died. Honestly, I didn't have a clue, so I sent him to social services for the answer. He stayed for an ice water and said he'd let me know what they said. I felt sorry for the guy thinking he was probably worried about what would happen to him when he passed," she said. "The next time he came was maybe a week later. He wanted to know how much everything cost—caskets, burial plots, cremations—that sort of thing."

"Did he get his answer from social services?" I asked.

Carla gave an *I don't know* shrug.

"You have to remember, this was in the middle of my busy workday, so I was a bit distracted while answering his questions. And, he was very much alive. There was no reason to think his questions were any more important than the hundreds of other things we talked about. Anyway, on one of his visits, he asked to see the caskets."

Carla described how she had taken Chester down to the room where they keep samples of coffins and urns for clients to choose from.

"Chester immediately pointed out that we should display them in a more inviting way, and offered to rearrange the room. I'd been thinking about the same thing so I thought, what the heck? What's the worst that can happen—I'd have to put it back the way it was if the bosses didn't like it."

According to Carla, the bosses loved the new look. Eventually, Chester was stopping by at least once a week to do odd jobs.

"The last time he came was just a day before he died." Carla's normally serene face did a deep dive.

"Can you remember what you talked about that day?"

Carla closed her eyes as she tried to retrieve her last conversation with the murdered man.

"He wanted to know how we were notified about which plot to dig, and if there was paperwork exchanged between the funeral home and the cemetery.

"What did you tell him?"

"I told him that when you buy a plot, you get a contract, but that he should call one of the local cemeteries for more information," said Carla.

"Do you think he did that?" I asked.

Carla frowned, as she studied a chip in one of her black glossed nails.

"And, I just got these done," she muttered, before looking back at me. "To answer your question, I have no idea if he asked anyone else about anything. It wasn't like twenty questions, which *you* are beginning to sound like. It was more of a conversation—multiple conversations. We talked about everything from casket colors to have we ever mixed up a body for burial. All of it was woven into normal conversation between two people, one of whom was very busy working."

Carla held up her hand, signaling *stop*. "And before you ask, the answer is no, we have not mixed up any bodies. We are careful about people's loved ones."

"What about cremains? Ever mix up the ashes?"

"*Really?*"

I shrugged. "I had to ask."

Carla couldn't remember any other specifics about her conversations with Chester except to say that no matter what they talked about, he was always interested. No alarm bells had gone off when he asked questions because they were always interwoven with other normal topics, like *have you been following the Yankees* or *I hope the storm doesn't knock out the power.*

"We both shared a love of puzzles, so sometimes we'd see who could do the *New York Times* mini crossword the fastest. He loved a good mystery, and once told me that if he ever built a house, he'd have a secret room. He was a pretty observant and inquisitive guy, which is why I wasn't all that surprised to find out he was a private eye."

"Can you remember anything else he asked about?"

Carla squinted, trying to relive her conversations which hadn't seemed important then, but were critical now.

"One day, he asked if the cemetery deeds had to be recorded with the town."

"Do you think Chester was onto something having to do with the plots?" I asked.

Hiding behind his homeless persona gave Chester the opportunity to watch people without others noticing—unless you were the Nosy Parkers who rarely missed much. It also allowed him to ask seemingly innocuous questions—just an indigent guy curious about the inner workings of the town.

"At the time, I just thought he was a little fixated on the process, because he was getting up in age and wanted to be sure funeral homes knew what they were doing. Now, I wonder if he thought something shady was going on—like maybe, people weren't being buried in the right places."

I tried to imagine the mess that might cause. People paying respects to the wrong deceased. Ugh. *How would you even unravel such a thing?*

"And, what does all this have to do with Arthur Willings? You said he was a collector. That doesn't have anything to do with the end-of-life business," Carla continued.

I had a sudden thought. "Do you suppose Arthur Willings collected caskets?"

"Doubtful," said Carla. "Unless he has a really large warehouse and what would be the purpose? It's not like people like to display antique caskets."

"I knew someone in high school whose dad had an old pine coffin and he made it into a coffee table. We all thought it was so cool in a creepy way," I said.

"Thankfully, that's the exception, not the rule."

Chapter Twenty-Three

With Chester's obituary scheduled for the local paper on Thursday, and the online versions on hold until funeral arrangements were finalized, I polished my write-up and got ready to submit to the paper.

My first call would be a sheepish one to Amanda, who had managed to work nothing short of a miracle in getting my name removed from my client's obituary.

Niggling at the back of my brain, the way an off-key ear worm might, I worried that maybe someone did intentionally alter the copy. Start-up sabotage maybe? My client was still unreachable on her cruise and Amanda might be the next best person to provide the submission details.

* * *

On Monday, I took the train into Manhattan to meet with a man named Wilks West. He had been the CEO of a company he had started in the nineties, during the dot com bubble. He, his company, and his marriage, finally crashed and burned in 2000, when his venture capital ran out and his company failed to thrive. He resurrected all of the above, including his defunct bank account by starting over, this time to do something for what he called the betterment of society. Twenty years later and he was a success story in a different way. He used his ample checkbook to work with homeless people, finding them a way to get them a safe and warm bed at night and a good meal by day. For those who wanted it, he also offered counseling and a way to get them permanently off the street.

I had listened as he told his story of his transformation from "entitled idiot," his words, to responsible human being. His eyes glistened as he said, "Winter, I want to tell my story to save others from making my egotistical mistakes. And, I hope this will call attention to my cause of helping the homeless get off the streets and into the warm beds that everyone deserves."

I had gently asked him the awkward question—was he just putting his affairs in order and wanted to write his own obit, or did he think that his earthly days were numbered. At that he burst into a very contagious laugh and said, "I like you girl."

Such is the nature of my business, and I was left to remain curious. He did add something when he said goodbye. "I have a lot of friends who want their stories told. If I like what you write, I'll send them your way."

I wasn't arguing. The Living Legacy segment of my business was beginning to be increasingly lucrative because my clients were all successful people who wanted to leave something behind for their children besides money.

* * *

On Tuesday morning, I spoke with Betty Willings. Her son's autopsy results were still not in, though the State of Connecticut was sensitive about getting bodies back for burial, and so, Arthur was on his way home for his final journey. Mrs. Willings and her daughter were coordinating the memorial with Anne Halliday, so as to avoid a conflict.

"My Artie and Chester were friends and we don't want people to have to choose between one service or the other," she said. "Plus, it would be downright inconvenient if they were on the same day because my daughter and I want to attend Chester's memorial. He was so good to my boy."

Part of me wondered if Mrs. Willings was still worried that Arthur wouldn't win out if people had to choose between the two farewells. With a promise to have the arrangements to me by tomorrow, she disconnected.

* * *

I spent the rest of the morning drafting obituaries and living legacies. I managed to get a good solid draft sent to Wilks West, and I didn't expect to hear his comments for a few more days. That's the advantage of prewriting a legacy—there is no urgency.

It was soupy on the lake, with an occasional drizzle, and while the rumble of thunder stayed in the distance, Diva was pacing and panting like a runner who just finished a marathon. The front of her furry chest was matted with drool, and her eyes darted between me and the window. I moved us to the kitchen hoping that might help but the dog's acute hearing picked up even mother nature's slightest growl.

"I can't fix the weather." I kept my voice soothing as I reached beneath the kitchen table, where she hid, to give her a pat. Diva stayed glued to my feet, which were now the recipients of her salivating waterfall.

By afternoon, I had done all the writing I could. I spent an hour updating my website and social media pages, and then closed the lid on my laptop.

By the time Scoop called asking that we meet downtown for a cup of tea, I had opened and closed the refrigerator door at least ten times, dusted the already shiny engines in the train room, and was about to consider vacuuming the downstairs.

Horace opened his door in greeting when I knocked, and Diva bounded inside.

"Poor thing," said Horace. "Did you try those antianxiety pills I suggested?"

"They actually had the opposite effect on Diva. The only thing that calms her enough to keep us all from drowning in drool, is a visit with Max."

As if on cue, the mammoth German Shepherd came into view, his huge ears and large presence dwarfing his furry friend. Diva immediately leaned against him and he led her into the kitchen.

"Time for tea?" asked Horace.

"Rain check?" I asked, and explained about my meeting with Scoop. "How about I bring some shortbread for dessert tonight?" Horace had a sweet tooth for Tazza's heart-shaped cookies.

Horace patted his stomach. "I'm not arguing."

I reminded Horace that Richard was cooking tonight and we had invited him, Scoop, and Kip to join.

"How's that working out with Richard spending more time with you? Are you two getting along OK?" He said it laughingly, though there was a note of concern in his voice.

"Why wouldn't we?" I asked.

"Oh, I don't know. Maybe, it's because the two of you used to have major standoffs, though I supposed that ended almost a decade ago."

The silence hung between us like the soupy fog outside. Ten years ago, when Summer died of an undetected aneurism shortly after her twin daughters were born, it had been the worst of times, to say the least. Prior to that, Richard and I disagreed about a lot of things. He thought I should get my teaching certificate in case the tough world of journalism didn't pan out. I wanted nothing to do with educating what I thought of as a bunch of disinterested kids. I didn't even know what I would teach.

Once Summer was gone, and my mother went to work as her grandchildren's surrogate mother, Richard and I were left to mourn alone. We had Horace, who had been the glue that held us together while we went through the motions of life. The silver lining was that Richard and I stopped arguing and began listening to each other. He honored my desire to study journalism and even helped me get an internship at the local newspaper after I graduated. I ended up staying until last year, when I was laid off.

"I'm sorry. Sometimes my mouth overrules my brain and just blabs away, forgetting about all the suffering that took place back then." Horace put an affectionate hand on my shoulder. "Ignore this old man."

I smiled my forgiveness. "Sorry to dump Diva on you . . ." I started, until Horace interrupted.

"Don't be," he said. "I like having both the dogs. Come on, I'll walk you outside because I need to get the mail."

The pickings in my mailbox were slim because most of my business comes via the internet or from the phone. Between the stacks of advertising flyers, I did get a nice deposit from my New York City client—he was old school like that—no Venmo for him.

Horace had an enviable pile. "What is all that? It looks like you're doing one of those old-fashioned chain letters my mom used to talk about. You know, you send one letter and you get fifty in return."

He was sifting through and he shrugged. "Fan mail. I'll tell you about it later."

I frowned at him. I'm a huge Horace fan, although the truth was, the guy rarely left his house, never mind the lake. I doubted he had any fans that would be writing.

The letter on top looked familiar. I had seen something with the same logo recently, although where was just out of reach, like that allusive dream you couldn't grasp.

I let it go. Not my business, though, just like the Nosy Parkers, I was incurably curious. I reassured myself that, at least, I had respect for privacy.

* * *

Outdoors, the wind was whipping up fast, blowing the light rain around and spraying the fine mist over the windshield of the car. By the time I found a parking space and made my way to Tazza for my rendezvous with Scoop, the skies had opened up, and I felt like I'd just climbed out of the shower. I hugged my puffer jacket close to my body and hurried into the coffee shop where Scoop had secured a table near the window.

"Ugh," I said, grateful for the hot cup of chamomile he slid in front of me. I shook my head Diva style, which let loose a spray of droplets.

"If I wanted something to cool my drink, I would have asked for it." Scoop put his hand protectively over the top of his cup.

I smiled inwardly. Despite his troubles, my friend was still as sardonic as ever. Maybe, things had improved. I could only hope.

I filled Scoop in on my conversation with Betty Willings.

"I don't know if she is worried about competing with Chester's service for guests, or if she really thinks it would be inconvenient for people if both were held on the same day," I said.

"I'll tell you what's inconvenient." Scoop dunked a small wooden stirring stick into his hot chocolate and came out with a dollop of whipped cream which he licked. "Murder is inconvenient. The building where Chester was found has been taped off since last week, and now it looks like Pop's Place has to be *'aired out'* before it can re-open."

Tazza was abuzz with loud conversation because unlike even the chilliest of days when people couldn't wait to snag one of the outdoor tables, today's dismal weather ushered everyone indoors.

Thunder grumbled like an empty stomach, not the overwhelming sound that sometimes shook my house. Still, I did a quick check of my phone to see if Horace had sent an SOS, because in this kind of weather, Diva could be a lot.

"Missing your buddies?" I asked, probably a little too snidely. For the past week, Scoop had changed the subject every time I brought up Pop's Place, Chester, Arthur Willings, and the arsons. Frustrated as I was over his refusal to name his source, that was at least something I could understand. Not sharing what he knew about the connection between Chester, Arthur, and Pop's Place felt like betrayal.

Truth be told, despite the punch I felt from being kept out of the loop, it was clear to me that he was being protective—that much I got when his cousins came to my rescue. His urgency and voice on that day convinced me that my friend had been acting out of fear. What I didn't understand is why everyone who hovered around me, didn't realize that I could better protect myself if I knew who the enemy was.

"Just worrying about Jimmy," he said, sullenly.

Scoop was right about murder being inconvenient and not just for the deceased. Murder obviously created all sorts of problems for those left behind, like Jimmy, the poor guy who owned Pop's Place. Scoop had said it was a financial hardship for him to be closed, especially with Halloween right around the corner. Apparently, Jimmy hosted an annual ghoulish celebration that packed the house.

Then there were other shop owners that shared the building and needed to reopen their businesses. Economic survival depended on it.

That got me thinking about the fire itself. Whoever tried to burn the building down should have taken an Arson 101 class, because even I knew that the sprinklers in the closed-up office space, where there was no incoming oxygen, would reduce the flames to embers before a lot of damage could be done. *Open the window*, I wanted to scream to the would-be arsonist, before realizing that, *thank goodness*, he hadn't. The fire department had little to do to knock it down and hence, there was little water damage. Smoke was another story. According to Scoop, the place stunk like the town dump.

There had been a separate back entrance to the building, and had it been only the fire, the fire marshal could have cleared the structure in just a day or two. Add the yellow crime scene tape, and the building was being held hostage until the scene could be released, which depended on everyone from the State Medical Examiner to the State Police Detectives, that our town police chief would no doubt have invited down to weigh in on the dead body.

"Jimmy says they got cleared for restoration at least. He's got a buddy who's repainting, but it's the smell. It still reeks," said Scoop. "A bunch of guys are going over to help."

Just then, the door swung open and Abby and Gabby Parker burst inside the tiny coffee shop. Both wore matching floral rain hats that looked more like shower caps than something designed for style, and they filled the space in a way that had all patrons' heads turned toward them.

"Whew, what a day. It's blustery. I think this drizzle could turn to snow," said Gabby, in a voice loud enough to stop sound in the small café. "Oh goodness, look who's here—Winter and Scoop—plotting another fire?"

Gabby giggled at her joke and even as the other customers squirmed uncomfortably, they leaned in to get a better look at us.

"Sorry, left my matches home," I said.

Failing to fan the fire, Abby tried again on her sister's behalf.

"I'm surprised you aren't in jail," she said, pointing a finger at Scoop. Now, the Nosy Parkers had the attention of every person in the café, including the wait staff.

And, while I'd never say it aloud, I secretly wondered the same thing. It had been nearly a week since Kip told me that he couldn't protect Scoop any longer. Scoop, who had no-one to confirm his alibi for the first two arsons, had no lawyer, and had enough inside information to suggest he was the pyromaniac, couldn't look more guilty.

Scoop offered a disarming smile to Abby and Gabby. "I don't wear orange well."

"They're not usually so venomous," I said, watching the Nosy Parkers curiously as they huffed away to the counter.

The gossipy sisters placed their orders, and a moment later, were carrying steaming cups to a small table at the back. Both greeted someone who was out of my line of vision.

"Be right back," I said to Scoop.

To get to the restroom at the back of the cozy café, I had to pass the display with mouthwatering sweets and sumptuous sandwiches reminding me that I promised Horace shortbread cookies. Beyond that, and right before the restroom, was my target. A table for three.

The ladies had taken off their hats and jackets and slung them over their chairs. Gabby's pink hair dye job had paled and Abby's had now faded to a light blue. So much for the new trend.

The man the women were sitting with had his back to me, and I couldn't see his face without making a big show of crooking my head back to look at him as I passed. All I could see was short dark hair peeking out from beneath a baseball cap, dark jeans, and oddly, buckskin shoes the color of vanilla fudge that seemed out of sync with the nasty weather. A large hand, with an oddly familiar ring, held a cup to a face I couldn't make out.

Thinking I could get a better look on my way out, I headed into the empty bathroom and thought, *when in Rome,* and used the facilities. After the happy birthday song hand scrub which irritatingly stuck in my head whenever I washed up, I headed back out. This time, I would be facing the man. Unfortunately, he wasn't at the table, and too late I realized that he had been standing, back to me, studying his phone while he waited for me to exit the unisex bathroom.

Asking Gabby and Abby about their tablemate would only stir their curiosity. Still, I wondered who they had been so intent in conversation with, and more importantly, was he the reason their normal pot stirring banter had suddenly turned so toxic?

Chapter Twenty-Four

Scoop was fiddling with his phone when I returned to the table.

"What was that about?" he asked, without looking up.

I told him about the guy with the Nosy Parkers.

"Maybe, he's the reason they've suddenly gone from *gossip girls* to *mean girls*," Scoop said.

"I really wanted to get a look at that guy's face. I know I've seen this guy somewhere, lately." It wasn't the hair or the slump of his shoulders. Maybe, it was his hands that looked familiar. I closed my eyes and envisioned the hand holding his cup. Thick fingers with a ring on one finger. Not a wedding band, but maybe a school class ring? I couldn't be sure.

"Let's wait him out. They can't stay here all day." Scoop pointed out that there was only one exit and they would pass right by our table.

"Well, I can't stay here all day either." Waiting for me were marketing deadlines that hung around my shoulders like the proverbial albatross.

If I was going to drum up more business, I had to spend a fair amount of time selling myself. The *How To* book on best obituary writing practices that I hoped to indie publish sat unfinished on my computer. Who knows, the examples of obituaries from funny to outrageous, sensitive, and sad, might even attract the attention of a publisher that specializes in self-help books. I'd never find that out unless I finished writing.

Then, there are the public speaking engagements. Trying to convince people to pre-write their obituaries made me a Debbie Downer, as Mrs. Willings had pointed out. A lot of my outreach was met by comments bordering from "Yuk" to "What kind of upbeat talk is that?" Speaking at Village Square had been a real boost, and in fact, Henny and his terminal wife wanted me to meet with them later today to help them write both their obituaries. My biggest business boost, however, was the living legacies I'd been writing with most of my clients living in New York City, and I wanted to increase my marketing there.

A good part of my business also relied on leaving flexible time in my day, because when a client called, they usually wanted to meet right away. Aside from making sure their loved one's obituary was a proper sendoff, it was also a way to notify the public of any upcoming memorials or funerals. Many families even used obituaries as a way to announce a death to distant friends or acquaintances.

Bereaved clients who were dealing with unexpected or untimely deaths were by far the hardest people to deal with. I had to make sure the pain that each felt, didn't seep under my skin. Plus, one wrong word, and their raw emotions surfaced like a shark on the hunt. They pondered over every phrase as if their own lives depended on it. I had a very simple form that helped get them through all that, making sure that they didn't forget to add Aunt Sue to the next of kin, although many still wanted someone to guide them through every step.

"Knock, knock, anyone home?" Scoop had put down his cell phone to rap his knuckles on the table, and was now staring at me with a very quizzical look.

"Sorry, I was just thinking about all the things I had left to do today."

Just then, Gabby and Abby made their way toward the front of the store. They wore smug expressions as they wove past us. For good measure, Abby gave a salute and said to Scoop, "Orange is the new black. Get used to it."

"You'd think they would be trying to help rather than spread their nastiness," I said, as I watched them go.

Scoop tapped his fingers on the table, a nervous gesture he sometimes had when he was deciding on a course of action.

"They aren't wrong." He trailed the two women with thoughtful eyes as they put on their shower caps to exit, and then turned a large brown puppy dog stare to me. "I'm about to be arrested."

I had been watching for the man with the white buckskin shoes to exit, though he didn't follow the Nosy Parkers. Now, however, Scoop had my full attention.

"*What, when? How do you know?*" I was sputtering rapid fire, leaving no space for Scoop to reply.

"I've been in touch with Kip," he said, and savored a long sip of the hot chocolate he had been nursing.

"You don't seem all that upset." In fact, my friend didn't have a worry line on his face. There was no evidence of the pasty pallor I had witnessed the other night, when he unfolded his threatening letter.

Scoop's tight smile and *oh well* shrug suggested that he had known this was coming. My heart sank as I studied him. His boyish looks and slight frame made him seem so young and vulnerable. Yet, he also looked like being arrested was no more than a walk in the park. Maybe, guarding all those secrets was a heavier burden than spending time in jail.

"There's something I need to tell you," he said. "I saw Chester the night he was killed. We had drinks together."

How had the Nosy Parkers found that out?

Scoop took a deep breath and then, let it out slow and easy, as he began his story. The night Chester died, Scoop had been at Pop's Place having a beer and playing darts.

"Most of the regulars were there, and when Big Joe arrived, I bowed out of the game."

Big Joe, Scoop explained, was a firefighter who dominated the dart board. Scoop steered clear whenever he was there, so Scoop was sitting at the bar when Chester came in and sat down next to him.

"It's customary for us to buy the guy a drink, so I offered him one." While the two companionably nursed their IPAs, the dart game had grown louder, so they shifted farther down the bar and away from the crowd. Chester had waited until they were out of earshot of others, and then, leaned in toward Scoop.

"He said he had been very interested in the arson stories," said Scoop. '*Such detail, maybe too much detail,*' is what he said. At first, I was confused and didn't understand. It was then that it hit me. The police had been coming down hard—maybe, they had good reason."

"You were writing about things that hadn't been confirmed yet. Like naming the accelerants," I said.

Scoop nodded.

"Horace was right. I was so excited to have such a good source that I overlooked the fact that the fire marshal hadn't even completed his investigation or testing. Anyway, I told him to stop talking in riddles and tell me what he was getting at."

"And?"

"And, he said that if I was as good a reporter as he thought I was, then I would figure it out. Then he said, 'and do it fast.' When I asked what he meant by that, he looked over his shoulder. There was some guy hovering close and we both figured he was trying to listen in."

"What guy? What did he look like?"

Scoop closed his eyes, trying to retrieve the description and then shook his head.

"I was in such shock over what I had done, I really wasn't focused on him. He was pretty much in shadow—Pop's Place is very dimly lit."

"What did Chester do then?"

"He stared the guy down and he backed off. Then he said, 'stay out of here for a while until things die down.'"

When Scoop asked how he knew all this, Chester had replied that when people think you're homeless, they treat you like you're invisible.

"You hear stuff is all is what he said," added Scoop.

Should I tell Scoop about my theory that Chester did more than odd jobs for Arthur Willings? Did Chester's scamming case have anything to do with the arsons? And if so, what?

"A lot of people saw us deep in conversation and I could feel them watching—you know how you sense when someone is staring at you?" Scoop continued.

"Anyone in particular?"

"Big Joe, for one. He's got eyes in the back of his head. A bunch of other people. Like I said, there was that one guy hovering, but that wasn't what was on my mind."

I asked Scoop if Arthur Willings had been there and he said that he thought so, although he couldn't be one hundred percent sure.

"Anyway, given that someone was trying to cover up Chester's murder with a fire, and because so many people saw me talking to him the night he died, I've become a person of interest—in other words, the prime suspect."

"Scoop, do you think that someone thought Chester was confiding in you? Maybe, giving you information? Is that why you've been threatened?"

"Possibly," he said. "Anyway, I could wait for a formal arrest, though Kip said it would be better if I avoided all that and turned myself in voluntarily. Which is why I asked you here. I'm ready to go up to the PD and I need your help."

"The cats?" I ventured. My heart was sinking for my friend whose adored pets would miss him as much as he would miss them. *Why, why, why* was he so vehement about protecting someone who he must now realize either knows the arsonist, or is the arsonist himself.

"The cats are taken care of. Carla is going to stay in the apartment until I can get home and if she can't, she'll at least feed them and change their litter. Or if I have to go to jail, which is likely because I won't be able to make bond, she'll stay until I figure it out. What I need from you is something else."

I was dreading his ask. If he wanted me to try to persuade Kip again of his innocence, that was a long shot. While I couldn't imagine my friend setting fires just so he could write award-winning stories, the fact that he knew things he wasn't supposed to know made even his most loyal friends uneasy.

"How can I help?" I asked.

"Do some housekeeping, will you?"

I had been leaning in to hear more of what Scoop had to say and was staring at the floor when a buckskin shoe jumped into my periphery. I looked up to see a man, donned in a black rain jacket with a hood that was now pulled up over his head. He was hunched over enough to obscure his face and as I focused my attention on him, he turned his head toward the opposite wall.

Scoop saw him too. Glancing at his watch, he jumped from his seat.

"I've gotta be at PD shortly—I don't want to be late and have them hunting me down." He then nodded in the direction of the guy who had exited, and was now passing in front of the window, walking briskly toward the crosswalk.

"I'll see what I can see," said Scoop, getting ready to hurry after him.

"Wait, what do you mean I can help by doing some housekeeping?"

Scoop grinned at me.

"You'll figure it out," he said, and followed buckskin shoe guy out the door.

Chapter Twenty-Five

Richard's slow cooker turkey chili wafting through the house did little to improve my spirits when I arrived home. Diva's tail thumbed like a metronome, until she got up and nuzzled my legs for a pet. Half an hour later, the scene was complete when Horace and Max arrived. Max and Diva did a little roughhouse dance which I immediately put to a halt. A huge German Shepherd playing games in the kitchen was akin to a bull in a China closet.

"Will Kip and Scoop both make it for dinner?" asked Richard, as he pulled a tray of Melillo's corn bread from a bag on the counter. "I know how they love this stuff so I got extra."

I told Richard about my conversation with my friend in the coffee shop.

"Tough one," he said. "I'll freeze the extra corn bread for when he gets out."

In the past two weeks while he camped out in the over-the-garage guest suite, having a family dinner when possible had become our ritual. I didn't see much of my uncle by day, as we both went about our routines. Richard had been deep into prep for the advanced calculus class he would begin teaching in January. He also spent a lot of time at his bungalow, overseeing the new kitchen he was having installed. He was determined that it would be perfection by the time Mary returned from sabbatical.

Carp had finally repaired all the Diva damage, and had then pointed out that my deck needed a refresh. We agreed to the bartering terms and he was trying to get it done before the winter weather set in, so unless it was raining, I left the distractions of my home to work in a reserved room in the library. Diva stayed with Horace or Richard during the day. Such had become our routine. And whenever possible, by unspoken consent, the day ended in the kitchen where we prepped a meal and caught up.

Tonight, Horace was as frisky as the dogs with a new toy when he burst into the kitchen. His wide grin, along with the large black envelope he carried, clued me in that he had something big to share.

"What's that?" I asked, as I peeled avocado for the salad.

He smiled, nudged me aside, and said, "I'll tell everyone at dinner. Right now, this salad is mine."

Kip arrived a little later, looking surprisingly relaxed for someone who had just arrested my best friend.

"Scoop will be staying overnight in one of the jail cells," he said, though surprisingly there was no accompanying brow rub.

"What, no lawyer? Is this a formal arrest?" I asked.

"He declined representation for the moment," said Kip, plucking a flavor bomb tomato from the salad Horace was making.

Who gets arrested and doesn't call a lawyer, I thought.

"And Winter, please don't give me that look. I'm doing enough self-loathing for both of us," added Kip.

"That was my sympathetic look."

Something about Kip's words were not jiving with this demeanor. He looked as if today were any other day of the week rather than the day he had to fingerprint Scoop.

"Then, I pity your clients," he said.

"OK, kids, let's not argue," said Richard.

My jaw ached from clenching it so hard. When Richard handed me a glass of Matanzas Creek Chardonnay from the collection he was continually accumulating in the wine fridge, I took it gratefully. Kip accepted a glass of Flowers Pinot Noir, one of Richard's favorites. He sipped and sighed.

"Winter, I apologize. I didn't mean to take my bad day out on you."

"You should count to ten before you lash out," said Horace. "I've practiced that all my life and it really works."

"I know how badly you feel about all this. Scoop knows it too. It's tough when the job throws mud at you," I said, relenting somewhat.

Kip nodded and by the time we sat down to dinner, things had thawed between us. Kip could be moody, though he was the kind of person who after he voiced his frustration, he'd let it go.

I reached over, touched Kip's hand and the familiar electricity between us brought some warmth to his eyes.

"Are we talking about Kip's job or yours?" interrupted Richard.

"Mine was hard today. Visiting with a couple that will soon say farewell after seventy years, is a real gut twister."

"That's your terminal client?" Kip asked.

"Yes, and the thing is, both of them seem more OK than I feel. They were comforting me saying they've had wonderful lives and all that. It was disconcerting at best."

Henny, the man I had met at Village Voices, and his wife, Eleanor, lived in the assisted care segment of Village Square. Looking through the French doors toward an expanse of lawn and a medley of color from the woods beyond, acted like a brilliant painting in the otherwise stark unit. It was as if the normal things that people have in their homes like memorabilia and photographs had been packed up, leaving behind a room that was as drab as a low-end motel.

On the other hand, the Hendricks had been as upbeat as if they had been planning their wedding rather than one of their funerals. As we sat with a plate of cookies between us, they talked about the final vacation that they planned to take after all the end-of-life arrangements were complete. Even as the couple held hands and ogled each other like two teens in love, I couldn't help but wonder at the wisdom of having a very wilted looking Eleanor travel. She looked as frail and vulnerable as a preemie in NICU.

"Where are they going?" asked Richard.

"Vermont, why?" I asked.

"Because Vermont has lenient medically assisted dying laws," piped in Kip.

That revelation stunned me into silence. Is that what they were doing?

Suddenly the empty house, the trip to Vermont, the persistent handholding, and the loving looks between them all made sense. Henny would make sure his wife had access to a medically assisted departure. What about him? Would he return to Village Square? The barebones living space said no. Somehow or another, I realized that Henny, who had no children and no ties to anything worldly, would be joining his wife.

This time, Kip reached for my hand, and gave me a reassuring smile. "That's true love."

With the certainty of death and taxes, I knew that despite the wedge Scoop's problems had driven between us, Kip was still there for me.

Horace cleared his throat. "This is probably a good time to tell you my news."

Richard, Kip, and I turned toward him in horror. Was he about to tell us that he too was in his final days? I felt my breath catch as I looked at my elderly neighbor in fear.

Horace held up his hand as if to say stop. "Whoa," he chuckled, seeing the look on our faces. "No, no, nothing like that. I'm fit as a fiddle. What I wanted to show you is this."

He pushed out his chair with a screech making both dogs perk up from their attack on squeaky toys. Horace stooped to give each a reassuring pet and then returned to his seat with the large black envelope in hand. The slow deliberate undoing of the string clasp made me want to snatch it from him.

"Arthritic fingers," he said, still amused at our assumption.

"Arthritic my butt, you can chop an onion faster than Bobby Flay. You're drawing this out on purpose," complained Richard.

"Don't all those famous chefs have sous chefs to do their chopping?" asked Horace, still working the string.

"Exactly. Give me that thing." Richard reached for the envelope, and Horace turned away enjoying the drama caused by his continued efforts.

"Now, kids, stop the arguing," I said, and we all got a laugh.

Finally, after what seemed a lifetime, Horace removed a sheath of papers with a proud smile.

"This is my pre-written obituary," he said, proudly holding up a form he had downloaded from my website.

In neat careful print, he had filled in the blanks and as an attachment, had added anecdotes from the highlights of his life.

"What else do you have in there?" asked Kip.

"I have a copy for Richard and Winter. I also have a copy of a pending contract for my burial arrangements."

"Pending?" Richard's face was a deep scowl of concern.

Grave Words

We both knew that Horace lived on a modest pension along with his social security. He always felt it was enough, though often worried what would happen if he had to go into a nursing home. His dream of having his house torn down and leaving his land to open space would be thwarted because his house would be sold to cover the costs of his end-of-life care.

"I have life insurance and apparently, there is a way for me to use that. I'm still looking into it."

"Just promise to check with us before you sign any papers." Kip bore a Grand Canyon sized crevice between his brows. "There are a lot of scammers out there just waiting for a chance to separate you from your money."

Kip would know. The PD was repeatedly called when some poor soul became a victim.

Horace had deflated slightly, though he nodded his agreement.

The first page had been the pending paperwork for something called Plot Plans, which I shoved beneath the two pages of stories Horace had written in carefully printed handwriting. I skimmed in awe.

"Some of these stories—you've never told me that you were recruited to play major league baseball!"

Horace looked as if he had just been knighted by the King, as I read aloud from what he called his life highlights.

"You have a brother?" I asked, incredulously.

How had I known this man for most of my life and not known about a brother?

"A brother, a mother, and a father too. I wasn't just dropped here by a stork, you know," he said, in an amused voice.

"I guess I thought you didn't have anyone but us," I said.

A shadow passed over Richard's face. "He doesn't," he said.

"No nieces, nephews, cousins?" I persisted.

Horace sighed deeply. "My brother never married and passed a long time ago. I do have a cousin, and I haven't seen him in years. I'm not sure if he's even still alive."

Horace's family tree intrigued me. I had known about the kindly woman he had been married to for fifty years. She used to bake us cookies and look out for Summer and me when Richard was in California and my mom was at work. She'd been gone for over ten years now.

"Any other surprises, like children?" I asked.

"Just you," he said, and patted my hand.

"Horace has a lot of secrets and I'm guessing that they aren't all in those pages. I think he's holding out and we should get to the bottom of it." Richard loved nothing better than to avoid serious conversation by poking fun, though I could see Horace wasn't playing along.

"I do listen when you tell us how important preplanning is," Horace said, and then turned to my uncle. "Richard, what about you? It turned out to be a lot of fun filling out the form from Winter's website. I can help if you want."

"Good idea, uncle. You have a lot of good stories to tell."

"And, a lot of secrets that should not go to the grave with you," added Horace, proving he could give as good as he got.

Richard did his professorial stroke of the chin and shook his silver headed dome.

"Winter, you can just surprise me. Now, who wants more turkey chili?"

Translation—Richard had no intention of talking about it—not now, not ever.

* * *

After dinner, Horace invited us all to his cottage with the promise of breaking open the Old Granddad that Richard had lost in the lottery bet. Kip and I begged off, and the two took the dogs for a walk before ambling over to Horace's place, where I suspected they would end the evening at the kitchen table hashing out world problems.

"I'll be back in a sec," said Kip, who disappeared out the front door.

I turned on the gas fireplace in the living room and snuggled into one of the abutting chairs. When Kip came back, he was holding a box. Still raw from my worry over Kip producing a ring, my heart fluttered at the sight of a gift from him, but judging from the box size, I'd have to be an elephant for it to be jewelry of any sort.

"Open it," he said, and took the seat opposite, ready to tear the package apart himself, he was so excited.

"It's not my birthday."

"I know that. This is more like a peace offering."

I peeled away brown paper bag wrapping and stared.

"If you think you can win my forgiveness for sending my best friend to jail with a Broadway Limited HO vintage steam locomotive, you might be right," I said, and remembering Arthur Willings and his collections, I carefully opened the package before lifting the beautiful train from the box.

I wasn't really shallow enough to let Kip off the hook because of a fabulous gift like this, however, I wasn't naive. Scoop had been the one to step in quicksand, and I knew it wasn't fair to keep making Kip my scape goat for the pent-up frustration and fear that I felt.

I held the engine and tender gently in my hands, admiring the detail. It would be my first foray into digitally-controlled locomotives and I couldn't wait to try it.

"Nah, you're not going to forgive me for that." Kip laughed, which seemed so contrary to how he should feel about arresting Scoop.

I looked at him suspiciously. "What's going on?"

"Listen, Winter, I'll tell you as much as I can. As for the rest—you really do have to trust me, even if you don't think I deserve it."

As Kip talked, I saw the start of something sinister beginning to unwind. According to my boyfriend, the police had done extensive background investigations when Chester first arrived in town. They were well aware that the man had been only posing as someone without a home, and it didn't take long before they pegged him as the successful owner of Eyes See, a private investigative firm.

"Apparently, Chester had confided in our Social Services Director when they tried to intervene. That's something they do when we find someone sleeping on the park bench."

I looked at Kip in surprise. "Is that a common occurrence?"

"Not an everyday happening, although we have a lot more homeless folks passing through than you might think. For a while, we had a guy camping out near the Great Swamp. He made a regular home there, tent, fire, food, clothing—the works."

Kip went on to explain that many of those without homes refuse intervention.

"One guy was downright prickly about the food that was offered. You'd think he was in a five-star restaurant interrogating us about the preparation. Plus, he turned down any canned items because they weren't light enough to carry in his backpack. Social Services ended up giving him a gift card to the grocery store."

This was an entire new world to me. I knew there were occasional folks down on their luck who might be seen pushing a shopping cart around town, however, they never lasted long in the streets. As altruistic as the interventions by town leaders were, I'm sure they were also motivated to keep our town looking Hallmark perfect.

"Social Services arranged with landlords for Chester to stay in their empty offices or apartments. They kept it under the radar."

"Why the cloak and dagger?" I asked.

"He was working undercover and wanted to stay that way. The fewer people who knew that he was here on a mission, the better."

"What mission was he on?" I asked.

Kip didn't know and explained that all Chester would tell them is that he was there at the request of someone who thought his mother had been scammed out of a small fortune.

Arthur Willings, I thought.

"We wanted to get involved—to help. I mean if one older woman has been scammed, then think of what ripe pickings the approximated 15% of our population might be. In the end, there was nothing we could do. Chester wasn't doing anything illegal and it wasn't like he was sleeping in the gazebo at Ballard Park."

I tried to imagine what the community spirited Elizabeth B. Ballard, who deeded her property to the town for a park, might have said if she had found Chester curled up on a bench for the night. The park, in the heart of the village, was a place that drew many families and even on a dreary day, it bustled with kids on the jungle gyms, teens tossing Frisbees, and families just gathering. There wasn't a Ridgefield parent who would tolerate a loiterer who might present stranger danger.

"You'd think his moral compass would have kicked in. If he thought people were being scammed, letting the public know might save someone else from losing their life savings."

It still prickled me when I thought about a phone call Richard received, seemingly from one of his nephews saying that he needed money to get out of a jam. The impersonator, who did a pretty good job at mimicking my young cousin, had pleaded for help and begged Richard not to tell his parents because in his words, "they would kill me." Instead of wiring half his savings to some offshore account in the Cayman Islands, Richard called his estranged younger brother and said, "Bail your own kid out."

Not exactly the best approach for mending fences, although it did open the door to conversation for the first time in years. Now the brothers talk a few times a year and Richard keeps in touch with my cousin, who had been sitting in the same room with his dad all along. When the imposter called back pleading for funds, Richard promised to help. He took down all the Western Union wiring instructions and handed all the info to the police. They couldn't catch the bad guys, though they did run a successful campaign warning townsfolk against what is known as the Grandparent Scam.

Kip recently gave a talk to the members of Founders Hall, our senior center, and I had attended. He explained how it was important to follow through with a loved one by calling them back on their own phone, because AI makes it easy for scammers to replicate voices.

Kip had advised the group to call the police and the loved one's parents, despite the warning. Most likely, a grandchild or niece or nephew is sitting at home, glued to a screen of some sort. He had then asked if anyone had ever received such a call, and half the hands in the room went up. He didn't bother asking if anyone had become victim of the scam because he already knew that a significant number of them probably had.

"Chester was definitely worried that others would fall into the same trap as his client's mother," said Kip. "The problem was, he was hired by a lawyer whose client needed a PI, and that made Chester bound by attorney-client privilege."

"Meaning he couldn't reveal the scam without revealing his client because that's where the proof lay."

"You got it. Right before Chester died, he planned to meet with both client and attorney to get permission to share what he had learned with us. Apparently, Chester felt that between his client's information and what he had accumulated, we might be able to make an arrest."

Thinking that the attorney/client privilege was set in place to protect the client, rather than protecting some random scammer, it didn't make sense that Chester would delay. I said as much.

"Chester didn't expect to die last Wednesday night. He had been methodically building his case, and he planned to meet with his client and his lawyer just to follow protocol before he talked with us. We were set to meet on Thursday."

"And then, the client also died in the wee hours of Thursday morning—both taking their secrets to the grave," I finished.

"So, you knew that Arthur Willings was Chester's client?"

"I put two and two together. Betty Willings mentioned that Chester was well-paid for the odd jobs he did around the house. Then, Anne Halliday told me about Eyes See when I visited her last week."

Kip stared at me for a moment before speaking. "You didn't tell me you spoke with Anne Halliday in person. So, you've known about Chester for, what, almost a week now?"

I nodded uncomfortably. I hadn't told Kip about Anne Halliday because I was afraid he would warn me off Chester's obituary. Now I could see Kip's wheels turning, as he calculated how many times we'd been together when I could have shared what I had learned about why Chester had been in Ridgefield.

"Who else did you tell?"

My stomach clenched as I confessed that Carla, my uncle, and Horace had all been privy.

"I see," he said, nodding slowly. The fact that I had trusted the three of them and not him, hung like a black cloud.

"Chester's obituary has references to Eyes See," I said, thinking that it would be better to tell Kip now rather than have him see it on Thursday in print.

"Which you were supposed to hold until I gave you the all-clear," he said.

Oh boy, my freckles left no room for any spin I could put on this now.

"It's coming out in the Thursday paper," I admitted. "Mrs. Halliday wants the digital versions held until the final arrangements are made."

"Can you pull the obituary?" Kip rubbed his brow until I thought it might fall off.

If last week's efforts to remove my name from my client's obituary had taught me anything, it was that even twenty-four hours ahead of press time, making a last-minute correction was like asking for a stay of execution. We were way past the Tuesday noon deadline and no way would Amanda be willing to work her magic again at the eleventh hour. Besides, I had an obligation to Anne Halliday who was now my client. I said as much.

"I can't believe it. You've kept this information from me for an entire week and now you're printing it in the newspaper while we're investigating the guy's murder. You might as well have painted a target on your own back that says *shoot here*. You're worse than your buddy Scoop!"

Ouch!

The bottom line, as Kip would see it, is that I had withheld information critical to his case—information that I didn't know he already had. Instead of helping my boyfriend solve a murder, I had confided in Richard, Horace, and Carla. It was pin drop silent as I held my breath and looked to the lake for the reprieve I knew wouldn't come.

Finally, Kip cleared his throat. "I'm not sure what all this says about us."

There it was. The trust issue which hovered overhead like the cliffs casting shadows over the lake.

The thought made it hard to focus.

"I suppose you told Scoop also."

"I never told Scoop about Chester being a private eye. Although, he knew about my trip to Nyack and also knew there was a connection between Chester and Arthur Willings. And, he suspected that Chester was only pretending to be homeless. That I got from our conversations."

"Nyack?" Kip jumped at the word, and I knew I was digging my grave deeper and deeper.

I explained how I had found out Chester's last name and that prompted my visit to Mrs. Halliday. I also came clean about Scoop's apologetic phone call, that led to his subsequent role as GPS replacement during my efforts to ditch the black SUV that had been following me.

"His cousin tried to get a photo of the license plate, but I haven't heard anything about it yet, and now that Scoop is in jail, I'm not sure I will hear."

I almost felt sorry for Kip as I revealed my deception. If the panic attack didn't send him in the other direction, I was pretty sure my duplicity would.

"Scoop suspected that Chester was posing, though he wouldn't say where he got that information—maybe his arson informant also told him about Chester," I said.

Unless he had multiple informants, I thought.

Kip put his head in his hands.

"So, now you're on someone's radar. That's just great, Winter."

"I'm sorry Kip. I'm just doing my job. If I didn't submit Chester's obituary, Anne Halliday would have found someone else to do it."

"But probably not in Ridgefield, where Chester got himself killed because the scammer figured that he was on to him. Now, the murderer will know that you too, are on to him."

"But I'm not on to him."

"Tell that to the killer."

Chapter Twenty-Six

Kip looked at me dully. "Winter, we need to talk."
Maybe so, though right now, all I wanted was to follow the train of thought that was tickling my brain.

"I know," I said, gently. "Can we try to figure this out first?"

There was something critical in this conversation that remained just out of reach. If Kip and I could just keep our emotions from clogging the drain, we might be able to figure out what Chester had been investigating and whether the other two arsons—now three, counting the garage fire on New Street—were related to his death.

Think, Winter, I ordered myself.

I looked at Kip who didn't seem in the mood to help me solve the case. He was probably still too busy wondering why he had fallen for a woman who spent more time pushing him away than nurturing the relationship.

"Kip," I said, sharply. "I want you to listen to me."

"All ears," he said, though he didn't seem that attentive.

"Scoop told me that his source wanted to make sure no-one confused the first two fires with the one that was started at Pop's Place."

"When did he tell you that?" Was that a little spark of interest I had just heard in Kip's voice?

"It was just something he dropped into one of our conversations."

I couldn't remember exactly which conversation because at the time I thought it was pretty obvious to everyone that the Pop's Place fire was different. No ventilation to feed the flames, a poor effort at doing any damage, and no financial benefit to the owner. I recounted that to Kip.

"So, you think that the arsonist was afraid that if we ever caught him, we'd also accuse him of murder?" Kip asked.

"Yes."

"What else aren't you telling me?"

Resigned that if I had any hope of convincing Kip that I could be trusted, I had to start by taking the first giant step. I took a deep breath and started from the beginning. I told him about Scoop's threatening letter, recapped the conversation, and even described the disruption I had seen in Scoop's normally orderly apartment the day after we had caught him in my study.

Before Kip left, he had mellowed somewhat, as he held me in a long embrace.

"We still need to talk," he whispered, and then before I could answer, he gave me one of his full-on kisses that left me weak-kneed and craving much, much more.

"And, Winter," he added, after another kiss that chased all reservations away. "I beg you—please be careful."

* * *

Once Kip was gone, I carried the locomotive he had given me to the train room, and carefully placed it on the track. I thought about Mrs. Willings, who had a son more interested in packaging sometimes, than the gift. A son who had become a multi-millionaire because he knew the difference between what to save and what to toss. Carefully restoring the box to its original condition, sans train, of course, I put it in the small closet where we kept the train supplies. Someday, maybe, someone would return the locomotive to its box for resale. Not me, though. It was one of the most thoughtful gifts from Kip that I had ever received.

I then slumped into the study chair and thought about everything I had learned, starting with Scoop's first phone call letting me know about being a person of interest in the fires. From there, it was Chester's murder, Arthur's suspicious death, and Scoop's arrest.

I had only told a few people about Chester and his company, Eyes See. Scoop's source, who knew everything about the arsons, might also have known that Chester wasn't just a random guy without a home. He obviously suspected that a death in the burning building could be linked to him, which made him nervous. Hadn't Carla's brother known that the man had been Chester? Maybe, he knew Chester was undercover.

If Richard and Horace knew about Chester being murdered, then it wasn't the state secret the police hoped it was.

My head was spinning and I got up to pace. None of this was making sense. There were just too many unknowns. I circled back to who I told about Chester and Eyes See.

Richard, Horace, and Carla.

Who else knew about Eyes See?

The police, social services, the murderer, and just maybe, Scoop's source because they knew enough to worry that all the fires would be lumped together.

It was unlikely that Scoop's source was part of the PD because the cops were more about keeping secrets than sharing them. Someone who Social Services had told? Also unlikely—those people were like a locked safe when it came to client information.

I would bet my life that neither Richard nor Horace had anything to do with starting fires or sharing information. That left only one person that I had told about Chester's undercover operation, who could have then told Scoop.

Could Carla be Scoop's Deep Throat?

Chapter Twenty-Seven

My duplicity had made Kip go radio silent and I couldn't blame him. He wouldn't understand how I would trust my friends with vital information and yet not trust him. He was right to wonder what that said about us.

There was no news from Scoop on Wednesday and the last thing I would do was call Kip to ask. Instead, I decided to confront Carla. If she admitted to being Scoop's informant, I would then pass the information to Kip.

I felt like a traitor as I drove to the funeral home and yet, I had convinced myself that Carla was Scoop's source and that her brother, Tony, was feeding information to her.

The parking lot was full when I arrived, so I parked behind the firehouse. The proximity to the funeral home and Scoop's apartment boosted my resolve, as I hurried across the street. The somber looking man, who met me at the front door, assumed I was there to pay my respects and before I could explain, he ushered me quickly toward the viewing room.

I was about to reverse directions to seek out Carla, when I felt a hand on my arm, guiding me into the room and toward an open casket.

"You must be one of my mom's aides," said a woman, who looked to be my own mother's age. "I'm sorry, I don't remember your name."

"So sorry . . . it's a mistake . . ."

"Oh, tell me about it. My mother should have lived to 100. A little better care might have gotten her that far—not blaming you dear—the facilities these days, not up to par."

"I mean my mistake . . ."

"Stop blaming yourself. My mother had quality of life until 99 and all because of her aides. She loved all of you. What did you say your name was again?"

"Winter," I mumbled. "I don't think you understand. I shouldn't be here . . ."

The woman frowned and interrupted. "I don't recall all her ladies, sorry, my memory isn't what it used to be. Here, let me introduce you before you pay your respects."

In horror, I was passed from one family member to another, and by the time I reached the last of the receiving line, I was described as one of the deceased woman's most trusted aides.

I was about to slip away when the ever-attentive daughter was suddenly back at my arm and ushering me toward the casket. "She looks lovely, doesn't she? Pink was her favorite color," she said, as she reached into the casket to adjust the dead woman's collar. "After you pay your respects, meet me in the back of the room. We have a small token of our appreciation for all of you wonderful aides."

What could I do but kneel in front of the pale pink coffin to say a final farewell to a ninety-nine-year-old woman named Gladys Night. And oh my, did she love pink—even the pillow surrounding her blush tinted coif looked like she was sleeping in a garden of pale roses.

I choked back the nervous laugh that threatened to escape, as I thought about Richard's oldies echoing off the lake. This woman could have endured a lifetime of teasing over her name. *Midnight*

Grave Words

Train to Georgia from Richard's seventies playlist began spinning around in my head. *Gladys,* I mentally whispered, *where are the Pips?*

Reeling myself in, I said a quiet farewell to Gladys and offered a prayer that she had had a good life. And then, my eyes darted to the closest exit. I was almost there when the dead woman's daughter stopped me.

"Winter, we're doing a little tribute to mom's aides." She swept her hand toward the back of the room where a number of people had gathered.

I tried to be discreet by holding back, though it was impossible with Gladys' daughter pushing me forward. I landed in the center of Gladys Night's other aides, who looked at me as if they had just eaten something that had turned.

And, I could see why. They were dressed in clothes that suggested they were there to pay their respects to a woman that they cared for, and also cared about. My jeans, sweatshirt, and Timberland boots looked more like I was about to work in the yard then attend a wake.

"Thank you," said Gladys' daughter, as she handed me a small pink box with an oversized white bow.

"Oh no, I couldn't," I said, horrified, as she thrust it into my hand, not taking no for an answer. She dabbed her eyes, suddenly at a loss for words, as she handed each aide the gift. When she reached the last of the group, she whispered a thank you and hurried teary-eyed from the visitation room.

* * *

"You stole the gift?" asked Carla, when I called from command center a la commode, a few minutes later.

"Just meet me at your office and put it back in the gift pile, *please!*" I said.

When I finally managed to exit the rest room and meet Carla, she took the box from me in a huff. "Did you open it?"

"No, why would I do that? And, why are they giving out gifts anyway?"

"Last wishes," said Carla, peering at the little pink square. "I wonder what's inside."

"Just put it back for me," I hissed.

We were standing outside her office and while there was a small alcove separating it from the mourners, we were still visible from certain angles.

"Too obvious. It's going to look like you or worse, *we,* stole this thing. I can't risk that."

We both stared at the box.

"OK, I'll slip out the back door once I see the coast is clear and you can wait until the right moment to return it."

Gladys had been popular but not enough so that I'd be hidden in the crowds. Getting out of their sight unseen was going to be difficult, especially because the woman's daughter had a bead on me.

"Here, you take this and hide in the restroom until things thin out." She thrust the box back into my hands. "And, I think it's up to you to return it."

"What if someone has to go?"

"Flush a lot. People tend to avoid bathrooms after multiple flushes," and here, she scrunched her nose.

I challenged the town's water system as I repeatedly pressed the toilet lever down anytime I heard someone near the restroom door. Finally, things grew quiet and I determined, from the steady drone of one voice, that the minister was giving a final farewell to Gladys. I cracked the door, saw no-one, and raced toward the open back exit, leaving the little pink box behind.

A few moments later, Carla met me outside near my car where she triumphantly handed me the gift. "I had to check to make sure the restroom was, you know, fit for people, and I saw that you left this."

I groaned. "It does *not* belong to me."

"It does now. Turns out they had one of these for everyone who attended. Let's see what it is."

I glanced back at the funeral home where apparently the mourners were still in prayer.

The small pink box with its overpowering white bow screamed OPEN ME. I slid the bow off and then slowly lifted the lid. Inside was a pendant the size of a silver dollar. The piece was half gold and half silver. Embedded on the gold was a silver rope knotted in the center. The rope turned gold when it reached the silver side. A David Yurman style to accommodate all jewelry preferences. A card was placed below with a message that read, *"He who does not trust enough, will not be trusted."*

I turned the pendant over. The back was the reverse of the front, only this time, the symbol was a closed loop and three knots, something I didn't recognize.

"Wow, a Pikorua," said Carla, fingering the unusual pendant. "It's a symbol for eternal emerging life paths. It embodies the life bond of friendship, love, and loyalty. I haven't seen one, in like, forever."

"I recognize the rope and knots, though I don't think I've ever seen this," I said, pointing to what Carla called a Pikorua. "It's quite beautiful the way it's all put together, isn't it?"

Carla looked at the piece of jewelry with a soft smile and turned her head back and forth in wonder. "I'm sorry I didn't know this lady because she definitely had her priorities straight."

"You take it," I said, trying to push it into Carla's hand.

Carla snapped out of her reverie and rolled the sleeve up on the coral sweater she wore to reveal her tats.

"I don't need it. I have these." And then, she looked me straight in the eyes and said, "Winter, it's karma, because if ever there was a message you needed to hear—this is it."

Carla then sent her eyes heavenward and said, "Well done, Gladys."

After that, how was I supposed to ask Carla if she was Scoop's informant and possibly the arsonist, or at least the person covering for the fire starter.

"Was there some reason why you wanted to talk to me?" she asked, as she walked me to my car.

"Do you have time for a drink?"

"Tomorrow," she said, with a wide smile. "Tonight, I have plans."

And then, she hurried back inside, leaving me to wonder about the secrets Carla kept.

Chapter Twenty-Eight

Thursday, and still no word from Kip or Scoop. By now, Chester's obituary had hit the paper and I was pretty sure the next time I saw the Nosy Parkers, there would be a smug *I told you so.*

Don't do it, I willed myself, as my finger lingered over Kip's number in my contacts list. Instead, I pushed the button on the side of my phone that made it inactive, thereby assuring that I didn't make an inadvertent butt call.

I plowed through the day working at the library, worrying over just about everything. Kip, because our relationship was on the rocks and I didn't know how to fix it. Scoop, because I didn't know where he was or how bad things were for him. Add to that all the other life worries, like Richard's secrets, Horace's sudden need to make end of life arrangements, and Carla's possible involvement, I was a basket case. Plus, I had this shiny new gold medallion with a message that haunted me and an obligation to call Gladys' family to confess.

On my way home from the library, I finally called Carla.

"What's wrong with your voice?" she asked, when she answered.

"It's my portable handsfree device—it makes everything sound . . . I don't know . . . tinny," I said.

"It creates an echo on my side, so I can hear two of all parts of the conversation. It's weird."

"I'm just calling to see if you want to meet me for a drink at Pop's Place," I said.

"Did you say Pop's Place? I thought with the fire and all, it was still closed."

"The police gave the all-clear and I guess Jimmy—that's the owner—is desperate to re-open; tonight's the night."

"I don't know, isn't that a guy hangout?"

"Which is why I need another woman to go with me," I said. "I don't want to look too out of place."

"You're not going to blend in with all that testosterone, no matter who you bring along," she said. "What time?"

* * *

I stopped at home to change out of the black wool hoodie I had thrown on earlier. That, and a fleece vest, had been enough to ward off the daytime chill, though now I shivered as the afternoon waned. Instead, I put on my eye enhancing royal blue sweater and added a little makeup. I grabbed my old leather jacket—just vintage enough to be in style, and hoped that the look would be a lure for anyone who might have information I was trying to wrangle. Passing through the kitchen, I stopped at the cooktop where Richard was stirring a pot of sauce loaded with a batch of newly created miniature meatballs. Stabbing one with a fork, he handed it to me.

"You've got to eat," he said. "I'll leave some of this in the fridge for you for when you get back. You can cook some pasta to go with it."

"Why do I have the sense that you are trying to take care of me?" I asked, between bites. "Hmmm, this is good."

Diva sat at our feet looking longingly with those hard to deny eyes. Richard leaned down, gave her a pet, and then served her a tiny meatball which she gobbled in one quick bite.

"Somebody has to, because you don't always take care of yourself," he said.

What had he meant by that?

Richard was busying himself with a container for the sauce, so I let it slide.

"Where to tonight?" he asked.

I told him about my plans to have a drink with Carla.

"Why Pop's Place?" Now, he eyed me suspiciously and I knew I might as well come clean, or I wasn't getting out of there any time soon. I explained about my idea that Pop's Place was the one thing that all these mysteries had in common. Scoop frequented there. Chester and Artie were regulars, and that's where Chester had died.

"So, you are thinking that Chester's scam investigation has something to do with Scoop's arson stories?"

"Maybe." I told Richard how Chester had sought Scoop out and warned him about his stories the night he had died.

"He even told Scoop to stay out of that place for a while."

"All the more reason that you should stay out of there too," my uncle said.

I kissed my uncle on the cheek and told him not to worry. I gave Diva a pet. She would stay with Richard at his bungalow tonight. With the clock ticking toward Mary's return and the renovation approvals up in the air, he wanted the rest of the bungalow shipshape.

Like a first-time mother, I felt a wave of apprehension at the thought of Diva on an overnight, though I could think of no safer place for her than with Richard or Horace. I was never a dog person, though since I inherited her, she has wormed her way under my skin.

With her large expressive eyes and her keen intelligence, she didn't need a voice to let me know what was on her mind.

* * *

As I had told Richard, I really believed that Pop's Place was the common denominator in the mysterious murder of Chester and the potential murder of Arthur Willings. It was also a place that Scoop frequented and where he had been the last to see Chester alive. I felt my resolve bolster. This had to be where I'd find something that might help my friend.

Then, there was all the stuff about Scoop's source feeding him info on the accelerants before they were even verified by the fire marshal. Was that related to Chester and his death? I didn't see how and yet, Chester had been warning Scoop the night he had been murdered.

If Carla was Scoop's source, which I was beginning to believe, then tonight would be an opportunity for me to pry it out of her.

Pop's place was alive with a serious dart tournament happening on the far side of the large room, the rest of which was taken up by a long-arced bar and surrounding high-tops. Through an open archway, I could see a pool table and two men intent on their game. The décor was dark, paneled, and heavy with pub vibe.

When I entered, I felt the quick appraising eyes of the other patrons. Apparently, my wardrobe efforts weren't enough to warrant more than a quick look because everyone went back to what they were doing, as I made my way to two empty bar stools. A moment later, Carla entered, and the room grew quieter, as a number of heads assessed. And, continued to assess, as she slid into the seat and out of her black wool pea coat to reveal a hot pink sleeveless tank tucked into faux leather jeans. A rhinestone belt and stiletto heels accented the look, which landed somewhere between hooker and biker-babe.

"I said we were going for a drink, not on a pick-up mission." I lowered my voice because the room had fallen very quiet.

"I'm thirty-one years old and my biological clock is ticking," she whispered back and then, with a smile, turned to the bartender who was waiting to take our order. "I'll have a Ketel One Martini up, with no vermouth and two olives, please." Again, the huge brilliant white teeth flash.

"Why do you call it a martini if it has no vermouth? Why not just ask for a straight vodka without ice?" I asked, after giving my order, a glass of the house Chardonnay.

"I like the shake with the ice, so the vodka is really cold and especially the olives. Plus, I feel like I'm in a *Sex in the City* scene when my adult beverage comes in a chilled glass."

The noise level hadn't yet returned to full pitch and I could feel eyes on us. I wasn't sure if the gawkers were looking at Carla's ample cleavage, or the tattoos that covered her arms, neck and snaked down to her chest.

"You should be wearing the pendant," she said, as she did a subtle room scan.

"It's not mine. I'm going to give it back." I looked around too.

Carla had a way of lowering her thick lashes seductively as she surveyed the room, without people realizing that she too was evaluating. I know her well enough to know that her situational awareness is as sharp as it comes.

"Three o'clock," she said, giving a slight lift to her shoulder. "There is a guy pretending not to watch us. Not bad looking, though very conventional—more your type than mine."

"My type? I'm not looking for anyone," I said.

"Well, maybe you should. Your biological clock is ticking too and I don't see you making much progress with Kip." Thank goodness Carla was too busy sizing people up to notice the sucker punch she had just delivered.

"Oooh, check out the bartender. He has an adorable behind."

"Carla, we're here because I want to find out who Chester and Arthur hung out with."

And, to find out if you're the source Scoop refuses to give up, I thought.

Carla turned her big, beautiful eyes my way, pale intense glistening pools radiating a million thoughts.

"Are you thinking that Arthur's death was suspicious? I thought it was . . . expected," she said.

Since my trip to New Jersey, I had brought Carla up to speed, and, in fact, she was more of a confidant than Scoop these days. A flicker of Kip's face, when he learned that I had confided in others rather than him, flitted across my memory. I wanted to tell Carla what I had done and how it might have destroyed my relationship with him, and yet I couldn't. The thought that she could be Scoop's source was making me less certain about sharing my inner most feelings.

"Mrs. Willings thinks it's just too much of a coincidence that both Arthur and Chester died within hours of each other," I said.

A shadow fell over the bar and I looked up to see the bartender. Carla was right. He was cute with dark hair, dark eyes, and fit build. A young Keanu Reeves, with a disarming smile he directed at us.

"The gentleman over there would like to buy you ladies a drink." He nodded at a man at the end of the bar—the same one Carla had noticed earlier. I was about to say no, thank you, when Carla sent her own million-dollar smile his way, fluttered her lashes, and blew him a kiss.

"Great, we'll have another round," she said. "Just give us a little time to finish this one!"

"What are you doing?" I hissed.

"Sleuthing."

Chapter Twenty-Nine

The man at the end of the bar moved around to the empty seat near Carla when our second drinks were set in front of us. He introduced himself as John Smith.

Which one, I thought to myself, though I smiled as though I really believed the alias. Carla and I used our first names only, though with my name, I wasn't exactly undercover.

"Winter, unique name," he said, as he turned to me. "Are you that obituary writer that people talk about?"

While my business was fairly new, I had gotten a good bit of media attention a few months back when Diva's former owner took a tumble down the stairs, that started a chain of events leading to murder. It's possible that this guy had read about me.

"Guilty," I said.

"And I'm Carla—I manage the funeral home." Carla reached to shake, and I saw the look of surprise as he took in the tattoos, that dressed her arms like a long sleeve shirt ending in a soft hand with ghoulish black polished nails.

John Smith didn't hide his wince. "The Grim Reapers out for a drink?"

Carla flashed her neon smile. "Just taking a break."

The conversation was pleasant enough. John Smith was in sales, and the wave he gave when he mentioned his job, made it clear that he wasn't going to tell us what he sold. To me, he was selling some heavy-duty BS and I was pretty sure Carla saw it too, though she was chatting him up as if being in sales for some vague product was as exciting as being an astronaut scheduled for a trip to the space station.

"Did you hear about our poor homeless man, Wandering Chester?" she asked suddenly, which startled John Smith enough to splash his drink.

The bartender was busy with other customers, so Carla took the cocktail napkin out from under her glass and used it to dab at his shirt, while never missing a conversational beat. "He died right here in this very building—upstairs. Winter has to write about him and I have to make the arrangements for his journey to his final resting place."

Carla's door opening efforts didn't seem to be paying off, because John Smith was looking around and no longer rapt by my friend's attention. The bar activity had picked up with people coming and going and our bar mate was becoming increasingly uncomfortable, looking as if he wished he could disappear. Maybe, crowds weren't his thing, because his initial wolfish appraisal had been replaced by only casual interest. When I pressed John Smith about Wandering Chester, he mumbled something about seeing the man around town though said he had never met him.

"Did you know Arthur Willings by chance? I know he hung out here and I'm writing his obituary also."

"That's why we've invaded this male dominated hangout," added Carla. "We're trying to meet people that might have known Arthur or Chester . . . to help Winter out."

John Smith shifted on his stool and looked even more uneasy. His eyes darted around searching the room. For what? A rescuer? It was like talking to someone who was intent on his cell phone. The bartender broke the awkward moment by setting a bowl of pretzels down in front of us.

"I knew Arthur a little bit. Everyone did. He spent a lot of time here." John Smith sipped, fidgeted with his napkin, and looked longingly at the door. "Nice guy, as far as I could tell."

Carla continued chatting John Smith up while I scoured the room. Impossible to tell if anyone had eyes on us. The amber sconces in the dimly lit space created an aura of mystique around the bar, and people in the room were mostly in shadow. The adjoining game room was brighter because of the pool table light which spilled into a portion of the barroom, though not enough to pick out familiar faces.

Finally, John Smith seized his opportunity and said, "Oh, look at the time. I've got to run."

The bartender handed him his check and before making a fast exit, John Smith dropped some very large bills on the counter.

"That was like telling someone you had to wash your hair when they asked you for a date," said Carla. "That guy couldn't wait to get rid of us."

"Maybe, he was put off by our professions."

Carla, ever the observant one said, "Not that. It was something else—some room vibe that changed. Maybe it was that guy who came in right about the time John Smith sat down near us—you know the one who looked like the place belonged to him?"

"Sorry, I was too focused on John Smith. Do you see him now?" I swiveled on my stool to take in the room.

Carla swiveled me back. "Don't be so obvious and no, I don't see him from my vantage point. In a few minutes, you can go to the restroom and check things out though in this light..." Carla gave me a *who knows* shoulder gesture.

When the bartender came to collect the bills, Carla asked him if the guy always paid in cash.

"Don't know," he said. "I've never seen him before." He then confirmed that he was the regular bartender.

"There's a guy who fills in when I'm off, which isn't very often," he said.

Where, then, did John Smith know Arthur Willings if not from Pop's Place? Didn't he say Arthur was a regular? How would he know that if he didn't frequent the place? And, what was he doing here now?

"I heard you ask about Chester and Arthur," the bartender said. "I knew them both pretty well. I can try to help you. My name is Ramone."

Not quite like Ramen noodles, though I could see how Mrs. Willings thought so.

"You're Arthur's friend. The one who he was helping to get into Westconn," I said, reaching to shake the hand he offered.

Ramone smiled, bright white teeth and dimples lighting up an otherwise solemn face.

"That's me."

As Ramone talked about Arthur, I realized that he had the insightful qualities of a good bartender. He had recognized Arthur right away, as someone who was awkward in his own skin. While his mother sugar coated Arthur's popularity at Pop's Place, Ramone said he was the kind of guy that bullies considered prime pickings.

"He was always nice when he came in here and I thought he tried so hard to belong—too hard. The guys aren't exactly school yard bullies, but there are some macho types who think the F word is the only one in the dictionary. They picked on Artie—subtly, which made it all the worse, though I'm pretty sure Artie knew it and ignored it."

"How do you pick on someone subtly?" asked Carla.

Ramone thought for a minute and then, said, "It'd be like someone who is passive aggressive. Like if Winter said, 'I love your skirt,' and you answered, 'It would look really good on you—it's pretty fitted so you might want a large.'"

Carla choked out a laugh. "Winter would look like she was wearing my hand-me-downs in a large."

"Or you might say, 'You look so pretty today—I didn't recognize you at first.' Or my personal favorite, because my mother used to say it to my sister—'You've done a lot with what you've got.'"

"What they call a backhanded compliment," I confirmed.

Ramone nodded his head, acknowledged someone who was waving for a drink by holding a finger up in a *one-minute* gesture, and continued. "Artie was always buying the guys drinks, and they would slap him on the back like an old friend, whenever he was here. I could see that they were just using him though. And, when he'd ask if he could get in on the dart game, one of the guys would say, 'You know we'd love to have you but this round is just for the firefighters.' And, then, the next time it would be only for the Vets—always something they knew a guy like Artie would not qualify for. He could never have served his town or his country—not with his physical disabilities . . . they just played him along like he was one of the guys, and then shut him out in a way that reminded him of who he wasn't and would never be."

"How did they even know about his health issues?" I asked.

"Ahh, and now we get to the crux of that group. They know everything about everyone or at least they *think* they do. Politics, local government, heck, even how Jimmy runs his place—they make it their business to know it all."

Competition for the Nosy Parkers.

"You say it like it's one group of guys, not the entire clientele of Pop's Place. Was Chester also in the group?"

"Chester was quiet and hung back, though he was never far from Artie's elbow." A dark look travelled across Ramone's face. "They pretty much ignored Chester, though he didn't ignore them. He was a watcher, that one."

"What do you mean, a watcher?" I asked, remembering that the Nosy Parkers had said the same thing.

Ramone explained that he never bought into the fact that Chester was a random homeless guy that Artie took under his wing. He'd sit in the corner of the bar, nurse the same drink for a couple of hours, and watch.

"I read the obituary in the paper and I wasn't the least bit surprised that Chester was a private eye. You just knew the guy was absorbing the scene, sucking up info like a sponge, and storing it in that mysterious brain of his," said Ramone.

"What about Scoop, you know him, right?" Carla leaned forward and grabbed the pretzel bowl, took a hefty handful, and then slid them back over in front of me.

The thought of Scoop mixed up with the mean guy group made me think how easy it was to be swayed by your peers. It's one of those universal parent worries.

I had a flashback of my sister in a standoff with my mom. My mother had insisted that one of Summer's friends was a bad influence, always encouraging her to break the house rules. Summer's retort, "Did it ever occur to you that I might be the bad influence?" After that, my mother backed off.

Before Ramone could answer about Scoop, he was summoned by one of the guys near the dartboard who asked if he was too busy flirting with the interlopers to do his job.

"I'll come back when I can," he said, and hurried off to wait on customers.

"I thought you said that Arthur—I mean Artie, was accepted here? Isn't that what his mother told you?" Carla asked. "Sounds to me like he was bullied. Why keep coming?"

"I guess Artie told his mother something she wanted to hear. Unless, he thought he was accepted and all the insults flew over his head. Maybe, the guys yanked his chain just enough, but not so much as to lose Artie's open wallet?"

"Maybe," said Carla. "This Ramone seems sharp though, and we haven't even gotten to the part about how he and Artie got to be friends. I can't wait for Chapter Two—Ramone to the rescue!"

Suddenly, a loud yell, followed by a string of swear words cursing someone's mother. Despite the fact that Carla is streetwise, her eyes were saucers, as we looked toward the dart board.

"Hey, sorry man," said a beefed-up guy, with hands the size of boats raised as if in surrender. "How was I to know you were going to walk into my line?"

A slight man with dark framed glasses was holding his shoulder. A stain began soaking through his shirt and when he pulled his fingers away, they were red. Ramone rushed to his side and handed him a clean cloth to press against the wound, now uncovered by his rolled-up sleeve. It had obviously been caused by a well-timed and well-aimed dart, because it landed in the fleshy part of his arm where there would be no mortal damage.

Ramone glanced our way and then gestured to the two arguing men, as if to say, *now, do you see?* Guys were quickly moving from the pool tables and high tops to see what the skirmish was all about. Through the crowd, I thought I recognized a few faces, including Winfred Thomas III from the bank, though it was hard to tell between the low-lit room and the crush of patrons, who seemed to be choosing sides.

"I think we should go," I said to Carla.

"No way, this is where the action is."

I dragged Carla out of Pop's Place, though not before sliding my business card across the bar to Ramone.

"Can you call me?" I asked. "I want to do right by Artie."

He glanced around the room and then slipped the card into his pocket with a nod. There was a lot of finger-pointing from the crowd encircling the two men, and several of them started chanting "Big Joe, Big Joe."

Hadn't Scoop said that Big Joe was the guy he avoided when it came to dart games? No wonder. I wouldn't want to be on the receiving end of one of his tosses.

"Just when the action was starting," Carla pouted.

While I thought I'd learn a lot by seeing who chose to support which guy, I also thought we could get caught in an ugly scene.

"Action we didn't want to be part of," I said, and caught a mischievous smile from her cherubic face.

"Speak for yourself."

* * *

"So, what did we learn from tonight, besides that guys can be jerks," Carla asked, as we climbed into my car.

"I'm seriously worried about that chip you have on your shoulder," I said. "One break-up shouldn't make you so rabid when it comes to men."

Carla popped a piece of gum into her mouth and then offered me a stick. I shook my head no, so she liberated another piece from its wrapper and started chomping on that one as well.

"There's the pot calling the kettle black—you act like there's a fox in the hen house whenever Kip is around," she let out a half hiccup and half giggle.

"You're mixing metaphors," I said.

"I know, and it's so much fun," she said, giggling even more.

Carla had left her car at the funeral home. Her plan was to drive back to her place after checking on Heady, Topper, and the kittens.

"You can't drive," I said.

The protest I expected, never came. Instead, she said it was just as well, because Scoop's feline compound needed adult supervision. Besides, she often crashed at Scoop's apartment because when Carla was out on the town, she never drove.

I applauded both my friends—one for letting others decide if she was too intoxicated to get behind the wheel, and the other for always giving people a safe landing spot.

"We need to focus," she said, and stared at the ceiling intently as if focusing was out of reach, which I thought it just might be.

Carla began ticking off her fingers. "Here's what we found out. First, and this is a biggy, we found the Noodle Guy."

"Ramone," I offered. "Nice guy, and I think he has a lot more to say. Though, did you notice how he was always scanning the room?"

"He's the bartender," she said. "It's his job to scan the room. What else?"

"We learned that Arthur . . . I mean Artie, wasn't popular with 'the group' at Pop's Place. I wonder why he kept that from his mom?"

"A lifetime of worry can pile up. From the sounds of it, Artie was a sensitive guy. Maybe, he just wanted his mom to think he was accepted—you know, like you said, take the worry off her shoulders," said Carla.

"What did you do with my inebriated friend?" I asked.

"A couple of drinks and I'm a shrink," she said, with a laugh. "That John Smith was growing on me, though I think he got freaked out about something."

"Probably by your black nail polish," I said.

"Lots of people wear black nail polish around Halloween."

"Point taken."

We had just pulled into the funeral home parking lot when a black SUV passed by. The sooner I got Carla inside with doors locked, the better off we'd be.

"Whoa, Winter, slow down. I might have had a couple of drinks, but I don't need an escort up the staircase. And by the way, I know that the last drink was slightly watered down. You should try to be less obvious if you want to fool someone. I saw the wink Noodle Guy gave you when he served my martini. I hope John Smith got a discount."

And suddenly, the opportunity I'd been waiting for presented itself. "How does someone who looks as innocent as you end up being so deviously observant? It makes me wonder if you might be Scoop's source."

Carla laughed and I realized she hadn't taken my comment seriously.

"Experience," she said, as she pulled her jacket tighter against the evening chill.

Once Carla was safely inside with the promise of keeping the doors locked, I hurried to my car.

And sat.

* * *

Doors locked, car started, and heat cranked, I stayed that way for a good ten minutes. *There must be hundreds of black SUVs in this town,* I admonished myself.

I pulled out of the funeral home and as I headed home, I thought about tonight's events.

John Smith, a good-looking guy in his mid-thirties, not a regular he wanted us to think he was, offered nothing except a possible lie. If he frequented Pop's Place, wouldn't Ramone recognize him? And, why the wad of cash in the era of credit cards, debit cards, Venmo, and PayPal? Hardly anyone my age carried much cash anymore. Richard was always on my case saying I should be more prepared. I'd usually held up my phone and said, "It's all here."

"A lot of good that will do you if cell towers are down and internet is scrubbed," he would say.

These days, everything seemed pricey and the drinks at Pop's Place had been no exception. John had paid for a round for us and two rounds for himself. I calculated with tip. His wallet was either always filled with large bills or he had planned ahead to have an interlude, and I thought Carla might have been his target. His hasty retreat said something had changed his mind. What had Carla said? The vibe in the room had shifted.

The piece of information that I found most interesting was that John Smith said he knew Arthur Willings. Why would he admit to that and deny knowing Chester? And, he knew of me. Then again, so did a lot of people.

I should have snapped his picture.

I checked the rearview mirror and in the light along Main Street, I could make out the shadow of a black SUV, one stop light behind.

I tried to replicate the meandering tactics that my rescue team had exhibited only a week earlier to see if the SUV followed. I quickly turned into the CVS parking lot, exited out of the Catoonah Street side, essentially putting me exactly where I had started, in front of the funeral home. By the time I wove up Catoonah and down High Ridge where it meets Peaceable and King Lane, the car was almost on my bumper. After I took a left and landed back on Main Street, the SUV was still with me.

Enough, I thought, and turned right on Governor. Next stop, police headquarters. The driver correctly got the message and disappeared.

I thought about both times that I had been followed. Neither had been threatening. The guy didn't try to push me off the road or block my exit. It was almost as if he just wanted to know where I was going. Of course, I wasn't going to test my theory by leading him on dark lonely streets. Maybe, all our encounters so far had been too public to threaten. Even tonight, there had been a steady flow of traffic.

Would he be waiting for me if I backtracked and headed home?

If there was one thing good about growing up in Ridgefield, it was that the roadmap of backroads remained etched in my brain. I took a very long and circuitous route, winding from East Ridge to Grove, and finally catching Ligi's Way, before a left-hand turn landed me in the Stop and Shop parking lot where I sat, blending in with all the other vehicles that were coming and going. Satisfied that there was no black monster tailing me, I exited via Copps Hill to North Street, past the cemetery, and finally cutting over on back roads until I was at the high school. I crossed North Salem Road onto Mamanasco and was relieved when I saw the warm glow from my cottage.

Chapter Thirty

The house was as quiet as an empty church, and I felt the pang of Diva's absence. Save for the two small lights Richard had left, the rest had pitched in the kind of darkness where you couldn't see a hand in front of you.

I made a cup of lavender chamomile, switched on some lights to create a path to the sliders, and wrapped myself in a throw I kept on one of the chairs, before stepping out on to the deck to reflect. The night hadn't brought me any closer to figuring out how to help Scoop, or if Carla was Scoop's source. Maybe, tonight was a wild goose chase, although I believed in following instinct. Just as some sort of sixth sense advises you not to get into that elevator with its lone occupant, I was sure I, at least, had the Pop's Place part right.

The moon and stars were hidden beneath a stream of steadily moving clouds and save for the normal ambient light we have in this part of the country, it was tomb-like dark on the deck.

Finally, the waxing moon threw a spit of light across the lake, and an eerie howl came from the deck next door. I squinted into the darkness trying to make out if there was a figure lounging in one of the creaking old rockers on my neighbor's deck, or if they were just blowing in the breeze.

"Horace, is that you?"

"Who else would be sitting on my deck at this hour with this giant German Shepherd?" came the reply.

I crossed twenty yards of grass that separated my house from Horace's cottage.

"You OK?" I asked, as I slipped into the rocker next to his.

"More than . . ." he answered. "What about you?"

Remembering Anne Halliday's comment about everything being all about me, I held back my need to tell all.

"All good," I said.

No-one can outlast my moments of silence better than Horace, and after what seemed a lifetime, but was probably only a minute, I gave up.

"Can I ask you something?"

"Always," he said, and I caught the hint of a smile in the strip of light funneling from inside his kitchen.

"Was I wrong not to tell Kip that I knew about Chester being a private eye? He's upset because I told you, Richard, and Carla, last week. Somehow Scoop found out—maybe from Carla or maybe his source knew . . . not sure." As my stream of conscious thoughts reached Horace, he frowned and his brows came so close together they looked like a mustache hooding his eyes. I suppressed a laugh because he looked like he was wearing some sort of bizarre Halloween get up.

"You already know the answer," he finally said. "It goes to the root of your problems."

"Because I don't trust Kip enough." So said Carla and Kip. Heck, even the pendant from Gladys Night was a reminder—*He who does not trust enough, will not be trusted.* I had googled it when I had gotten home from the wake, and now knew that it was attributed to a famous Chinese philosopher named Lao Tzu.

"No, it isn't that. You hold back because you don't think he trusts you. Sometimes, Winter, you act like a stubborn child. If he isn't going to tell you—which I've pointed out is because of his job—you aren't going to share with him which, by the way, makes his job even harder."

Knowing it is one thing, hearing the truth is another. I felt tears prickle the corners of my eyes.

"He thinks we should take a break," I blurted out.

"Is that what you want?"

I thought about New York City and the part-time move that I had been working toward.

"You can run, but you can't hide," Horace added, as if reading my mind.

We sat in companionable silence as I contemplated my neighbor's advice. I knew he was right and yet, I had no idea how to fix it. Or, if it even was fixable. I rose, and was about to return to my own house when Horace shivered, and for the first time, I noticed that he was wrapped in a lap blanket along with his winter coat.

"Richard put you up to this, didn't he?"

"Can't get much by you," he said, with a chuckle.

"You guys are incorrigible. How long have you been out here, freezing to death, in hopes that I'd step out onto the deck before bed?"

"You are a creature of habit, however, I sure would like to finish this conversation inside where it's warm. I've been out here waiting for an hour," he said. "Your place or mine?"

"We're here, so it might as well be yours." And, I carried my now chilled cup inside, as Max lapped at our heels.

Chapter Thirty-One

Horace's pot-bellied stove gave more than it took. My neighbor had already had it running, and from the carefully piled wood on the floor next to it, he stuffed some logs into the belly and stoked. It wasn't long before my chilled hands and cheeks tingled with warmth.

"OK, what's this about?" I finally asked. "Why are you on duty tonight?"

Horace had dumped my tea. He poured piping hot cups for both of us from his newly purchased continually warming kettle, his one concession to modernization.

I watched as he debated how much to tell me, and when I insisted he tell all, he heaved a huge sigh so audible that Max leapt from his bed in the corner of the room and came for a nuzzle with us both.

"We've been worried about you," admitted Horace. "There's a lot going on with Scoop, and your close friendship with him could put you in danger. You have a tendency to ask a lot of questions and people notice that. Plus, you keep pushing Kip away, so we started thinking we should keep tabs on you—be there when you got home, and especially if you needed someone to talk to, because we know you trust us to never share your secrets with anyone."

"Except with each other," I said. "And, sometimes with Scoop and Kip."

"Well, that, yes but what else would you expect?"

In truth, I wouldn't expect anything less. And, that sudden realization caught me off guard. My most trusted people were the very ones that I was deserting by moving even part time to Manhattan.

"Is that why Richard is spending so much time at the lake?" I asked.

Horace ignored my question and sipped his tea.

"It's beyond me how a person who writes obituaries for a living can find so much trouble to get into."

It was my turn to ignore.

"Did you, by chance, tell Scoop about Chester being a private eye?"

"No, why do you ask?"

I did a play by play of my conversation with Kip.

"Kip wondered if Scoop's source had told him about Chester," I said. "When he figured out that I had held back on him and shared with you, Carla, and Richard, he was so hurt that it didn't occur to him to finish his line of thought."

"You're thinking it might be Carla who is his source, because you knew that Richard and I would never tell."

"Possibly . . ."

We hashed that around for a while until Horace suggested we meet tomorrow with Richard and discuss next steps.

"I think it's time to bring Kip into the fold," he said.

"I'm not sure Kip wants anything to do with me right now."

"He'll come around."

"Maybe," I said, remembering the lingering kiss and hug that ended the evening. "Meanwhile, you and Richard need to stop hovering. I'm not in any danger."

I wouldn't tell either of them about the wild ride to New Jersey and back, or about the black SUV that followed me around tonight. That would only worry them.

"If everyone is so worried about me being on someone's radar, then more information might help me to protect myself."

"Did it ever occur to you that if Kip gave you information, he might put his career in jeopardy? What if he was told NOT to reveal the victim's name? Good cops like Kip take the rules seriously because they know they are in place for a reason."

"OK, maybe I get that," I said. "What about all the secrecy about the death itself? How he was killed, who he really was . . . all that? If you and Richard knew Chester was murdered, then it wasn't classified information and yet Kip wouldn't tell me anything."

Horace laughed. "Are you hearing yourself? Your boyfriend is a cop and he is caught between a rock and a very, very hard place—meaning you continue to ask him to break the rules—something that puts him in real conflict. Just because Richard has his own sources, it doesn't mean that Kip should blab around. Two wrongs don't make a right."

Like one of my trains, slowly chug chugging at first, I rolled Horace's comments around in my head. And then, like an engine reaching the apex of a hill and picking up speed on its way down, I caught up.

I hit my head with a slap of my palm. Looking at it from Horace's point of view made me feel like a jerk. *Had I just pulled an entitled move on Kip—give me info and trust me or I can't trust you?* I thought of Gladys' pendant. *Trust was a two-way street.*

I put my head in my hands. Max's wet nozzle nudged me and I buried my face in his fur, reminding me that I hated not having Diva home with me tonight.

"You do know that you and Richard share that self-pummeling gene?" Horace added another log and patted my shoulder before settling back into his chair. "This is so much more fun from the watching point of view. Going through growing pains is agony. Glad it's not me."

And then, he chuckled again, his merry eyes crinkling in well-honed creases at the corners.

I felt the chest hug I had given myself loosen because Horace had that way of putting wisdom first, making everything else feel inconsequential.

The pot belly continued to warm what the night chill had seared to the bone. Max nosed me, adding even more heat.

And then, suddenly, we were both laughing.

After the stress releasing moment, I sighed audibly and said, "I guess I'll head to bed."

Horace smiled, and stood and outstretched his hand to pull me out of my seat. "I hope by tomorrow you'll start telling us what's really bothering you."

* * *

I strode across the small patch of lawn that reached beyond my ankles. Horace and I shared the mowing, and I cringed in horror with the realization that my turn was way overdue. As I thought about it, I was behind in all my housekeeping.

Housekeeping. The word niggled and then, I remembered.

When Scoop had asked me to help, he had said, "do some housekeeping." At first, I thought he meant tidy up the loose ends. Now, I wondered if he wanted to be taken literally.

Once inside, I took the stairs two at a time, put on my night clothes, a silky knee length tee that felt soft against my bare skin, and climbed into bed. Five minutes later, I was up again and headed downstairs, because I couldn't shake the idea that Scoop had left something for me.

I studied the living room. The last time Scoop had been to the house, he had been sitting in one of the chairs by the fireplace, and then had joined everyone in the kitchen for dinner. On his way out, he had passed through the living room again to pick up his computer bag. I went from room to room, retracing his steps and searching. I lifted pillows, looked under chairs, and found nothing. When I got to the front door, I suddenly recalled the tense moment in the study with Kip, Scoop, and me on the night of Richard's food fest, when he appeared to have been searching my computer. I walked slowly into the small space, letting my eyes travel over the bookshelves, and landed on the open door of the train room. I had been in that room many times since then and nothing seemed amiss, though it didn't keep me from entering and searching.

The trains were still polished, the buildings dusted. Everything looked just as I had left it. The engine, Kip's gift, sat just where I had placed it on the track.

Back in the study, I let my eyes slowly roam the built-in bookshelves, landing on every novel, best seller, and children's book that was crammed into the space.

I fingered oldies my sister and I used to binge on . . . *The Lion, The Witch and the Wardrobe* . . . *The Lord of the Rings* . . . books my mom and uncle carefully preserved for us and for my nieces when their turn came. To the collection, I've added others like *Harry Potter* and a signed copy of *Where the Wild Things Are* by beloved children's author Maurice Sendak, who lived in Ridgefield until he died back in 2012.

Grave Words

More current books—best-selling James Patterson, Louise Penny, Annelise Ryan, Richard Osman, Amor Towles, Percival Everett... obvious clues to my reading preferences.

Nothing appeared out of place.

Frustrated, I plunked down on the desk chair and stared. A cup, that normally held my pens, had a photo of two smiling tweens on it and had been a gift from my sister's twins on my last birthday. The pens I usually stuffed into it were still on the floor from when Scoop knocked it over. My foot landed on one of them with a crunch, and I hoped the ink wouldn't spill out on the carpet.

I got down on my hands and knees and began picking up the writing implements. One at a time I placed them atop the desk, studying each as I went.

No clues there.

Finally, I let my hand fan the carpet to see if I missed anything. I couldn't shake the thought that whatever Scoop was trying to tell me about housekeeping had something to do with the night he had invaded my study.

I was about to give up my floor trolling, when in one last ditch effort, I laid my head on the carpet and studied the area beneath the desk where the pens and pencils had fallen. It wasn't long before my eyes began to water and the carpet itched through my flimsy night shirt. I bumped my head as I pulled back to sneeze.

How long had it been since I vacuumed the cottage?

I wiped my eyes and refocused. There, almost invisible behind the base of the wood desk, was a small dark colored piece of plastic.

Squeezing my hand beneath the narrow opening below the cabinetry, I inched out a small thumb drive. Why didn't Scoop just tell Kip and me that he was leaving something in my study.

Because Winter, at the time, it was something he wanted only you to see.

I thought about my friend and all the secrets he was keeping. No wonder he looked like a skeleton these days.

My MacBook Air didn't have a USB port and somewhere, I thought, I had a convertor. I couldn't find it in my desk or in my satchel. Tossing things around in search was making the room resemble Scoop's upended apartment, and as I was about to put things back together, my cell phone shrilled. When I checked the caller ID, I thought, *this can't be good.*

Chapter Thirty-Two

Carla's photo had popped up on my screen, sending off alarm bells. Why wasn't she safely tucked into Scoop's bed, sleeping off the two martinis?

"Chester left us a clue," she said, when I answered.

"Why are you whispering?" I asked her.

"Oh, I don't know, maybe it's because when I'm here at the funeral home, I never feel like I'm completely alone."

"What are you doing there? You were supposed to go upstairs and take care of Scoop's cats. Then, you were supposed to drink three glasses of water, have something to eat, and go to bed. You promised."

"I know. But I picked up the mail and there were some things I wanted to leave on my desk for tomorrow. And then, I got distracted with answering a long list of phone calls. Those things can't always wait, you know, and sometimes, an urgent call gets mixed in with an everyday ask."

"And?" I asked, hoping to hurry her along.

"Someone else obviously listened to the answering machine, thought a message from Chester was routine, and left me a note to follow up. I transferred that note to my to-do list, but never listened to the actual recording until tonight."

"From when?" I asked.

Carla gave an exhausted sigh followed by a yawn, which immediately caused me to do the same.

"That's the thing," she said. "The time on the phone says it was the night he died. You need to come over here and listen, because I'm going crazy trying to figure it out."

"Now?" It was nearly 10 PM.

"I think it's important."

* * *

I reluctantly pulled on some tights and zipped a fleece over the silky tee, hoping my trip to the funeral home would be short and sweet. I was relieved that Diva was with Richard, because I was running out of bartering power with Carp. His reels had created a long wait list of customers and he was now a very busy man.

I left my computer sitting on the desk in the study, though I stuffed the thumb drive into one of the drawers.

Keys, crossbody bag with license and ID, I was about to head out the door when I had a moment of pause. Should I tell Richard, Horace, or Kip where I was going? There was the matter of that black SUV.

Kip would tell me not to go. Richard would want to meet me there, and Horace would be buckled into the seat next to me, with Max breathing down my neck as we drove off. No, this was probably only a martini influenced quest.

All I had to do was listen to the answering machine downstairs in the funeral home before escorting Carla to bed upstairs to Scoop's apartment. I would reassure her that whatever the message she had, was not part of some sinister plot mulling around in her alcohol infused brain. I might have insisted that we wait until morning except that Scoop might have a converter lying around in his apartment that I could borrow.

When I arrived, I drove to the back of the funeral home where Carla had said she would leave the door unlocked. I pulled my Subaru into the space next to Scoop's empty one and glanced up to see his dark apartment, which expanded the hole in my heart. His scooter was being stored at Marty Motors where the great guys over there were sympathetic to his cause. The funeral home didn't require him to give up his space during events, however, Scoop was sensitive knowing how precious those spaces were. Parking elsewhere meant that he would be leaving additional room for a bereaved family member or guest.

That was Scoop, and a slow ache crept through my body. He'd been locked up for several days now and I hadn't seen or talked to him. I hoped they were at least feeding him.

Eastern Standard Time wouldn't begin for another week, however, the days had quickly grown shorter, and between the overcast night which kept knocking out what little moon we did have and the lateness of the hour, I might as well have been in a ghost town.

The noise from my dangling keys that I had clipped to my crossbody bag made me cringe because I thought it could wake the dead, although when I knocked on the funeral home door, there was no response.

A small light twinkled down the hallway. The door was ajar so I crept inside, shutting it securely behind me, and the loud bang made me jump. A funeral home by day can be a calming place. By night, with no lights save for a tiny flicker in one window, which I knew to be Carla's office, my imagination conjured it into something downright creepy.

I made my way in the direction of Carla's office, where she was sitting dreamily at her desk with her ear buds in. She had changed from her glam clothes to sweatshirt comfy.

"Carla?" I said, loudly, as I marched in front of her.

She slammed her hands on her desk, whipped out her ear buds, and then looked up like she had just seen one of the ghosts I imagined haunted the place.

"Oh my God, could you just not sneak up on me like that?"

"Sorry—you didn't answer the door."

The room Carla sat in had a comforting vibe. It was painted in pale blues—the color that invites you in, and yet asks that you don't stay too long. The credenza was laden with handouts with various papers and brochures fanning over the desk. One caught my eye. It was done in vibrant eye-catching color and read Plot Plans. I flashed to Horace's letter and then to another bold red logo I finally remembered seeing fluttering on a bulletin board not too long ago.

When I sat down opposite my friend, she glanced over my shoulder, as if someone might be watching her move some papers on the top of her desk to uncover a bright orange notebook with a ribbon dangling page-marker.

"I keep all my *to-do* lists in this book. When I'm working, I can end up with a hundred scraps of paper all over the place, so I transfer them all at the end of the day into this book. Then, I check them off as I complete each task or return each phone call."

"OK," I said, letting her know I was following.

"And here, look at this." She pointed her finger to her to-do list. I squinted at the barely legible handwriting.

"I know, it's bad, right? Sometimes, I can't read what I've written myself and I promise, it has nothing to do with the two very yummy martinis."

Carla scrolled her finger upward to last week where a notation read *call Chester in the morning.* It was dated the day he died.

For Chester, morning never came, so Carla had just run a pencil strike through the notation.

"Then, when I was sorting my mail and cleaning off the desk, I found the original note which said to check the answering machine for a message from Chester. I had this idea that I wanted to hear his voice one more time . . ." Carla's own voice trailed and not for the first time, I realized that she had some feelings for the man.

"I told myself I was just listening and processing old messages—you know, in case there was anything urgent. When you manage a funeral home, you have to get back to people right away. It can't always wait."

The same was true of obits, so I got that.

She jabbed at the page in her orange notebook, where number ten on her to-do list had taken shape. Chester's name, asking that Carla call a number, which she had taken the time to neatly enter.

"Should we call?" I asked.

"I already called it." She pointed to the paragraph below, and this she had printed carefully. "I wanted to make sure I could read it especially because when I called it again, it said the phone was out of service."

The message read: *If you're calling this number, it means that I can no longer be reached here. I'm partial to the neon green casket because of the way it mirrors images. Thank you, Carla, for being who you are.*

I pulled the book closer to study it. Were these Chester's last words? Had he been threatened and was trying to leave a clue? Or was it just his fun puzzle way of telling Carla she had been a good friend to him. My eyes wandered to the list of items above the notation about Chester, and Carla, sharp as she was, slapped a hand over the page.

"Private," she said, and gave the wad in her mouth a nervous snap. "A lot of this notebook has things I don't share with anyone."

That was like dangling a piece of steak in front of Diva and telling her she couldn't have it.

"So, did you reserve the neon green casket for Chester?" I asked.

"No, his sister-in-law chose one of the eco-friendly models. The bamboo, I think because she said that Chester was very into protecting the environment. I worked with the funeral home in Nyack, a beautiful place by the looks of it."

"So, why leave this message about the neon green one if his casket wasn't even going to come from here? Did you look at the casket? Maybe, he left some sort of message—like in a fun way."

"I was waiting for you," and again the gum smack, which I was beginning to suspect had less to do with nicotine withdrawal and more to do with nerves.

Carla grabbed her keyring from the desk, and we retraced the earlier steps I had taken toward the back of the funeral home, where she unlocked a door. At the bottom of a staircase, we landed in a large dimly lit room where I could make out caskets lining the walls. Upper shelves held urns of all sorts of shapes and sizes.

"These are empty, right?" I was hopeful that Gladys Night was in her final resting place below the grass, and hadn't been awaiting burial down here.

Carla laughed, as if I hadn't been serious, and moved comfortably past a glistening white casket that reminded me of my patent leather first communion shoes.

"This one was a special order for a very large gentleman." She pointed to a more pedestrian casket with something akin to paternal pride. "I helped design it. We call it the double-wide. Our client has been cooling his heels in the freezer for quite some time, and now that it is finally ready, the funeral is scheduled in a few days."

I glanced at a wooden casket, twice as wide and deep as its sleek contemporary neighbors. Unlike the rest, the lid on this one was opened, revealing a cushion of gray velvet. The man who had passed, Carla explained, had had a pituitary disorder and his family wanted him to have a lot of room because it was his pet peeve in life—always being squeezed into places designed for someone half his size.

"Nice story, right? Anyway, I, for one, will be happy when he has a roomier resting place," she said, and ran her hand fondly over the soft gray fabric before crossing the room to stop at a bright green casket that looked like it belonged in a sixty's psychedelic scene.

"Would you call this neon? I think of it more like Shamrock or Kelly green."

"Looks pretty bright to me. Is there a better light in here?" I asked.

"Sorry, I should have switched it on from the top of the stairs. Right now, we just get the little glow given off by those sconces that we always leave on."

Even in the faint light, the green casket made me wish I had brought sunglasses. "Who would ever want to be buried in that?" It looked like a reason to stay on the good side of your relatives.

"You'd be surprised. People get very creative about their burials these days." Carla did a slow 360 studying the shelves and walls. "You know why I like this room? It gives the grieving a chance to choose something that suited their loved one's personality. I've seen people come in here weeping, and then end up smiling when they leave. One time, I had a couple and their grown daughter, who were on a limited budget, and were choosing for the husband's sister. The couple kept picking outrageously expensive caskets and the daughter kept reminding them of their limited funds. Finally, she marched right over in front of this neon green one and said, 'if you two don't behave and pick something affordable, *this* is what I'm burying you in when you go.'"

I couldn't help but smile at Carla's story. She really was the right one for this job.

"Just look at all these choices, especially the urns—comforting, right?" she added.

I tried to remember getting any comfort from our choices when my dad died, and later, when my sister Summer followed. I could never do Carla's job.

"So, have you picked yours?" I said with a nervous laugh.

"Of course," she said in a way that said, *shouldn't everyone?* "I change my mind periodically. Right now, I'm fixated on that high gloss black model with a crisp white satin interior. It would be a nice contrast with my dark hair, though not sure about my pale skin, although it should show off my tats pretty well."

"Well, hopefully by the time you need one, you'll be white haired and withered."

"I hadn't thought about that." Carla put a finger to her lips. "Maybe, a pale pink interior with . . ."

"How about we concentrate on the neon green and see if Chester left us any kind of message?"

Carla fiddled with the side of the shiny casket and began to unlatch it so we could lift the lid.

"Why go to all this trouble," I frowned.

"I told you. We both liked puzzles."

"If his message is important, it was risky leaving it down here," I said. "You might never have found it."

Carla nodded her head in agreement, and then said, "Although, Chester knew that if he left me a mystery, I wouldn't rest until I solved it."

Still risky, I thought. We were about to open the casket when a sound resounded throughout the room. It felt like someone had taken a hammer to one of the upstairs walls.

"What was that?" I asked, feeling my already rattled nerves upping their game.

Carla went rigid.

"The back door," she whispered. "You have to bang into it because it sticks, and I haven't had a chance to find someone to repair it yet."

"It opened fine for me." I was trying to process why anyone would be coming to the funeral home's back door at this hour.

"That's because I left it ajar. Once it's fully closed, you have to keep bumping it until it opens." Carla's eyes were darting around the room as she spoke. "Winter, no-one should be coming in here now."

I looked around for an exit or a place to hide but the room had only the entrance we had entered, with no hidden doors or closets we could slip into. The space-conscious caskets, arranged tightly against the walls, offered nowhere to conceal a person.

"Maybe it's the owner, coming to check on things," I said, hopefully.

Carla shook her head no. "He was working another wake in Danbury tonight. I talked to him after we got back from Pop's Place, and he said he was beat and would see me tomorrow."

No worries, I thought, *we weren't in any danger down here.*

As if reading my thoughts, Carla said, "Doubtful they'll come down here unless . . ."

"Unless they see the book on your desk, read the note, and decide to investigate," I finished for her.

"Quick, over here," said Carla, who had crossed the room and was now climbing into the double-wide.

"I'm not getting in there. What if we can't get out?" I said, as I fumbled with my crossbody bag, with keys dangling noisily from the carabiner. I began rummaging for my phone.

"Shhh, could you be any noisier?"

A few hours earlier, my friend had been the giggly girl making jokes about our adventure at Pop's Place. I hadn't even trusted her to drive herself home. Now, she wanted to hide us from a potential murderer by climbing into a casket, and I wondered if her judgement might still be impaired.

The main floor had grown quiet.

"He's in my office."

A moment later, the footfalls thudded overhead, moving more quickly now, with the sound of doors opening and closing letting us know that the intruder was getting closer to the casket room. I held up my phone and squinted. Barely a bar. I tried 911 and got nothing. I moved closer to where Carla was now inside the double-wide. One bar. I tried again. It still wouldn't go through.

The door at the top of the stairs had opened and I could hear the first tentative step coming off the landing.

Carla was now deep into the coffin and beginning to test the lid. Despite the fact that Mr. Big would have plenty of room inside, I didn't think the two of us would have much breathing space once I joined her. Thank goodness, it was sitting on the floor so I wouldn't have to hoist myself up.

Carla frantically waved at me as I heard the intruder taking the steps more quickly now. What choice did I have? If this was Chester's killer, we were in deep trouble.

"Get in here or I promise, I will have you buried in the neon green," hissed Carla. "And, hand me your bag."

I reluctantly hoisted myself over the edge, and sunk into soft velvet fabric while feeling tears of fear filling my eyes. It wasn't being dead that scared me, it was my claustrophobia. Diva had nothing on me.

Winter Snow, 29, suffocated in a double-wide casket . . .

Carla took out the wad of gum from her mouth, and I thought it was her first reluctant moment when I saw her put it in the latch, so when the lid was down, something would keep it from catching. The lid was heavy, but between the two of us, we were able to lower it enough so that Carla could also slip the edge of my bag into the space, leaving a small gap for air. Fortunately, she had the sense to let my keys hang on the inside so as not to catch the light.

As if uncertain, the footsteps had halted. *Listening? Had he heard us?* "In this light, it should look closed from the outside," Carla whispered into my ear.

The new car fresh smell of the casket didn't keep my vivid imagination from conjuring up all sorts of images. I looked at my phone in relief. We were, now, two bars. I was about to send an SOS text and stopped. I knew what that meant. I'd done it once by mistake and suddenly my phone had been lighting up like fireworks in an inky sky.

Carla slapped her hand over my phone and mimed for me to put it away. In the tiny stream of light, I could see her vehemently shaking her head, no! Carla was in survival mode, and I had to admire her instincts. Maybe, she should team up with the Nosy Parkers and write mysteries.

As I hid the phone deep in the pocket of my fleece, my elbow knocked the casket and the footsteps paused again, this time at the bottom of the stairs. After what seemed a lifetime, the intruder finally came cautiously into the room. Fortunately, they hadn't known any more about the light switch at the top of the stairs than I had. From the gap between the lid and the base of our prison, I could see feet crossing the room, not even pausing to look at our oversized hiding spot.

Buckskin shoes, I mouthed, and pointed to the feet that had stopped in front of the green coffin, confirming that their owner had read Carla's notation. Carla blinked her understanding.

He, or at least from the size of the feet I thought it was a he, was fiddling around, struggling to lift the lid before it creaked open. As his feet moved slowly from one end of the casket to the other, I imagined his hands searching for whatever clue Chester had left.

It was then that the sudden overwhelming feeling of a sneeze seized me.

Find the damn clue and get out, I willed the perpetrator. But he was taking his time. Either he hadn't found what he was looking for, actually what we had been looking for, or he was making sure Chester hadn't left anything else in there.

I sucked in air and stifled my sneeze, leaving my eyes watering and my nose running. My body was drenched with perspiration and the fleece I wore only added to my discomfort. Suddenly, my heart started racing and my body turned clammy—a panic attack in the making. I was about to burst out of our tomb, regardless of the consequences, when I felt Carla's hand grip mine and her black nails dig in. Was she actually trying to draw blood?

The distraction was enough to keep me in place. Suddenly, the feet moved to the neighboring casket and the intruder began his investigation of it. As he moved on to the next, and farther away from ours, I could make out more details, although the face remained out of view.

And then, with clarity, I recognized those hands as the same ones holding the cup at Tazza yesterday—the Nosy Parkers' tablemate. A flash on thick fingers, a ring probably, as hands moved to lift the lids. Little by little, I watched in horror, as he circled the room. *How long before the bad guy would get to our hiding spot?*

Carla had aborted her attack on my hand, and instead now, grasped it the way a child reached for a parent for comfort. The tremor I felt worked its way straight through my body.

By now, our eyes had become accustomed to what little light seeped into the casket. I pointed to the pocket where my phone was tucked in question—*send an SOS text?* Carla shook her head no. I knew she was right. Activating my phone even for a text would be like a lighthouse beacon. Buckskin shoe guy would see us and would have plenty of time to make sure we were permanently locked in our tomb, before taking my phone someplace far away from the funeral home to be tracked. We stayed quiet, hands entwined and hearts pounding in sync.

The footfalls grew closer, until I knew he was investigating the casket just a few feet from the double-wide. The only plan I could think of was to burst out of our hiding place when he reached us, yell loud distracting accusations, and run for the stairs. Maybe, one of us could make it to get help.

And then, I had another idea, one that stemmed from something Horace had done, not too long ago, to scare away another intruder. I could see the carabiner with my keys dangling from my crossbody bag. I pointed at them and mimed pressing a button to Carla.

She mimed back steering a car. I nodded, and she slipped a keychain worthy of all keychains from her pocket. A slight jingle made us both freeze, though buckskin shoe guy was too intent on his investigation to hear.

I reached across Carla, grabbed my car key, and pushed the alarm button. Carla was only a second behind with hers.

Suddenly, loud car alarms screamed from the parking lot outside. It wasn't as loud as I might have hoped, given that we were downstairs in the basement, but enough to make buckskin shoe guy pause and consider. Between the fire department across the street and the numerous residences nearby, someone would come to investigate.

The quick and heavy footsteps exiting on the stairs, and the loud slam of the door, let me know that the intruder probably agreed.

"Let's go," I said, pushing at the heavy lid.

Carla pushed too. It budged and then came down again with a thud, squishing my purse even more. I unzipped my fleece and with Carla's help, managed to get it off. When we tried again, I slipped it on top of my bag to make the crack slightly larger. The lid, however, wouldn't open wide enough for us to escape.

"No use, it's like a log," said Carla.

"We should try again," I said, feeling my panic attack symptoms resume.

Carla's sixth sense kicked in and back came the nails, digging hard into my skin. A moment later I felt her breath, slightly sour from her martini night, blowing in my face.

"911 or SOS—we don't have to worry about the light," I croaked, indicating my fleece where my phone was tucked into one of the pockets, hopefully not the one dangling precariously outside the casket.

Carla carefully reached her hand into the pocket.

"Other one," I said. "Be careful."

I thought the whites of Carla's eyes were as bright as the patent leather coffin next to us, though she successfully managed to remove my phone and hand it to me. Thankfully, this time my call went through.

* * *

"What do you mean you are stuck in a coffin? Is this some kind of joke? We take it very seriously when someone abuses the emergency system," said the dispatcher.

I had been trying to explain, giving too much detail, and she thought I was pranking her.

"I'm going to forgive this call because it's Halloween, but it better not happen again," said the dispatcher, before disconnecting.

"Oh, for God's sake, Winter, give me the phone," ordered Carla.

I did, and she hit 911 again. When the dispatcher came back online, Carla was succinct in her explanation, saying that we had hidden in one of the coffins to stay safe from an intruder but were now trapped.

"I apologize for my friend," she said. "This is not a Halloween prank and we really need help."

Grave Words

The dispatcher told us to hold tight and she'd have help there in five minutes.

All I could do, besides gasp through the crack for air, was to distract myself with what I would say to Kip if he responded to the call. Meanwhile, we chose to keep the car alarms blaring until help arrived.

Chapter Thirty-Three

It took two firefighters and some heavy-duty tools to get us out of the coffin, because the strap to my crossbody bag had gotten so tangled in one of the hinges that no amount of coaxing would make it budge.

Carla's brother Tony, one of the responders, calmly explained that he'd have to snip the straps on my bag. When the liberated straps stayed stubbornly spooled in place, still hindering the hinge from completely rising, he muttered something about removing them completely.

"Don't damage the casket," hollered Carla. "We have to bury our client in just a few days."

With light filtering from the now brightly lit room, I could see Carla gnawing on the inside of her cheek. "Winter, my boss will kill me if we ruin this casket—it took so long to get it."

"Don't worry. Carp will fix it."

My hands were trembling as the firefighters continued to work, though I found talking about something unrelated to our problem calmed me somewhat. I babbled on about all the dog damage and how it had been restored better than new. "Carp can fix that back door too."

"You really think he'll help? I see his reels. He must have a million customers waiting for him."

But only one named Carla, I thought.

"He'll come."

By the time the lid was finally raised, my body was frozen and cramped, and I needed the help of Big Joe from Pop's Place to get me out. Carla's brother was already checking her from head to toe for signs of injury.

"What do you have on?" asked Carla, casting a disapproving frown at my flimsy night shirt, which did little to hide what was beneath.

I flushed, though I was so relieved to be out of there that I doubled-over, and the EMTs, worried that I might vomit or faint, were wrapping me in a blanket.

"I'm fine," I gasped, though I shivered as if I had just crawled out of a freezer.

My initial relief at not seeing Kip was short lived, when he materialized behind one of the beefy firemen and beelined it straight for me.

With her soft dark curls only slightly matted from having her head pressed against the pillow, Carla looked as if she had done nothing more than take a quick power nap. I, on the other hand, had no doubt from the look on Kip's face that I looked akin to something Heady or Topper had dragged in. I was drained and craved bed, a side effect of my aborted panic attack. My body had vacillated between sweat drenched and clammy while in the casket, and I caught the whiff of perspiration. Now, outside in the unheated basement, I couldn't stop shaking. I was still taking enough deep yoga breaths to make me dizzy, and despite my protestations, an EMT was assessing me with his blood pressure cuff and stethoscope.

My cheeks flamed as Kip approached, and I knew my freckles smothered like a bad case of chicken pox. He scowled as he grabbed my shoulders, letting his eyes roam over every inch of my body.

"I'm fine," I assured him.

"You don't look fine."

"It's not every day that you get buried alive," I said.

He tightened the blanket the EMT had wrapped over my shoulders, and began stripping off the sweater he wore, to give me warmth.

I pointed to my fleece, which he retrieved and helped me into.

"Not funny, do you want to tell me what you two were doing in there?" He nodded toward the casket with its lid dangling haphazardly askew. In the process of the hinge removal, the wood had cracked and left a patch of splinters in its place. I was pretty sure coffin repairs would be added to my already tight budget. Maybe, if Mr. Big's family knew that he had probably saved us from injury or worse, they'd at least understand any delay in his burial.

I wasn't sure how much to tell Kip, although after Horace's reprimand earlier this evening, I had a sense that it should be "all." On the other hand, Carla would have a fit if she had to relinquish her bright orange leatherbound book with all its secrets. Still, someone had broken into the funeral home and might have stolen a critical clue to finding Chester's killer, and I couldn't hold that back. I glanced at the neon coffin, now brighter than ever since the downstairs lights had been turned on.

I omitted any reference to Carla's book as I explained about Chester's unusual message on the answering machine, the number Carla called, and the message he had left for her. I would leave it up to Carla whether or not to show the police the notes she took.

"Carla asked me to come so we could look inside the casket together," I said.

"And, it didn't occur to you that it might be a good idea to call the police to join in that little search?"

"It might have been nothing. Maybe, he really did want a neon green casket," I said.

Kip blew out a breath and gave me one of the head shakes I was now becoming accustomed to receiving from him. "Let's check it out."

He waved over an officer talking to Carla, and as the two studied the neon green, Carla leaned in to ask what I had told them.

"The truth," I said. "It's up to you whether or not you want to tell them about your big orange book and show them the notes you wrote."

My fleece and the blanket didn't completely eliminate the tremble that now seemed to invade my entire body. Kip turned to study me and then waved an EMT back over, who suggested that I might be in shock from our near encounter with a potential murderer.

I didn't bother to tell him that if I was in shock, it was probably from the claustrophobic encounter with the double-wide. Another layer of blanket smothered my body as I watched Kip and his fellow cop pour over the green casket, looking under the pillow and the drape, checking all around it to see if there had been a message taped or etched into it.

"If Chester wanted to leave a message, why didn't he just leave it on the answering machine?" I asked Carla. "And, when would he have been in here to even know about the casket?"

"Oh, that part's easy, I told you he did odd jobs around here, and one of them was to keep the caskets looking bright and shiny which he did every time he came. As for the answering machine, I told you he liked puzzles and clues. Plus, he would have known that the other employees wouldn't have bothered calling that number. I was the only one who dealt with Chester."

"Could you tell if the intruder found whatever it was that Chester left?" asked Kip, after aborting his efforts to find a clue.

"If he had found it, why not take it and get out? It was as if he was still looking, hoping that maybe, it was with another of the caskets. He was doing a slow steady canvas of the room until he heard the car alarms go off."

Kip hadn't been on duty when the call came in over his scanner, and yet his cop gut told him if the funeral home was involved, Carla or I might be also. Now that this might be relevant to his murder case, he wanted to get back to the PD to sort things out. I declined his offer to have an officer drive me home because I was feeling almost normal by the time things were clearing out. One of the cops would at least stay with us until Carla locked up—just in case the intruder returned.

I accompanied Carla upstairs. She was going to call her boss and see what she should do about the casket. At this late hour, I didn't envy that task. After a trip to the restroom, I headed to Carla's office where she was wrapping up her phone call.

"We're still here. Any chance you can come over right now? Five minutes? Great. There's a cop out back and I'll let him know you're coming. Yes, Winter is with me." Carla put the landline back on the cradle. I noticed that her orange notebook had disappeared from her desktop.

"Who were you talking to?" Her boss lived in Danbury and definitely couldn't be here in five minutes.

"I took your advice. Can you believe it? Carp is coming right over even at this hour. I owe him big time if he can fix this."

If Carla had asked him to fly to the moon, he'd be in the next rocket. As for owing him, if she only knew.

True to his word, a few minutes later, Carp arrived from the house he owned on Silver Birch Lane, a tiny dead-end slip of a road just off New Street. While we gave him the abbreviated version of our coffin adventures, Carla showed him the double-wide with the cracked wood and broken hinge.

Carp gave a slow whistle as he investigated. "No wonder Winter looks like she just climbed out of the bottom of the laundry basket."

"Didn't your mother ever tell you that if you can't say anything nice . . ."

". . . don't say anything at all." Carp and Carla finished in unison, and both laughed.

While the two had heads together, pondering the rescue mission for the double-wide, I stared across the room at the neon green casket. In its reflection, I could see the oversized coffin and a moment later, the heads of my two friends popped up. Carla was again laughing at something Carp said and the two looked like they were having a moment.

"Carla, can you remember Chester's exact message?" I interrupted.

She looked up with a frown as if surprised that I was still there. Then, she closed her eyes to retrieve the message from afar and recited what she could remember. "*If you're calling this number, it means I'm no longer reachable. I want you to know that I'm partial to the neon green casket because of the way it mirrors images.* Anyway, something like that."

She left off the part about her being such a good person.

"When was the last time Chester worked?" I asked.

"The day before he died, why?"

"That's probably when he left his clue."

I studied the reflection and turned to see my two friends in their odd communion.

Maybe, he hadn't been sending us to the neon green but rather whatever reflection was mirrored in it.

"Was the double-wide here then?" I asked.

By now, Carla had popped more gum into her mouth, and it sounded like she was talking around marbles.

"Yes, delivered, but we were waiting for the interior fittings to be done. They were doing those on site."

"Don't coffins usually come with the fittings already inside?" I asked.

"The family had something custom made—didn't you notice how soft that fabric was when we were in there?"

The only thing that I had noticed was how trapped I had felt.

According to Carla, the interior fabric had been professionally tacked down and wasn't completed until after Chester died. If there was a clue inside, I'd have to pull out the innards and my friend would have a fit if I was wrong.

What were you trying to tell her, Chester, and why leave a message in a casket?

I had another thought. If he wanted to leave a message for Carla that she would find, he wouldn't leave it in something that might be six feet under before she figured out where it was. That meant it couldn't be in the double-wide.

I went back to the neon green and stared, trying to conjure what was in the reflection, Carla and Carp bobbing up and down as I'd seen before. They had since lowered the lid of the casket so Carp could inspect the damage to the hinge's inner workings.

"Can you two bend down for a minute so I don't catch you in the reflection?" I called back to them.

Carp frowned, letting me know he didn't appreciate the interruption as they both crouched behind the casket. I moved slightly so the light would catch the reflection better, and I was looking beyond the double-wide at a neatly lined shelf of urns.

"Were these like this when Chester was here?" I asked.

Grave Words

Carla stood and looked at the shelf, taking stock. "Chester dusted and rearranged them last week."

One by one, I carefully lifted each urn from its perch, looked inside, and then returned each. Midway across the shelf, I came to a warm green urn, the shape of a honey jar. I removed it and peered inside where a scroll was tucked.

"Look guys, this must be Chester's message."

With two people breathing down my neck, I unrolled what appeared to be a sheet of paper with a list that made no sense to me. Cemeteries, dates, and numbers crowded the space. The messy print looked as if someone had dashed them down in a hurry. Also with it, was a brochure from Plot Plans, the same one that Horace had received in the mail.

"Remember, I told you Chester had a lot of questions?" asked Carla. "Well, this was one of them."

Carla tapped on the Plot Plans brochure before continuing. "He saw this on my desk one day and asked about it. I was helping a client preplan. She had put money down on a burial plot from this place, and I was to follow through with all the details like location and process to be ready when needed."

"And, did you?"

"I'm still working on it. They never answer their phone and they never return emails. I gave them an ultimatum in my last phone message—call me back or I'm reporting them to the Better Business Bureau and also calling the police," she said. "Even after that threat a week ago, I still haven't heard a thing."

I thought about the intruder. Maybe her calls were finally being answered.

"Is it OK if I take this to Kip?" I asked Carla, because technically, the message had been for her.

"Please do," she said, and then after taking one final look at the hastily written note, turned back to wrap up the hinge discussion.

As I pondered Chester's message, I could hear Carp telling Carla that with a little sanding, stain, and varnish, the double-wide would look better than new.

Chapter Thirty-Four

"Are you people finished down there yet?" hollered the police officer who was acting gate keeper.

"Just about," yelled Carla in return, as I slipped Chester's note into my fleece pocket. I wouldn't be able to search Scoop's apartment for a converter at this late hour with the police officer hovering. I would just have to get to the Apple store, first thing in the morning, to get a device that would allow me to connect the thumb drive to my MacBook.

I felt a twinge of guilt at not contacting Kip right away about the thumb drive, and now, this note. I justified my actions with the thought that neither Scoop nor Chester had shared their information with the PD.

* * *

Once home, I spread Chester's cryptic note out on the kitchen table and stared at what looked like gibberish. Chester had written his note on the funeral home stationery, leading me to believe he had done it in a hurry while he was there on his last day. Whatever message he was sending to Carla was lost on me. The one thing not lost was that he was entrusting her with something that he wanted to leave behind for safekeeping.

I thought about the trust pendant still tucked away in the little pink box.

"Come-on karma," I whispered. "Get to work."

* * *

Morning on the lake, regardless of the weather, usually feels like renewal. Not today. My funeral home adventures had left me tired and stiff, and even the vibrant autumnal rainbow outside my window couldn't coax me out of bed.

Until I remembered today's errand.

I checked my cell phone which was sitting on the table next to my bed, and groaned. 8 AM. I sunk back into the covers and tried to close my eyes.

No such luck. A ping sounded, letting me know that I had incoming mail. I was a sucker for ringing phones and all the pings and notifications that mobiles emitted, so despite the fact that it was probably news or junk, I opened it anyway.

Surprisingly, this notification came in over my business email, which meant someone had been on my website. I was hoping for an obituary or a living legacy writing job, when the message emerged:

Destroy Chester's message, or else.

I looked over my shoulder, which was a joke because all I had behind me was a mound of pillows and a bedframe from the Ethan Allen store in Danbury.

How did anyone know that I had found a message from Chester? And then, I remembered Carp. Like the Nosy Parkers, he loved to share a good story.

* * *

Grave Words

The Apple store in the Danbury Mall was worse than busy. I thought the steady background noise of classes running in the center of the room, at the same time customers were considering the purchase of iPads, phones, Macs, and a myriad of support items, was distracting to the point of being annoying.

"What can I help you with today?" asked the friendly tablet holding gal who greeted me at the door. I had a concentration lapse, as I considered the floor to ceiling screen showing an example of how to reorganize your address book. I shook off the distraction.

I explained what I needed, she spoke into a mic and a moment later, a young man who looked barely old enough to work, led me to the wall and went into great detail about which adapter I needed.

Back home again, I fired up my computer, inserted the adapter, and stared at it.

Five minutes later, I was still staring at the computer with the unplugged thumb drive and Chester's note sitting next to it.

"Damn." Horace's words of wisdom weighed on my shoulders like a load of bricks. My conscience was doing battle with my justifications.

If Scoop had wanted Kip to see what was on the drive, wouldn't he have just given it to us the night we found him invading my study? On the other hand, a lot had changed since then. Scoop had been arrested and apparently, Kip had tried to delay that process as long as possible. And, Scoop had asked me to do some housekeeping. Whatever was on that drive might explain why Scoop was getting threatening letters. Could this also help determine who had sent me a threat?

As for Chester, I had no reservations about sharing that info with Kip, though why in the world had Chester entrusted it to Carla instead of the police when he knew full well that the PD was on to him. And then, I realized. Did he leave it for Carla in case he got hit by the proverbial bus before he had a chance to get permission from his client to share the information with the police? That meant that whatever this was, it had to be important enough for him to entrust her.

I wanted to talk this through with someone besides Richard or Horace because I didn't want them to know about my threatening note.

My mother answered on the first ring.

"Are you OK?" she asked, in an urgent tone. Apparently, the paranoia apple didn't fall that far from the tree.

"Yes, I'm fine," I lied.

Two minutes into the conversation and I realized that there was no way I could burden my mom with my problems. She immediately launched into the long-overdue Christmas visit with the twins and could I get Nutcracker tickets, and while the girls were beyond Old Saint Nick, she wanted a photo, so where would we do that?

"Ok, Mom, I'll put it all together and can't wait to see you," I said, as way of goodbye. We signed off with the familiar "love you" and then she was gone. And I was back to staring at the computer.

I punched in Scoop's number though I already knew it would go straight to voicemail. *Hope springs eternal* and all that.

Finally, I took a deep breath and called Kip. After several rings, it too went to voice mail. *Probably in the shower*, I thought. I waited, and after fifteen minutes, giving the guy some cleansing leeway, rang again. Voicemail. Apparently, I was still getting the silent treatment.

I didn't bother to leave a message. Instead, I sent a text.

Can you call me right away because this is really important.

* * *

I didn't know how I'd stand the wait with both Scoop's thumb drive and Chester's note staring at me like invitations waiting to be opened. Making a note to add a robotic Roomba to my *if I ever win the lottery* list, I lugged the Miele from the closet and began hitting every dust bunny I could find. Dusting, cleaning, and even hitting the bathrooms, sucked up an hour and still no return call from Kip.

I headed outside to a clear cold morning. A tiny shed attached to the side of Horace's house held our shared mower, which I now put to use. I hoped the cranky belching machine wouldn't bother Horace, or the other neighbors for that matter. The unwelcomed noise of mowers and leaf blowers was a big discussion in Ridgefield these days. When my cell rang, I jumped to answer despite the fact that I had one more segment to go.

To my disappointment, it was Richard who wanted to coordinate a Diva return.

Where was Kip? I couldn't blame him for avoiding me. First, he finds out that I shared what he would consider vital information with everyone but him. Then he finds me stuck in a casket at the funeral home, dressed in my flimsy night shirt. And, if I had called him the moment we heard Chester's message, we never would have been in jeopardy in the first place.

I AM TRYING TO DO THE RIGHT THING, I shouted over the hum of the mower, which I had restarted to finish the job.

"Are you calling me?" Horace stepped partway on to the deck and leaned over, cupping his hand so I could hear him above the mower's sputter. Max, who wasn't a fan of loud noise, stuck his head around Horace's legs, his ears twitching at the offending cough of the machine.

"Just singing!" I called back.

Horace looked at me with question, and I knew without a doubt, that he would be on the phone with Richard as soon as he retreated indoors.

Winter is definitely losing it . . .

Grass finally trimmed to buzz cut length which would elicit more raised brows, I went back inside and with conviction this time, stuck Scoop's thumb drive into the computer.

It churned and finally, the drive icon landed on my desktop. I clicked it open and was met with five files labeled by date, beginning with the day of the first arson.

I clicked the first file open, and suddenly, videos and photos of the fire raged on my desktop. As I scrolled through them, they began telling the story of Mrs. Means' house from the first flames to the fast and furious finish.

The second file didn't name the source but quoted them extensively. Every detail of the story was documented and attributed to the source. Even their meeting place, which turned out to be the location of each fire.

12 AM: Fire gets put out and fire department leaves behind a skeleton crew to watch for flare ups.

12:30 AM: Talked with source at fire site. Scene now taped and structure completely destroyed. Firemen on the lookout for embers. Fire marshal still on scene.

3:15 AM: Filed story.

What was it that Scoop thought was in here that would save him? Was he trying to steer me toward his source? Finding out what Carla or her brother had been doing during his timeline, could eliminate them, at least, as the informants. Although, my guess was that Carla would say she had been home in bed, and Tony, if he hadn't worked the fire, would also be sleeping.

I followed that thread. If we could find who worked the fires and who lingered in case the fire reignited, we might narrow down Scoop's source.

The next two files on the drive were a record of the second arson. Scoop was meticulous in his research and had verified the contractor's alibi right down to the date, time, and duration of his visit to Florida. Receipts showing the use of his credit card had been scanned in as added proof.

Grave Words

I was about to open the fifth file when my cell rang. Caller ID said it was Kip.

Sure, now he decides to call back—just when I'm getting to some answers.

"Are you OK? You've been trying to reach me," he said, his voice urgent as if he just arrived at an accident scene.

"I thought you were ghosting me," I said.

There was a moment of silence on the other end until he said, "Well maybe just a little bit . . . you called so many times . . . I started to worry. What's up?"

"Can you come over?" I was about to lure him with news of my two finds when he interrupted.

"I'm at the rec center gym. Just give me time to hop in the shower. I should be there in fifteen."

Chapter Thirty-Five

Fifteen minutes later, Kip walked through the front door with his hair still damp.

Tempting though it was, I hadn't pushed play on the last file in Scoop's thumb drive. I explained what I had found and where. He pouted for a second, asking why I hadn't contacted him immediately. I took out my cell phone and showed him all the calls that I had logged in.

"You said you found it last night." His voice dripped with accusation.

"With no way to read the file, I was at the Apple store when it opened this morning to get an adapter. You can see here that I started calling the second I got home."

Apparently, I wasn't the only one with trust issues.

Kip settled in and scanned Scoop's files, and then took in the notes that he had written.

"He doesn't name his source," he said, with disappointment.

We were sitting in the living room with the gas logs burning. I had nudged my chair closer to Kip so we could both view the screen on my laptop at the same time. Kip's damp curls spilled onto the collar of the fleece he had tossed on and the lingering scent of his after-work out shower made me want to curl into his arms.

"Are you OK Winter, because you look a little . . . flushed? It's a panic attack, isn't it?" Before I could answer, he jumped from the seat and ran to the kitchen.

A few moments later, I was being smothered in iced towels and force-fed a sparkling water with lemon.

"What else can I do?" Kip asked, in earnest.

With my libido now sufficiently tamped, I smiled my thanks.

"I'm fine now," I said. "Let's open the last file and see what clues Scoop might have left."

As we hovered over my computer and waited for the file to open, I was acutely aware of Kip's leg touching mine. Kip, on the other hand, seemed rapt with the screen.

"There," he said, pointing to the file that had just opened.

We both peered at it in surprise. A video of two men in animated conversation had been captured just outside the bank.

Chester and Winfred Thomas III.

"Why do you think Scoop left this for you?" asked Kip, eyeing me suspiciously.

"You can see how detailed his notes are. I'm guessing he hoped it was proof enough that he hadn't had anything to do with the arsons."

Scoop's notes listed dates, times, and locations of each encounter with his source. The detailed conversations had obviously been recorded because my reporter friend had transcribed them right down to every *um* and *F-bomb* dropped. In addition, his source repeatedly asked for reassurance that Scoop would not reveal his name.

"We know that Scoop is not the arsonist," said Kip, confirming the obvious. "We also know that his source probably is or knows who is."

As I studied the screen, a pattern emerged. Scoop's initial conversations with his source took place shortly after the flames were knocked down. To me, this confirmed that he was talking to someone who worked the fire or had stayed to make sure there weren't any flare ups.

I explained to Kip my theory that Scoop had arrived on the scene, cornered one of the firefighters for info, and then had his story filed just a couple hours later in the wee hours of the morning.

"That means that his informant worked both fires."

"It could still be anyone," said Kip. "The arsonist slash informer could have started the fire and might not have even been there while it was burning."

"What, and then show up at the burn site to give Scoop information? Unless the guy looked like he belonged, like a firefighter or the fire police, people might notice him talking to a nosy newspaper reporter, especially at that hour. With all the publicity and with Scoop's reputation for having inside information, it would be risky for someone random to show his face, particularly at the second fire."

Kip thought about this for a few minutes. "I need to get hold of the shift roster—see who worked both fires."

"There'd be a record of who was on that night, even if someone was taking someone else's place, right?"

"Definitely," said Kip.

"If you can narrow it down, would that give Scoop a get-out-of-jail-free card?" I asked.

"Unfortunately, no. He was also one of the last to speak with Chester before he was murdered." Again, Kip didn't seem to be the least bit distressed by this.

"Don't tell me having Scoop under arrest gives you a break from public pressure," I said, annoyed that he seemed happier to have the reporter in jail than not.

Kip gave me that look he has which said my comment didn't justify a response.

"Do you want to know what I think?" asked Kip, and then before waiting for my answer, he said, "I think Scoop wants to give up his source and is trying to figure a way to do it without doing it?"

I slowly started nodding my head getting what Kip was driving at.

Scoop wasn't snooping around in my computer or on my desk to get information from me. He was trying to find a clever way to leave his thumb drive in my office knowing when I found it, I wouldn't be able to resist opening it to see what it was. My friend knew me well.

His files don't list his source, although they sure left enough clues for even the most novice detective to figure it out. Scoop assumed that I would tell Kip who I thought the source was, especially if my reporter friend got himself arrested. Once Kip put the pressure on, the source would see that all fingers pointed at him or her. Was Scoop banking on a confession?

"We thwarted his plan when we caught him in the study," said Kip. "He tried to pick up the pens that had rolled under the desk and presumably, the thumb drive, when I stopped him. That's when he high tailed it out of there."

"That's why he kept asking me if I had picked up the pens yet and then pressured me to get some housekeeping done."

"No-one could accuse him of giving up his source if you somehow tripped over evidence and gave up the source yourself. How was he planning to explain the thumb drive in your study?"

That part was easy, and I explained to Kip how I had found Scoop's jacket in my office.

"He must have been planning to say the drive had been in his pocket and must have fallen out—that is IF anyone bothered to ask.

"Not a great plan," Kip said.

"He was getting desperate," I said.

I thought about my friend. He sure had a lot of faith that I would find his drive, though presumably, he would have left it somewhere more obvious rather than stuck in a dark corner under the desk. His jacket had been laid on my desk, so maybe, he would have pretended that it fell out of his pocket when he picked it up. He also had a lot of confidence that I would be able to put two and two together. Scoop had concocted this scheme as far back as the night of the deck party after Chester's warning, and the sloppy plan was probably because he had been in a big hurry once he found that Chester had died.

This had been Scoop's way of steering me toward his source without being the one to give him up. At that point, he probably didn't believe his source had anything to do with the arsons. My mind wandered to Carla. Had Chester determined that the good person he admired was Scoop's informant and was trying to find a way to help both Scoop and Carla?

"Your wheels are turning," said Kip, eyeing me with question.

When I held out the roll of paper still curled from being hidden in the urn, Kip frowned.

"What's this?"

I explained how Carla and I had lingered while Carp assessed the damage to the casket.

"Chester's message said something about liking the way the neon green mirrored images, and sure enough, I could see Carp and Carla conferring over the double-wide."

I gave an involuntary shudder as I remembered being trapped in the large casket. What would have happened if I hadn't thought to remove my phone before slipping my bag beneath the lid. Or if there hadn't been any bars? Or if it had dropped from my pocket when we had stuffed my fleece into the crack to give us more air? I don't think I would have survived that claustrophobic space until the next day, when presumably, the owner would have come to work.

Grave Words

Kip, who had been watching me closely, handed me the remainder of my water and said, "Don't think about it. It's over."

How could I not think about everything that had happened, especially the threat that had come in earlier? Not to mention the black SUV that had been following me around like an unwanted shadow.

Those without trust will never be trusted.

"I want to show you something," I said, as I changed windows, called up my business email on outlook, and turned the computer toward Kip.

"Along with this threatening letter, a black SUV has been tailing me around town," I said. "I see it everywhere, though to be fair, half of Ridgefield's moms drive black SUVs."

Kip gave me that *I told you so* look. And then, he abruptly stood and began pacing. Finally, in exaggerated calm, he slowly began ticking things off his fingers.

"Let's just review for accuracy's sake. You were warned off Chester's obituary which you pursued anyway. You were followed to Nyack—oh I take that back—somewhere in New Jersey where you lost the tail, and then you went to Nyack to visit Anne Halliday, wrote an obituary with key information about an ongoing investigation that the PD didn't want released, which you then shared same information with your friends and family, followed by nosing around at Pop's Place where you were followed home."

I winced as Kip's voice rose with every accusation. "Let's see what else. Oh yes, you got yourself trapped in a casket while hiding from a would-be murderer who probably got a bead on you at Pop's Place to begin with. All this was followed by a threatening letter which tells me, somehow, someone knew you found the note that Chester had hidden. Have I missed anything?"

"Well, when you put it all in a list, it does seem like a lot."

Kip waited with his hands on his hips.

"There might be a teeny tiny bit more," I said, pinching my thumb and pointer together. "Did I mention the Nosy Parkers?"

Kip was swaying one foot to the other, with his body moving like the pendulum in a grandfather clock, but he said nothing as I told him about my original conversation with the gossip queens and how they had steered me toward Arthur Willings' connection to Chester. I talked about their venomous streak when Scoop and I had seen them with Mr. Buckskin shoes, and I mentioned that the intruder in the funeral home wore the same kind of shoes.

"There's also this ring that he wears with some kind of logo, though I can't think what it reminds me of because I didn't get a close look at it."

Kip stopped moving and he leaned into his hands.

Big breath, big sigh and then, he said, "Tell me about the shoes."

"Some guy who was meeting with the Nosy Parkers had on these buckskin shoes, straight out of the 1950's."

"Buckskin shoes? I'm not sure if I know what they are."

I got up and went to a long cabinet in the room where Richard kept a robust collection of vinyl. After a few minutes of sorting, I pulled an album cover and handed it to Kip.

"You know how Richard loves everything oldie? This is a Pat Boone album cover from the 1950's and check out his shoes." A photo of the former heartthrob had him sitting, legs crossed with his signature shoe choice front and center.

"These are the same kind of shoes the guy in *Tazza* wore when he was talking with Abby and Gabby, the day they turned from *gossip girls* to *mean girls*."

"And the ring?"

I explained how the man had his face mostly turned from me, and how I could see whisps of brown hair beneath his baseball cap. I described the man's hand and the ring that niggled at my memory.

"When we were trapped in the casket, he began checking each of the others. The farther away he moved, the more I could see, and I caught a glimpse of something that sparkled on his hand. Maybe a ring, maybe not."

Kip sat down on the double chair so that our bodies touched. He tapped the papers Chester had left.

"Who else did you tell about these?"

"Carla and Carp were there when I found them, and you know Carp—he probably announced it to everyone at Early Bird this morning over coffee."

Half the town probably already knew about our casket adventure and how Carp will be the double-wide hero when he restores it to perfection. Early Bird had a cast of regulars, among them the Nosy Parkers, our very own verbal *tik tok* whose magnified rendition of our adventure was probably already viral.

"Only one way to find out," I said, as I grabbed my phone and texted Carp.

With customer—will call later.

I held my phone for Kip to see. He nodded and indicated that I should hand over Scoop's thumb drive. I wanted to keep it, though I could see from the look in Kip's eyes that there would be no discussion.

"Can I just make a copy first—you know, in case something else occurs to me. You did say I have good deduction skills."

"Winter . . ." he started, in warning, when at that moment, the door burst open and Diva pranced in, tail swinging in delight with Richard trailing behind.

Kip smiled at the dog's enthusiasm as Diva sidled up to him for pets and Kip didn't disappoint. He was as fond of Diva as the rest of us. Richard held up a bag and I could smell the warm cinnamon buns from my perch on the chair. Kip was out of the seat in a heartbeat and leaning over to peer inside the bag which Richard had opened.

"Fresh out of the oven," he said.

"Your oven?" asked Kip, hopeful because he had been on the receiving end of Richard's favorite recipe many times.

"None other," said my uncle proudly. "I'll put some coffee on."

My stomach rumbled in response. It was already after lunchtime and I'd barely had any breakfast. With the dog jumping and Kip salivating over Richard's offerings, I used the distraction wisely and now had a copy of Scoop's drive on my computer labeled *October Obituaries*—just in case anyone was curious enough to check my desktop.

I had already scanned Chester's notes into the same file because I thought Carla was entitled to a copy. Kip had pocketed the notes with a grim face, and I knew he was thinking that this information might be what got Chester killed. Now, it might also put me and Carla on someone's radar.

* * *

Horace and Max must have smelled the coffee because they arrived a few minutes later, and the four of us sat around the kitchen table feasting on the warm cinnamon rolls.

I filled Richard and Horace in on the casket adventure and they looked like they wanted to lock me in a tower and throw away the key.

"Tell them everything," said Kip.

I glared at him wide-eyed across the table. I didn't want them worrying, couldn't he understand that?

Kip ignored me. "Winter is also being followed. A black SUV shows up almost everywhere she goes. I think if you two know what's going on, you can be on the lookout. I'm trying to get the tag number to run from Scoop's cousins but so far, they aren't answering my calls."

And, I doubted two people who probably skirted some of the legalese when they fixed things would be calling any time soon.

Thankfully, Kip did not tell them about the threatening email. I caught the furtive looks between my uncle and neighbor. They reminded me of the telling looks between Luna and Layla, the boxer, in those clever social media reels that could suck you in for hours. The salivating white boxer and her Aussie sister are always pranking their clueless mom, with the outcome usually resulting in aborted vet trips, stealing food, and entertaining Dakota, the baby in the house. The looks are always a signal that something's up, and I now studied Richard and Horace with unveiled curiosity.

"What?" asked Richard.

"You two are up to something."

Kip, who had resumed eating his second cinnamon roll, stopped mid bite with a questioning look.

"We will definitely keep an eye out," said Horace. "In fact, we were just talking about that last night, weren't we Richard?"

"Full disclosure, Winter. I have been spending more time here because I'm worried about you."

"Yes, Horace told me," I said. "And, it's totally unnecessary. Although I'm not complaining about being well-fed, I want you to go home and get that place of yours ready for Mary."

"Fat chance," said Horace, as he snuck a nibble to both dogs.

Kip wasn't doing a very good job of suppressing his smile. "I didn't know you had bodyguards."

If my growing suspicions were right, I had more than Horace and Richard keeping track of me. The fact that no-one was overly concerned about my SUV shadow suggested that one of the three other people in the room was getting daily reports about my comings and goings.

"I really need to know if Scoop is OK," I said to Kip, changing the subject. "Can I visit him?"

"He's not taking any visitors right now," said Kip.

"What do you mean, not taking visitors? It's not like he's in a hospital room picking and choosing who he wants to see while in his johnny gown. He's probably wasting away in his jail cell and might welcome a friendly face."

Kip shrugged. "Let's just say he wants to be alone."

"Well, so do I sometimes, although, look around me. I don't get a choice."

Richard and Horace laughed, got up from the table, and got ready to dog walk. That was to be followed by a day in town, getting all Horace's errands done, and ending at the Lantern for their traditional glass of beer. Kip rose too, kissed my cheek, and whispered for me to stay home and stay out of trouble.

"You're on dog duty so I assume you won't be going anywhere," added Richard, as he and Horace followed with a goodbye wave.

"At least the dogs don't talk back," I said.

* * *

The second the three of them exited and the door slammed shut, I was at my computer calling up the file I had named October Obituaries. Like the movie *Groundhog Day*, the fires burned again and again. Each time, I'd pause to see if there was anything that might be a clue.

I went back to the timeline and Scoop's notes.

An hour later, I came up with nothing. To get any closer to an answer, I would have to see if Carla could get Tony to fork over the shift schedules for those nights. I'd see who overlapped on both fires, and hope that the late-night duties of the firefighters eliminated the lion's share of the department as suspects. Kip wouldn't be happy that I was acting on my own, however, Scoop tasked me to the job and I would follow through if it helped my friend.

Grave Words

I was just about to call Carla when it hit me. I went back to the video that Scoop had sent, a panoramic of both nights. Scoop's reporter's voice gave a play-by-play overview of what I was seeing. I pushed pause.

The firefighters were in full gear, and it was hard to tell one from the other with their bulky clothing and heavy masks, except that, when he could, Scoop had zoomed in on their nametags. What names I could not read, Scoop provided as his fire stories unfurled.

I grabbed pen and paper and began scribbling the names of the first responders. Rewind, pause and pretty soon, I had identified most of them.

I did the same for the second arson and I began identifying certain career guys and volunteers by their photos.

Several names emerged and among them was one that sent my heart into a nosedive.

Chapter Thirty-Six

Carla was tied up with clients when I called so I left a message for her to get back to me ASAP.

The Nosy Parkers didn't answer either. I hadn't given buckskin-shoe guy too much more thought after my visit with Scoop at Tazza because everything that happened afterward made me feel like I was riding on a runaway train. However, now I realized that the person sitting at Gabby and Abby's table, heads together and maybe, influencing them in some way, might be the same person who had broken into the funeral home in search of Chester's clue. I mean how many people wore those 1950's relics?

As far as I could see, there were two things going on. The arsons that Scoop had been arrested for committing, and the murder of Chester which still placed my friend at the top of the suspect list because according to the Nosy Parkers, he was the last to see Chester alive.

What to do? Call Kip or wait for him to let me know who he had identified at the fires from the RFD roster? It was always better to have two sources, I decided. If Kip confirmed the people I now thought to be there from Scoop's video, our suspect pool would immediately shrink significantly.

Grave Words

Activity at the front door told me Richard, Horace, and the dogs were back from their walk. I put on my smiley all is fine face, accepted the dog turnover, and shooed Richard and Horace out the door for their downtown day.

Horace never needed much in the way of food, especially since Richard had been cooking at the lake most nights. Between that and the leftovers which Richard was never shy of, we always had enough provisions to survive an apocalypse. I knew from experience that their errands would also include getting household products, anything at CVS that Horace might need, and a visit to Village Square because Richard was always looking for opportunities to lure his friend to move there. The two wouldn't be back until dinnertime if that.

"How about a ride?" I said aloud. Diva probably understood the word because she snuck away to her bed upstairs. Max wagged his tail, always ready for an adventure.

By the time I had gotten the two of them in the Subaru, it felt like I was stuffed in the casket again. Diva's escalating pants sounded like a train racing along the track. Max let out a few happy howls. The two took up the entire back seat, with Max ducking his head so as not to hit the roof. With all the huffing and puffing, I was beginning to question the wisdom of this errand, although I knew it was something that had to be done.

I was going back to Ridgebury, this time to visit the home of the late Gladys Night to return the trust pendant. A quick look in the rearview confirmed my suspicions. No SUV today.

* * *

An hour later, we were back home, with the dogs walked, fed, and napping. I tried to reach the Nosy Parkers again and again, no answer. I would have to ask Richard to knock on their door, though not today. I wouldn't interrupt his Horace day and while I could do it myself, the thought of stuffing the dogs back in the car was unappealing at best.

I sat down at my computer, fingering the trust pendant that I now wore and thought about my visit with Gladys Night's daughter, Barbara. Barbara lived on a lovely property out in Ridgebury, not too far from Betty Willings. Passing by the now familiar landmarks of the Meetinghouse, I had stopped at the Sunrise Café for a tea to go. The delightful little oasis amidst the rural stretches in this part of town, opened last year, joining the only other commercial eatery in the area, the seasonal Odeen's Barbeque at the Ridgefield Golf Course. While I initially worried that one of the most untouched stretches of town might fall way to commercialism, that hasn't happened. The much-welcomed café and gathering spot is just one more way for neighbors who often have acres between them to get together.

Barbara lived on a road called Shadow Lake on a secluded property tucked at the top of a hill. When she had met me at the door, I was struck that without the makeup and mourning clothes, she looked more like a farmer's daughter than the socialite I thought her to be.

It had been by design that I chose this day to return the pendant because the dogs gave me a good excuse to explain my embarrassing impersonation of her mother's aide quickly and get out. Barbara had another idea, and she immediately opened the car's back door and gushed over two pets who loved nothing better than to be the center of attention. She led us through a farmhouse style kitchen with wide open space, butcher block countertops, and enough accoutrements on the counters to rival a kitchen supply store. She paused to reach into a large cookie jar and produced two dog biscuits, explaining that she kept them for visits from her "grand dog."

Grave Words

From there, we had gone outside where large arborvitaes flanked each side of a flagstone patio. Cushy outdoor chairs had lap blankets draped over each. By now, Diva and Max were glued to Barbara and she made each sit, gave a pet and then the dog biscuit reward.

"Winter, I was so delighted to get your call," she said, once the dogs were settled. "I hope you'll be warm enough out here. We try to harvest as much sunshine for as long as we can because the winters on the top of this rise can get pretty cold."

I wasn't sure if we were at the elevation of Pine Mountain, one of Ridgefield's highest points and just a short distance away, though I thought we might be close. With dogs settled and platitudes out of the way, Gladys Night's daughter looked at me expectantly. Without a word, I produced the bright pink box with the big white bow.

"I can't accept this," I said, as I slid the box across a glass coffee table until it was in front of her.

I took a deep breath and spent the next painful minutes explaining who I was and how I had been at her mother's wake by accident. I admitted to opening the box and by way of lightening the mood, said that if it had been a swan with candy coated almonds, I wouldn't have bothered to return it.

"I've been expecting you," she had replied, with a smile.

"Then you knew I didn't belong?" That surprised me.

Barbara laughed, a light tinkling of bells, and her eyes crinkled into deep crevassed crow's feet. "Of course, I knew you weren't one of her aides. My mother was demanding when it came to dress and decorum. No offense, dear, but you didn't fit the mold."

"Then why the charade?" I asked. "I have to say, I was mortified to receive this gift and I didn't know how to give it back without upsetting everyone."

"When I saw you take the time to say a true farewell to a woman you had never met, I wanted you to have this."

"Why did your mother buy trust pendants for everyone at the funeral?"

It had to cost a fortune and I couldn't fathom how she would even anticipate how many she might need.

"She didn't. There was only one trust pendant. The rest of the aides got small doves you can put on a chain if you like, and the remaining guests—well they received something akin to candy coated almonds." Barbara laughed again. She was clearly enjoying herself.

That settled it. No way could I possibly take the one and only trust pendant and I told her so.

"I read about you, Winter Snow. I knew you'd be back with this," she said, smiling as she took the piece of jewelry from the box in admiration.

And then, she did the oddest thing. With the dogs attentively watching her every move, she unfurled the long chain, slipped it over my head, and adjusted the silver and gold jewel ceremoniously against the sweater I wore.

"My mother would want you to have this," she had said, with glistening eyes.

And, with finality, she had closed the door on the subject.

* * *

With no news from Kip, and armed with some information that might help Scoop get out of jail, I was as restless as when I had been waiting for my sister to deliver her twins. It was late afternoon when Carla finally returned my call.

"I need your help," I said, as way of intro.

"That usually means I'm about to be asked something I don't want to do," she replied, through a gum snap.

"Can you ask Tony who worked the fires the night of the two arsons?"

Carla was quiet as she processed this. If I knew my friend, she would deduce that several of the career and volunteer guys would have overlapped, which would mean those were the most likely to be Scoop's sources.

"Why do you want to know?" Her voice sounded like she was picking her way through a bramble patch.

I already knew from Scoop's videos that Tony was one of the guys who had been there the entire night during both arsons. He was easily recognizable even in his gear, tall, formidable and he appeared to be very much in charge. Rumor had it when our current fire chief retired at the end of the year, Tony was one of the most likely replacements.

Tony could be Scoop's source, or even the arsonist, and it would be better if Carla came to that conclusion herself. Or he could have told Carla all and she could be the informant, though that theory was waning quickly. Scoop hadn't captured any video of Carla, and to my eye, he had done a pretty thorough sweep.

Unless, of course, Carla and Tony were in it together.

"Winter?"

I fingered the trust pendant. Both Barbara and Carla had said it was karma that I ended up with it. Well, let's just see, I thought.

"If we know who was at the fire, then we can eliminate those who were not," I said, honestly.

"Tony was at both. I hope you're not pointing the finger at him," Carla was ramping up her attitude.

"I'm not pointing the finger at anyone. I just think we should eliminate as many people as possible," I said.

Carla reluctantly agreed to call her brother and disconnected.

I drummed my fingers on my desk.

Now what?

Max was at my side nudging me, and Diva, who had recently learned to ring a bell hanging from the door when she wanted to go out, had just set the front door peeling.

Our walk was a leisurely one with no black SUVs or bears in sight. When I returned, Max bounded around the back of the house, and when I caught up, I found Carp crouched with his hands over his head while being smothered in kisses.

"Get him away from me," he whimpered, and it might have been comical had Carp not been so afraid.

Max looked confused as I led him back around and into the front door with Diva.

"Are you OK?" I asked, exiting to the deck.

"Just drenched in drool. Why does he do that?"

"He wants you to like him," I said.

Carp looked to the deck door where Max sat happily wagging his tail.

"Well, he has a funny way of showing it."

Carp had secured all the loose deck boards, and explained that the next steps were a power wash and a coat of stain which he would schedule as soon as he was sure it wouldn't rain.

"How's it going with the double-wide?" I asked.

"Better than new," he said.

"And, with Carla?"

Carp stuck his hands in his pockets and grinned. "She said she'd consider a date."

"Consider, what does that mean?"

"She's thinking about it," said Carp.

That was Carla, honest sometimes to a fault.

Back inside, I decided to call Plot Plans. Chester must have included that brochure in his message for some reason. Using the excuse that I was calling on behalf of Horace, I plugged in the number. The chipper recording on the other end, asking me to leave a message, sounded suspiciously like AI. Pandora's box had been unlatched and suddenly AI was everywhere.

I asked the company rep to call me so I could discuss my friend's interest in Plot Plans, and left my name and phone number.

* * *

Kip arrived after work and we immediately took our place at the front door to give out candy to the trick or treaters. The dogs were whining to join us outside. I ran inside for a piece of printer paper and scribbled a note which I taped to the basket of candy: *Caring is sharing.*

"I doubt that will keep someone from taking all, and you ending up with toilet paper strung all over the front of the house," said Kip. "Or worse, shaving cream."

"Two barking dogs and lights out should help," I said. "Besides, kids don't seem to do that anymore. Most of them spend the night in town."

Residents on Main Street go all out for Halloween with decorations, spooky audio emitting from speakers and even dressing up to dole out thousands of goodies to the crowds of families trick or treating.

Back inside, we pulled out leftover turkey chili, heated cornbread, and I made a salad.

"Did you get the roster for the first two arsons?" I asked.

"I did. And, did you?"

"No," I said, annoyed, because Carla had called to let me know that Tony couldn't provide it.

"I asked the FD not to release the information to anyone else," Kip admitted.

Here we go again, I thought. Kip was in information shutdown mode and I was again left in the cold. I tried to think of this from

Horace's point of view though it still annoyed me that I was the one doing all the sharing. The trust pendant, still dangling around my neck, was hidden beneath my sweater and I felt the weight of it. Gladys Night's message was tickling me right near my heart.

"Are you not telling me because it would be breaking one of the cop codes? Or are you trying to protect me by keeping me in the dark?"

Kip sighed. "To be honest, a little of both."

"Please Kip, tell me what you can because the only way I can protect myself and to help Scoop is if I have information."

He sighed again, a sound that no longer perked the ears of two inquisitive dogs. Both snoozed with low hums and occasionally twitching ears.

We dished out food which did get a perk up from both. I gave them each a dog treat and we carried our bowls to the living room to eat by the fire.

"The roster shows a fair amount of career and volunteer firefighters responding to both scenes. The number gets whittled down to a lot less for a couple of hours after the fire has been put out. I think I can narrow it down to a few of the guys who stayed and only two or three overlap both fires. I think that gets Carla off the hook," I said.

Kip suddenly shifted. "So, you too were wondering about Carla?"

"I know the way your mind works," I smiled. "She spends a lot of time at Scoop's apartment—always crashing after her nights out. She works just ten feet below him and her brother is a firefighter privy to inside information."

Kip didn't disagree and instead asked how I thought Scoop's information relieved Carla of any complicity.

"To start, did you even watch that video?"

Kip squinted his eyes. "You have a copy, don't you?"

I ignored him and continued. "The interviews Scoop had with his informant must have been recorded and then transcribed by a program of sorts, because they include every *um*, *uh*, cough, throat clear, and even a sneeze, in his notes."

There had been no effort to short cut with more succinct phrasing, something I do when I transcribe.

"I did notice a lot of pretty raunchy language," said Kip.

"Exactly, and Carla may look like a tough cookie, but the worse you'll ever hear from her mouth is 'damn.' Plus, I didn't see any reference to bubble blowing or gum smacking. Besides, it appears that Scoop interviewed his source at the scene and as many times as I study the video, I don't see her in it anywhere."

Kip thought about that for a minute and then said, "That doesn't erase Tony from the suspect list."

"Tony doesn't swear either," I said.

"Maybe not in front of you, but if you were ever a fly on the wall of the firehouse, your wings might curl."

Chapter Thirty-Seven

The black SUV showed up again the next afternoon as I traveled down to the library. I didn't bother trying to ditch it because by now it was beginning to feel more like an escort than something to fear.

Ignoring it, I thought about Scoop. My gut said I was getting closer to helping him, though I was miles from understanding what happened to Chester and how that connected to my reporter friend. That last video he left of Chester and Winfred Thomas had to be a clue, though I was out of ideas and would have to wait until I could talk with Scoop.

I put in a few hours at the library before succumbing to my lack of concentration. I was on the funeral home doorstep just as Carp was finishing up the back exit repairs.

"Hey, looks good," I said, noting that he had his sleeves rolled up and his hummingbird tattoo exposed. "Aren't you worried Carla will see that?"

"I told her about it," said Carp, with a frown.

"How'd she take it?"

"I'm not sure," he said, and turned to me with a look that I can only describe as wonder. "We're going for drinks."

* * *

Inside, Carla was hunched over her orange book and when she saw me, she snapped it shut.

"Don't worry," I said. "I have no intentions of invading your privacy."

She shrugged. "To what do I owe the *pleasure?*" I couldn't blame her for the chilly reception. She thought I was accusing her brother of being Scoop's source and probably the arsonist.

"Do you have time for me to pick your brain?"

Carla would never say no, so I rehashed what Scoop's file had revealed. Carla opened her orange book and turned the pages back to the dates of the two original fires. As she skimmed her pages, I watched frightened eyes land.

"Arson number one: I was in Rhode Island visiting a friend. Tony texted about the fire—I didn't get it until the next morning but he sent it when he got back to the firehouse."

Carla then tapped her finger to point out the next line.

Text from Tony—fire tonight—all safe.

"We have an agreement that if he gets called to something big, he checks in afterward so I don't worry about him."

She turned her orange book more toward me and placed her finger under another line for me to read. This timeline indicated that Carla had been home in Ridgefield because it read: *Met with landlords. Travel schedule in place—begin inhouse check and plant watering next week.*

"That was earlier in the day. The second arson happened that night. I remember because I stayed up late working on my calendar.

It's one of those painted-on-the-wall things that I can use a Sharpie on and then erase to reuse. I have three months staring at me in the face when I have my breakfast every morning. It's the only way I can keep track of my landlords' comings and goings."

"So that night while your brother was working the fire, you were filling in your schedule."

"With my handwriting, if I want it legible, I have to spend a lot of time. I worked well into the night."

Tony's text after the second fire was curious. Carla noted that it was written at 5 AM. *Another fire—all safe. Meeting with Scoop and then off duty. I'll be home all day.*

"Tony can't be Scoop's source. If he was, he would have talked to him at the fire and wouldn't be looking for him later. You said yourself that Scoop's stories were filed at 3:15 AM."

Tony could have talked with Scoop at midnight and then wanted to add something additional at 5 AM. Like a warning not to print the accelerants because he realized his mistake—TMI.

"Did Tony ever tell you why he was looking for Scoop?" I asked.

"No, and I never asked."

* * *

I pulled my laptop from my ever-present satchel and called up October Obituaries. Carla looked amused at my subterfuge, although she said nothing as Scoop's video began to run.

I paused and pointed.

"Tony, right?"

She nodded.

I pushed pause as each firefighter at the scene of Mrs. Means' blaze came into view and Carla, more familiar with everyone, scribbled their names on a piece of paper. She did the same for the video taken at the contractor's fire.

"Depending on the size of the fire, they might stay for a couple of hours to make sure nothing flares up," she said. "And, the fire marshal can always call the others back if he thinks there's a problem."

Carla's information jived with what I had.

When we finished the videos, I showed her the timelines and the transcripts from Scoop's interviews. She stayed wide-eyed and gum chomping while she read.

Finally, she turned to me and said, "I know you said Scoop knew stuff he shouldn't know, but this . . ." and here, she pointed at the laptop screen. "This is damning."

As she slowly closed the lid and slid my laptop back to me, I thought I might be getting a glimpse of what Carla's resolve looked like right before she marched into the tattoo parlor.

"So, we are inching closer to finding Scoop's source and the arsonist," she said. "And, Kip has all this, right?"

I nodded.

"Good, then we can move on."

"Should we at least confront Tony?" I asked.

"No. We should leave that to Kip."

Carla, survivor of many things, was not going to spend another minute worrying about her brother's involvement. If he did it, he did it. If he didn't, he would be proved innocent. End of story.

I pulled copies of the papers Chester had left in the urn from my satchel and laid them out in front of Carla.

"You didn't have a chance to look at these closely the other night so I made copies for you."

She looked at the papers dismally and then her eyes suddenly brimmed with tears.

"Chester," she whispered. "He was one of the good guys."

"Do you want to tell me about it?" I asked, and for once she did.

At first, she had discounted Chester as a homeless guy in need of a break. She gave him odd jobs and coffee while she worked. After a while, she began to look forward to his visits.

"So, you had a flirtation," I said.

"It wasn't as if he came in looking like a bum. He was cute in those mismatched clothes and very buffed. And, he was a great conversationalist. I now know he was probably fishing for information. Whatever he was trying to say with this . . ." She tapped the papers I had given her. "I don't know. Anyway, it never went anywhere, just a lot of looks and innuendo—you know, the fun part when you're still playing."

We spent some time studying the papers Chester had left behind and I told her about my threatening letter and the black SUV that seemed to be everywhere these days.

"What about you? Do you still feel like someone is watching you?"

Carla laughed. "Oh yeah, and my Stan is right there at the back door."

"Carp tells me you're going for a drink."

"He's cute in his own way," she said, and then pushed back the sleeve of her sweater to reveal the hummingbird. "I told him that if it doesn't work out, he can add a broken heart to his tat. The poor guy looked green."

* * *

By the time I got home, Kip, Horace, and Richard were already in the kitchen. Dinner was chicken cutlets and risotto with what I've come to think of as Horace's signature salad—mixed greens, cherry bomb tomatoes, avocado, and goat cheese drizzled with a Champagne Vinaigrette from Sur La Table, our gourmet take-out shop.

Grave Words

"What's going on with Scoop?" asked Richard, when we settled.

Kip, who had been shoveling food in as if he hadn't eaten in a week, put his fork down, wiped his lips with his napkin, and took a sip of water.

"He's cooling his heels. He's got his computer so he's content."

It hadn't occurred to me to try emailing him. I wondered if he was allowed access to the internet. I squinted my eyes. Something was off.

"And, how are you doing with the crime spree?" asked Richard.

No-one was eating now because we were all intent on hearing what Kip had to say.

"I wouldn't exactly call it a crime spree and we are getting closer to solving the arsons. I hate to admit it, but we are going around and around in circles with Chester's murder."

According to Kip, who was telling us what I already knew, they were aware of Chester's firm, Eyes See, and also his connection to Arthur Willings, who wanted him to look into a specific company.

"Plot Plans sells burial plots," said Kip, looking at Horace. "That was the brochure you showed us the other night, right? Where did you get it?"

"In the mail," said Horace. "You know how it goes. Once you start a search for something, you get inundated with related stuff. I was working on my end-of-life plan and all of a sudden, my mailbox was filled. This one looked interesting because it offered a reduced-price option for choosing plots."

"How can someone offer a plot for less?" I asked. "That's pretty expensive real estate."

"That's the thing we can't figure out and the company never answers our calls. We're still wading through layers and haven't yet found who owns Plot Plans."

"What about the papers that Chester left for Carla?" I asked.

"I suppose you have a copy of those too," said Kip, turning to me and thankfully, there was no telltale brow rub or scowl. The seas were calm.

"Guilty," I said, with a smile.

"Have you figured anything out from them? Because I can't find a pattern or a message, just a lot of cemetery names and numbers that don't make sense to me."

"Same here."

I explained how I gave them to Carla in hopes that she might make some sense out of them and so far, she too was in the dark.

"She's been calling Plot Plans since before Chester died because one of her clients brought her their brochure and asked that she follow through for their end-of-life planning. Apparently, the client visited the plot and then gave Plot Plans a lot of money to reserve it. They plan to pay for the rest in exchange for the deed when they get back from their European vacation next month."

Now, Kip did rub his brow. "I can't figure out what the scam could possibly be."

"It might be that you pay money for a plot that doesn't exist," I said. "Because, I've been calling them, Chester called, and Carla called. None of us can reach them."

"It can't be that," said Richard. "You said Carla's client visited the plot."

Something was staring at us in plain sight and yet none of us was seeing it. It was Richard who got there first.

"What if Plot Plans takes the money of reasonably healthy individuals for the same plot over and over? Maybe, they've sold it a hundred times by now. That's a nice return on a small investment—a nice plot for say $5,000 and reselling it numerous times at a discount."

"I wouldn't think you'd make enough money to outweigh the risk of getting caught," I said.

"Take it a step further," said Kip, getting excited. "What if this is one of many plots."

"And, maybe Plot Plans doesn't even own the plots," I added.

I read about a real estate scam not too long ago where a piece of property was sold and the purchaser, with forged deed in hand, started digging a foundation, when the real owner of the property stepped forward. The purchaser had been scammed out of close to $400,000. And, apparently, that was one of many such scams.

"What happens if someone dies—they risk getting caught," I said, thinking that unlike a big financial gain as with a single piece of property, a cemetery scammer would need multiple sales to make it worthwhile.

"Not necessarily," said Kip, warming to the theory. "As long as we never learn who is behind Plot Plans, all they have to do is start over with another company."

I finally remembered where I had originally seen the Plot Plan logo. It had been fluttering in the wind on Betty Willings' bulletin board.

"Have you spoken with the lawyer who hired Chester on behalf of Arthur?" I asked.

"Yes," said Kip. "He was supposed to meet with Chester the morning after he died. He too was waiting to hear about the scam."

For a moment, the room went quiet.

"What about the Nosy Parkers? Have you asked them who the guy was that they were sitting with at Tazza—the buckskin-shoe guy? If he's the same guy who broke into the funeral home, they might be in danger," I said.

"We can't reach them. We did a wellness check and they aren't home. And, their car is gone. None of their neighbors have seen them for a few days," said Kip. "In fact, everyone who seems connected to either that guy, whoever he is, or Plot Plans, has disappeared or is dead."

I jumped from my seat and pointed to Horace. "Do not let him out of your sight," I said to Richard. Kip jumped with me.

"Where are you going?"

"To find Carla."

* * *

"Still voicemail," I said, holding up my cell.

Kip had taken the back roads to reach Carla's home with caution. It was so easy to miss seeing an evening dog walker or a couple of kids still hanging out on the streets. When we reached her house, her car was gone and the only lights were the exterior floods that people often left on when they weren't at home. While it appeared that no-one was there, Kip wondered if he should do a well check anyway.

"Wait," I said. "Carp mentioned that they might go out for drinks." I quickly texted both and within moments I received a question mark from Carla and a *what's up* from Carp.

I texted for Carla to call and when she did, I told her she was on speaker with Kip and then I started to explain.

"Slow down, what brochure, what phone calls?"

"Chester's repeated questions about Plot Plans is probably why he ended up dead. Your threatening phone calls to the company and your association with him might have placed you in danger," said Kip. "Have you received any threats—I mean aside from the break in at the funeral home?"

"How to ruin a nice night," she said, in response.

By then, Carp had grabbed the phone, which apparently Carla also had on speaker.

"She got a note to mind her own business and she won't listen to me that this is serious."

Kip gave Carp instructions on making sure Carla stayed at Scoop's apartment tonight rather than in the secluded area where her landlord's property was tucked away off a private drive on Oreneca Road.

"She'll stay with me. I have an extra room and I won't let her out of my sight," he promised.

* * *

"Are you sure you can't remember anything else about the guy who broke into the funeral home, or for that matter, anything else about the man with the Nosy Parkers?" Kip and I were back at the house with Richard and Horace.

I didn't bother to answer because it was the umpteenth time he had asked.

"Why would Scoop have a video of Chester in animated conversation with Winfred Thomas the third on his thumb drive?" I asked. "It seems so random and not at all related to the arsons."

"It's time to ask Scoop," said Kip, and stood to leave.

"Now?" I asked. It was close to 9:30 PM.

"Yes," said Kip. When I rose to join him, he shook his head no. "Will you please stay here with Richard and Horace?"

I felt like I was the one in prison. Horace insisted on returning to his own cottage, and because Max, the marshmallow, would turn into a lethal weapon if any stranger approached, he felt safe.

"I wouldn't be someone they'd care about because like Betty Willings, all I did was receive a letter. It's the people who start asking questions that are the targets," said Horace, looking at me pointedly.

Richard looked from Horace to me, no doubt trying to decide which of us needed more protection.

"I have a million alarms and you'll be back in a while with Diva," I said, shooing him.

"I'll be back in a bit," he said, and followed Horace out the door.

* * *

"I'm going stir-crazy," whispered Carla, a little while later, into the phone. "I've decided to check on Scoop's feline family and maybe, drop into Pop's Place for a drink. Can you meet me? I think we should talk to Ramone."

"What about Carp?" I asked.

"Sound asleep," she said. "I'll leave him a note."

The lights were still on at Horace's cottage and Richard hadn't yet returned. I left him a note, letting him know that I was going to feed the kittens with Carla.

I debated a text to Kip and decided that if I couldn't talk Carla out of a drink at Pop's Place, I'd inform him then.

Carla opted to walk back to the funeral home only a short distance away, because she wanted to try out the new sidewalks on New Street, and besides, she didn't want to wake up Carp.

* * *

As we fed Heady, Topper, and their starving housemates, Carla and I discussed what we had learned.

"I never checked to see if Winfred Thomas the third wore buckskin shoes," I said.

"And, I never looked at John Smith's feet. However, it seems like every time I turn around, that guy is there."

"Maybe he's just into you," I said as I emptied an overloaded litter box into a large bag, scrunched my nose as I tied it against the odor, and refilled.

Carla was holding one of the kittens who was mewing loudly, no doubt, its version of protest for being left alone for so long.

"Scoop has got to get back here before these guys need psychotherapy," complained Carla.

Cats settled and apartment refreshed, we plopped onto Scoop's sectional.

"Let's go to Pop's," said Carla. "It's only 10:30."

"I don't think that's the best idea you've had. Kip told us to stay put and although I don't feel particularly threatened here together, I'm not so sure about going out. It'd be like saying 'here I am, come and get me.'"

"Think about it, who really wants us?"

"Besides the guy who thinks we found incriminating evidence in the double-wide?" I asked. "Or maybe the arsonist who thinks that Scoop might have told one of us who they are?"

As Carla thought about that, my phoned pinged.

"Oddest thing—I've been getting these notifications from Apple, telling me that an AirTag is moving with me."

"There's your stalker," she said. "Apple does that when an AirTag has been away from its owner for a while and is seen in your vicinity. Check your bag."

I rummaged around and saw no white round tracking device. I was about to dump the entire bag out on Scoop's coffee table when my cell rang.

"Are you OK?" asked Richard. "I got your note."

"We realized that Carla hadn't fed the cats, so we're here at Scoop's apartment."

I could hear some chatter in the background.

"Is Horace with you?"

"Yes, we heard your car leave."

"Go back to bed. I am fine." I said, suddenly feeling suffocated.

"Let's go," I said to Carla after I hung up and tossed my phone on the table in frustration. "I need to get out."

Chapter Thirty-Eight

Pop's Place had a much livelier vibe than I would have thought at this hour, and then I remembered that it was their Halloween bash. Tonight, there was a mix of men and women with a lot of them still in costume.

Move over Johnny Depp because Ramone was dressed like a pirate, complete with leather hat, headband, vest, and all the accessories, including a sheath hanging loosely from his waist. Carla looked like she might start panting the way Diva does when we go for car rides.

"Where were you? You're missing the best party," he said, by way of greeting. "Your usual?"

Carla shook her head, no, "Just a glass of red for me. Those martinis you make are life altering."

"They're a death sentence," I agreed, and Carla giggled.

"Nice broach, Winter," Ramone said, a few minutes later, as he placed a Chardonnay in front of me.

"You kept it," said Carla, in surprise. It was the first time I had taken my jacket off and it now glittered in the pendant lights that hung above the bar.

"I didn't mean to kill Chester. I intended to knock him out, take my papers, and disappear," he said, looking at his watch. "And, I had nothing to do with Arthur—his death was just plain old convenient."

"Who is we?" I asked.

Winfred smiled, and a moment later, I heard the soft footfalls of someone coming down the hallway. I had a wistful moment of hope that my stalker had followed me, but hope was at odds with reality because when the door opened, I was staring at the buckskin shoes. I followed them to a body and finally a face.

"You?" I asked, in surprise.

"I tried to warn you off, but no, you had to keep sticking your nose in it, didn't you?" said Teller Girl.

As she came deeper into the room and closed the door behind her, I took her in. She was a tall woman and I now realize that when I saw her at the bank, she was probably sitting on a stool. The next time I saw her, she was in and out of the crowds so quickly that I hadn't registered her size. I now flashed back to how large her hands had seemed when she reached for my phone at the bank. And the ring on her pinky, with its red rimmed center, looked identical to the one worn by the person sitting with the Nosy Parkers in Tazza.

Now that I thought back to the day at Tazza when I saw someone wearing buckskin shoes meeting with the Nosy Parkers, I assumed it was a man, although I could now see that it easily could have been a big-boned short-haired woman.

As she stepped over Ramone, his arm suddenly shot out, grabbed her foot, and the woman went plunging to the floor. Winfred sent a well-placed kick to Ramone's kidney and it appeared that the young bartender went "lights out."

Gun still pointed, Winfred pulled Teller Girl to her feet and did a quick inspection of her face, which now included a bloody nose.

Between her tears that poured as if from an open spigot, she kept repeatedly asking if it was broken. It was Carla who reached for a box of tissues and handed it to her.

"I'm sorry, you got involved," Winfred said to Carla and me.

Teller girl wiped her face with the tissues and dabbed at her eyes. She then rolled small pieces to stuff into her nostrils, which successfully kept the flow at bay.

She had recovered enough to ask if she should empty the files.

"Done," said Winfred. "There's nothing left but to wipe down."

"What about us?" asked Carla.

"Not another arson," I said, rolling my eyes. "You're pretty lousy at it, you know."

"I'm sorry, ladies, we're going for a very long ride. Meanwhile, your bartender friend will write a suicide note and succumb to an overdose."

I watched, as Teller Girl, whose name turned out to be Shirley, took a sheet of paper and printed out a carefully worded note. The handwriting looked very familiar and I flashed back to the threats Scoop received.

Ugh. How had I called this so wrong? She then pulled a bottle of water from her tote, doused Ramone enough to rouse him, and I watched in horror as she began feeding him pills from a small-tinted bottle she had removed from her bag.

"If our long ride includes some sort of accident, no-one will believe it," I said. I was banking on the fact that Winfred and Shirley weren't willing to walk away from their current lives in Ridgefield just yet. From the looks of that list, they were about to come into some sizeable returns on their scam. Several of the names, Horace's included, had notations on the possible checks they might receive. Others, like Carla's client and Betty Willings, had already paid significant deposits with the other half due within the month. A quick calculation told me that Winfred and Shirley would be leaving close to half a million dollars on the table and a distracting town tragedy would give them time to collect and disappear.

"Why not? Two women out for a night of fun, taking a joy ride, and ending up crashing their car," said Winfred, with a laugh.

"I never go anywhere without my satchel," I said. "And, everyone knows that."

I tried to smother my relief when Winfred held up my messenger bag and Carla's purse with a smirk. If there was a little white disk emitting locations in there, I wanted it travelling with me.

I felt Carla's shaking hand slip into mine and Winfred stuck his head out into the hallway. The music had died down and I was guessing that all that was left of the downstairs festivities was the clean-up. I thought we might make a run for it, but Winfred jabbed his gun in Carla's back.

"Let's not have any more casualties at Pop's Place," he said. "Poor Jimmy's business probably wouldn't survive."

Shirley was now wielding her own gun, this one a small revolver. She opened Artie's office door and waited while Winfred dragged Ramone inside.

"So, the scam was to buy a plot and then sell it over and over again?" Carla asked.

Her damp hand squeezed mine. Buying time?

"Don't be silly. That's like assuming everyone wants the same casket."

That piqued my curiosity and I asked, "So, how did you do it?"

Shirley glanced quickly at the door where apparently, Winfred was posing poor Ramone on the couch with the pill bottle. I'm not sure what he was doing about the ice cream that was probably now melting all over the counter, or the evidence that we had removed something from the bottoms of the cartons. If he were smart, he'd clean it up, but remembering the botched arson, he didn't seem that smart to me. I might be looking at the mastermind of this plan.

"Once we found out what cemetery they were interested in, we got a map of the available plots. We previewed the plots before showing them to our clients," said Shirley, proudly. "No-one ever questions anyone who is wandering around a cemetery, so it was easy to pretend we owned them. We were raking it in until Chester broke in and stole the pages from our ledger. And then, you came to the bank and began asking about him. That's when we started watching you two."

"So, you're my stalker? You followed me to New Jersey?" I asked, surprised, because by now I thought I knew who was following me and why.

"What? No. We just kept an eye out, noticed how often you two were together and Win saw you at Pop's Place. He also saw that reporter friend there with Chester. That's why we're wrapping up the business. I mean how many people can you get rid of without getting caught—you're going to make a mistake eventually, right?"

As Shirley continued boasting, I began forming a plan. One of them still had to go back to Artie's office, get the *Star Wars* collectibles and suicide note, which, no doubt, confessed to killing Chester. They had to bring the note, at least, back to where Ramone would be found dead in the morning. Then, there was the clean-up, with Shirley's blood-soaked Kleenex and all our fingerprints everywhere in their office.

"On the count of three," I whispered in Carla's ear. She looked at me with inquiring eyes.

Shirley urged us toward the staircase we had originally come up.

I tapped one, when Winfred poked his head out of the office and whispered, "Not that way."

Shirley glanced at him inquiringly, so I quickly mimed a pushing motion at Carla's back.

"I've got to clean up, so I'll be a few minutes. Wait for lights out and go down the back," he said. "By then, I'll be done here."

Moments later, as we perched near the top of the stairs where music had been blasting from just a short while earlier, things had grown quiet, and finally I heard Jimmy hollering goodbye to the last of the staff. I considered calling out and Shirley, anticipating this, stuck the gun close to Carla's temple.

"I'd have nothing to lose," she whispered, in warning.

When a final door slammed and all was quiet, we waited for what seemed an eternity.

Two, I tapped, as Winfred closed the door to Artie's office behind him, and hurried back to his own office to wipe things down.

By now, Carla understood the plan, nodded, and let go of my hand.

We were at the top of the back staircase with Shirley wielding her gun like a pro.

I tapped three, bumped her gun hand with all my might, while Carla moved behind her and with a hefty shove, pushed her down the stairs. Because I was partly in front of Shirley, she began taking me with her until I grabbed for the banister with two hands, felt her bump hard into my shoulder, try to grab my trust pendant to break her fall, and then began rolling head over heels until she landed at the bottom with a thud.

Not waiting for Winfred to investigate the screech Shirley had let out as she tumbled, we hurried down after her. Winfred was calling from behind us now as we stepped over a very contorted Shirley. I stared into lifeless eyes with a wave of sadness. Carla yanked at my arm reminding me that we could be next if we didn't get out of there.

I had no idea where the revolver might have fallen, and I grabbed a dart from the target as we passed. We both bolted toward the front door which was securely locked. With Winfred already on the staircase, I didn't think we had enough time to figure out the locks. Instead, I yanked Carla's hand toward the bar. We both hoisted ourselves up, climbed over, and crouched behind.

And then, I felt a hand clamp against my mouth.

I was about to jab with my dart when I heard the frightened whisper of John Smith, pleading, "Don't make a sound. I'm one of the good guys."

It was then that blaring sirens prefaced the strobe of lights that began blinking through Pop's Place.

Chapter Thirty-Nine

Ramone's face was swollen and one eye was black and blue. He still looked worn from his overdose. The sedative Shirley had shoved down his throat knocked him out and the bartender had remained unconscious through his entire ordeal.

"You're lucky we got to you so quickly," said Tony, Carla's brother.

We were all gathered at the Lake Mamanasco cottage waiting for Scoop to arrive. Richard and Horace were predictably preparing a buffet feast.

"It's a good thing I froze all these lasagnas," said Richard, carrying steaming Pyrex pans smothered in oozing cheese to the buffet table.

After helping in the kitchen, Carla and Tony joined Kip and I by the fire. The dogs were bouncing from one person to another enjoying the steady barrage of pets and shamelessly begging for more.

"Eat whenever you want," announced Richard, who poured himself a glass of wine. As Horace made a plate, Richard perched on the end of my chair and sipped his robust red.

"Thank you, Winter and Carla for figuring out who Scoop's source was. I was working every fire, hoping to isolate him myself, but honestly, I was too distracted to remember that the app we use handles scheduling and call response—that could have saved some steps," said Tony. "I have to admit, at first I thought Scoop might be the arsonist, but then Carla convinced me that it wasn't his style."

"Is that why you were looking for him after the second arson?" I asked.

"Yeah, I wanted to pressure him to see if he had talked to anyone in the department."

The names Kip had acquired narrowed the suspects down to only a few people who had worked both fires. When he compared his list with the firefighters Carla and I had identified from the pictures on Scoop's thumb drive, he realized his wasn't completely up-to-date. The guys on stand-by in case of a flare-up, had not been included. It was then that he noticed Big Joe front and center in Scoop's photographs.

"So, Big Joe turned out to be Scoop's source?" asked Richard.

"And, responsible for the arsons," confirmed Kip. "Once we cornered him, he admitted everything. He switched shifts at the last minute and made sure that he would be on stand-by for any flareups so he would be available to feed Scoop information."

"He must have had help," I said. "You can't start a fire and respond at the same time."

Kip nodded and explained that Big Joe was the broker who brought the contractor and a hired arsonist together.

"Apparently, the arsonist actually has a company called *Fire for Hire*."

"I can't imagine that little old lady hunting around on the dark web to find an arsonist," said Horace, who now joined the circle. Kip relinquished his seat so Horace could sit and balance his plate. The lasagna smelled delicious and everyone's eyes turned toward the buffet.

"She had nothing to do with it," said Kip, happy to be able to finally share details.

I listened as Kip repeated an alleged conversation at Pop's Place between Big Joe and the contractor who wished his problems could go away in a burst of flames. Big Joe, who hadn't yet seen a fire in his career—too many smoke detectors and sprinkler systems for anything to burn these days—saw an opportunity to shine.

"The two plotted together and whoosh, problems gone," said Kip.

"And Mrs. Means?" asked Horace, wanting reassurance that the old woman got off the hook.

Kip explained that the contractor had his eye on Mrs. Means' property but didn't want to pay a premium for a decrepit teardown. Once the fire obliterated the modest ranch, he swooped in and bought the property at a lot less than it was worth because the distraught older woman just wanted out. Between the insurance money and property sale, she was able to move near her daughter. The contractor then began building a much in demand downtown colonial.

"So, is the contractor under arrest for arson?" I asked.

"He's a person of interest, although it's Big Joe's word against his. Big Joe was paid in cash and arson is hard to prove. That's a wait and see," said Kip.

Richard asked if Ramone's apartment fire had also been started intentionally and Tony shook his head sadly. "It was a plain old electrical fire. The homeowner did some of the wiring on the apartment himself and didn't quite get it right."

The doorbell rang and I hurried to welcome Betty Willings and her daughter, Mandy. I had been anxiously awaiting them and at the moment, I felt the swell of pride at the role I had played in what was coming. Waving off our offers of food and drink, Betty strode into the room and immediately zeroed in on Ramone.

"So, you're the one my Artie wanted to help. You were a good friend," she said.

"He was the better friend," said Ramone. "And, I'm sorry about the *Star Wars* figures. Those idiots had no idea what they were doing when they removed them from the packages."

When he had recovered enough to speak, Ramone had told Kip about the action figures that had by now disappeared because Winfred had escaped out the back door before the police had surrounded Pop's Place. They had caught him pretty quickly, though the figures had been nowhere to be found.

Betty turned to me.

"Artie's autopsy did not show any foul play," she said, blinking back tears. "It was just those damn genes I passed along that killed my son."

I reached for her hand and squeezed.

Mandy opened her purse and handed me the letter from Plot Plans that I recognized as the one that had been on her mother's bulletin board. With it was an envelope, presumably my check for Arthur Willings' obituary.

"I thought you might want this letter to remind you of what a great service you did. Artie sensed something was wrong but he didn't want to disappoint Mom. She had been so proud of herself for buying plots for the family. So, Artie put a secret investigation into Chester's hands."

We all stayed quiet for a moment, acknowledging the man who had paid the ultimate price for his role in shutting down Plot Plans. If it hadn't been for Chester, we might never have found out about the scam to repeatedly sell the same burial plots—plots belonging to someone else. Judging by the spreadsheets Chester had hidden in the ice cream containers, there were a lot of people who had been duped into believing their end of life plans were settled. That alone was going to be a mess to unravel.

"Your son was a hero. Think of all the people he saved from losing their money," said Richard, looking pointedly at Horace.

"I was about to turn in my life insurance policy to secure a plot," admitted my neighbor. "My policy is for my end of life care, and I wanted to make sure none of the funeral burden fell on Richard or Winter."

Now *I* was blinking back tears.

Mandy smiled and put an arm around her tiny mother who dabbed at her eyes with a tissue. She then pulled an official-looking envelope from her purse and handed it to Ramone.

"Artie entrusted this to me and said I was to make sure these collectibles were sold on your behalf when you were ready," she said, and then with a nod from her mom added. "Winter told us about the *GoFundMe* account set up on your behalf and we've also included a contribution to that."

Ramone stood and gave each a hug. He then opened the envelope and peered at the papers.

"This . . . this is . . ." and that's all he got out before he burst into tears.

"Now, now, none of that," said Betty Willings, who again wrapped her arms around him. "Next week, you'll come to the house and help us start sorting things out. And, we'll need help with the memorial service."

The Willings left shortly after, intent on visiting Pop's Place to give Jimmy a nice tip, per Artie's final wishes. When they were gone, Ramone crumbled back into his chair, occasionally wiping his eyes, mostly just staring at the lake. Between the unexpected windfall, his near overdose, and his guilt about trying to lure Carla and me upstairs in hopes of discovering the list he had been searching for, he hadn't had much left in the tank besides his repeated apologies.

After an evening of lively chatter and plates of lasagna passed around, Tony rose to leave and when I walked him to the door, I bumped straight into my reporter friend. Tony gave Scoop a hefty pat on the back, said "I owe you," and then was gone.

With Scoop's entrance, the conversation pitch rose enough that I worried the neighbors might think we were having a deck party without them. More food was offered and Scoop, looking a little less like a skeleton since being imprisoned, wolfed his down and went for more.

And then, as if on cue, everyone stopped talking and stared expectantly at him.

"What?" he asked.

"Start from the beginning," said Richard.

Scoop confirmed that he had been trying to hint at who his informant was without officially telling me.

"I concocted this plan the night Chester warned me about the accelerants, the same night he was murdered. I couldn't believe how foolish I'd been."

"Why not just tell us?" I asked.

"Because, at that point, I didn't realize Big Joe played any role in the arsons. I didn't want to mess up his career."

"He did that all by himself," said Kip.

Scoop confirmed that he had no idea that Chester was anything but the homeless man he thought he had been until Kip questioned him.

"I suspected, though, and that's why I sent the file with him and Winfred Thomas. I couldn't figure out what a homeless man was doing with a bank manager. Then, when he was killed, I figured it'd be worth showing Winter the picture."

"Why me?" I asked.

"Because you were trying to find information on Chester to do his obituary and I thought maybe Winfred could help with his last name at least."

"Shirley and Winfred began closing up shop because they thought Chester was on to them. The truth was, he was only on to Plot Plans. That video was Chester probably asking how to follow the trail of the check Betty Willings had written on her account at the bank," said Kip.

"Chester wasn't about to ask Betty for permission to look into who had cashed the check she had written to Plot Plans, because he and Artie were still trying to keep her in the dark."

"How did Teller Girl . . . I mean Shirley, know to go to the funeral home to search the caskets?" I asked.

"It was all those threatening phone calls I made, wasn't it?" asked Carla.

Ramone sat up straighter and looking sheepish, interjected, "I think it was my fault. Winfred asked me about you two after you left the bar that first night. I let it slip that you were asking about Chester."

Kip confirmed. According to Winfred, who was apparently trying to push as much blame onto his dead partner as possible, it was Shirley's idea to break into Carla's office. They knew from Carla's repeated phone calls that there might be evidence pointing to Plot Plans and they wanted to find it so they could buy a little more time to collect their money before closing up shop. Once inside, she found Carla's book, saw the notations about Chester, and went in search of the neon green casket.

Despite the fact that I already knew most of the story, I didn't want to miss a word. Apparently, everyone felt the same way because none of us got up to clean the buffet until a persistent bell tingle made me realize that two dogs were waiting anxiously by the front door. Diva and Max wanted their walk.

Carla stood to leave. She was meeting Carp for a drink after he finished door repairs at Pop's Place that occurred when the cop's forced their entry. Ramone got up to go with her. Carp was putting him up in his extra room until the *GoFundMe* page started by his former landlord accumulated enough money for him to find a rental.

Kip, Scoop, and I cleaned up while Horace and Richard took the dogs for a walk.

"Was it Winfred who followed you to Nyack?" asked Scoop, as I laid out a plate of chocolate chip cookies.

I sighed. I'd been wrestling with what to do with that piece of the puzzle.

"It was John Smith. He was hired by Horace and Richard to follow me," I blurted out.

"You're kidding," said my friend, mid bite. "Why?"

"The usual," I said, "they were worried about me, and then they escalated. I hadn't told them about the SUV following me to New Jersey so they knew I was holding out on them. They decided they needed to keep an even better eye on me by starting up surveillance in Ridgefield as well."

"I'm surprised John Smith wasn't more discreet," said Scoop.

"Are you kidding me? The poor guy is an engineering student at Westconn. Richard was paying him for odd jobs. He had no idea what to do. He nearly freaked out the first night we met him because someone he knew had come into the bar. He couldn't get out of there fast enough—subterfuge will never be his strong suit."

"There's more," said Kip, with a smile. "Richard sewed an Apple AirTag into the seam of Winter's satchel."

Scoop just shook his head.

"They knew I was keeping secrets from them and worried over what else I wasn't telling them," I said. "It was probably that simple act of invading my privacy that saved us."

I explained how Richard immediately called Kip when he saw that the AirTag was still at Pop's Place, but according to John

Smith's phone call, I was not. By then, Kip had talked at length with Scoop and knew that the arsons and Chester's murder were unconnected. He had also finally reached the Nosy Parkers, who had returned from a mini getaway. They told him that they had been regularly meeting with a woman from the bank named Shirley who was helping them with their investments. We could only guess at Shirley's motivation for feeding vicious lies to the gossipers, although I suspected it was to deflect by trying to pin Chester's death on Scoop.

Kip explained that when he got Richard's call, he raced to Pop's, radioing the station on the way. "I asked for lights and sirens."

When the police broke through the front door, they found Carla, John, and me hiding behind the bar.

"By then, Winfred was in the wind and the first priority was to rescue Ramone," Kip said. "We caught up with Winfred at home, packing a duffel to disappear."

"Wow, talk about a potential award-winning story," said Scoop. "Did you confront your uncle and Horace?"

"Only about the AirTag," I said. "I'll let John Smith tell them his cover was blown. For now, why not let them think they got away with something?"

Scoop left shortly afterwards. Richard and Horace returned, letting us know that they would take Diva and Max next door where they would sip some of the lottery-winning Old Granddad, and congratulate themselves for saving my life again.

It was then that my cell rang, and finally! My client was full of apologies. She had been on a cruise and cell service had been limited.

"I'm so sorry, Winter, I thought I'd submit the obituary for my mother myself and then take a very needed vacation. I never checked to see how it read and I asked that they find a photo from their files. My mom was so well known in the community, I knew she had been in the paper many times for all her committees. I never dreamed . . ." I stopped listening, relieved that the chapter was over.

Kip and I ended the evening with a night cap in the train room where my new locomotive, tender attached, gleamed as it travelled the tracks.

"Digital," I said, clapping my hands. "I can't believe it."

We both watched for a moment until Kip broke the silence.

"Why did you go to Pop's Place when you knew you could be in danger?"

I fingered Gladys Night's trust pendant before answering.

"I was feeling . . . suffocated," I admitted. "First with Richard and Horace, because by then I had figured that they had someone following me. I didn't think that you would do something so invasive, although I wasn't a hundred percent sure."

Kip shook his head sadly. "I thought you knew me better. How did you figure out that they had hired John Smith to follow you?"

"First of all, no-one, you included, seemed overly concerned about the black SUV," I said. "Second, the guy was no threat. He just seemed to want to know where I was going. Then, John Smith started showing up at Pop's, pretending to be a regular when, in fact, he only seemed to go there when I did. And finally, who else could it be? If it wasn't you trying to keep me safe . . ."

"Hey, stop, I would never have you followed," said Kip.

I studied my upset and earnest boyfriend.

"I know that," I assured him. "I just got to thinking, who else would go to such extremes? Richard had practically moved back into the house and Horace was holding vigil every night on his deck making sure I got home, no matter how late or cold it got."

"I also suspected it was the two of them," admitted Kip. "They always had their heads together, conspiring and then trying to look so innocent."

"Did you know it was John Smith in the SUV?" I asked.

"I didn't even know he existed," said Kip.

"Poor guy. That's what happens when you're trying to earn a few extra bucks and your professor hires you. John was smart enough to begin to put things together at Pop's Place, and when Ramone said we had gone for the night, he called Richard who told him that my satchel was still somewhere in the building. So he hid, with the intent of looking for me after everyone else had gone," I said. "Anyway," I didn't know how to feel about Richard and Horace . . . having me followed and tracking me . . . ugh!"

"You were mad at them—"

"And you, I interrupted. "When were you going to tell me that Scoop was in hiding to keep him safe? He wasn't ever arrested or charged, was he? Just tucked away somewhere so people like the Nosy Parkers could continue spreading rumors in hopes that the bad guys would think they got away with blaming him."

"Chester was dead because Winfred thought he knew who was behind Plot Plans. Scoop was seen in deep conversation with him the night he was murdered and then he was being threatened. I wanted Scoop off the streets so when I suggested he get out of town for a few days, he went to Ridgewood for a long overdue visit with his cousins. How did you figure it out?"

"How could I not? You looked downright relieved the night you said you arrested him. Plus, as a former reporter, I'm fully aware that you can't arrest someone without having them arraigned the next day, unless it's a weekend, which it was not. No bond had been set, no court appearance, and just tons of rumors fueled by the Nosy Parkers that Scoop was an arsonist and a murderer."

Kip confirmed. "We wanted the bad guys to think we had eyes on Scoop."

Kip then reached out and fingered the trust pendant that dangled on my chest.

"We have a lot of work to do," he said, quietly.

The train was climbing the hill toward the tunnel. It was my favorite part of the route because I envisioned the passengers wondering what would be in store for them on the other side.

"I know," I said, wrapping my arms around him and feeling the comforting beat of his heart against mine. "Can we please wait until tomorrow?"

Kip pulled me tighter and I could feel the trust pendant press against my chest.

"Tomorrow," he agreed, and we both watched as the train emerged on the other side of the tunnel.

Acknowledgments

I should probably acknowledge the entire Ridgefield, Connecticut community for putting up with the writer's leeway I take when I create my fictional stories. To the Ridgefield Police and Fire Departments, I hope my imaginative twists in this book don't stray too far from the accurate depictions that have been so generously shared.

My town—I hope you can tell how much I love it. And love the people who continue to support me on this author adventure. Thank you to my friend Sally Sanders, former Arts & Leisure Editor for the *Ridgefield Press* for her keen editing eye. Thank you also to author and retired *Ridgefield Press* Editor, Jack Sanders because he is an encyclopedia of town history and always willing to share. Both are such great assets to our community for their dedication to keeping our history alive.

A huge shout-out goes to Emergency Management Director Dick Aarons, my go to person for everything disaster, death and recovery. Thanks to Tim Pambianchi, chief of our amazing volunteer firefighters whose 26 years of service and dedication earn him applause from the entire community. Tim patiently answered my endless questions articulately and promptly. Also thank you to New Canaan firefighter

Acknowledgments

Damien Sheerin who gave me an alternate perspective on how other departments do things. To Ridgefield Police Chief Jeff Kreitz who I've known since his high school days (not mine), thank you for opening your door despite how busy the department gets. And a big thanks to Patrol Officer Jorge Romero whose input rescued my plot, whether he realizes it or not. And a special acknowledgement to Beth Rosner who manages Temple Beth-El Cemetery in Stamford, Connecticut. A peaceful walk and talk and I learned enough about cemeteries to make my plot work.

To my beta readers always starting with my sisters, Leigh and Michele Karwoski. Leigh for her tough stance on plot discrepancies; Michele for making sure none of the things that annoy her about other books, land in mine. Thank you also to Lorna Nelligan, a beautiful writer; to Lesa Hocutt-Smith whose go-to "house gift" is my first book. Thank you to Rick and Camille Miller whose input I value and to my critique partners, Muffy Flouret and Cathi Stoler. You have no idea how helpful all your comments have been.

There are never enough kudos for Crooked Lane Books, my editor Tara Gavin and her amazing "dream team." All always in my corner. And almost last but NEVER least—Agent Adam Chromy who is responsible for this journey. One of these days I hope to thank him in person.

And of course, thanks go to my family. My son Christian whose guidance and input I could not succeed without. My husband Bob, who I thought might want to cut the ties after my three-month writing marathon but no–there he was handing out swag along with grandson Miles and inviting people to "meet the author" at a recent book signing. Thank you to my children, grandchildren, and extended family and friends who continue to be there for me. And to my readers, keep at it. You all make my heart happy.